PROJECT VAMPIRE KILLER

Also by Jonathan Raab

The Haunting of Camp Winter Falcon

*The Secret Goatman Spookshow
and Other Psychological Warfare Operations*

The Crypt of Blood: A Halloween TV Special

Camp Ghoul Mountain Part VI: The Official Novelization

PROJECT VAMPIRE KILLER

JONATHAN RAAB

MUZZLELAND PRESS

Project Vampire Killer
Copyright © 2023 Jonathan Raab
Cover art by Hellish Maggot
Edited by Steve Grinstead
Muzzleland Press logo and section break icon
by Mat Fitzsimmons

All rights reserved. No part of this work, save brief quotations for reviews, may be reproduced without the express written consent of the publisher.

ISBN: 979-8-9879688-0-2

This novel is a work of fiction. Any resemblance to real persons, events, or weird little freaks is purely coincidental.

Muzzleland Press
Victor, NY

*For James R. Moore
a son of the Island and a child of the night
whose sweet music and
vampire film recommendations
never fail to inspire.*

"It is a childish terror to fear death but not to fear sin."
Saint John Chrysostom, *Homily V on the Statues*

"If it's not in frame, it doesn't exist."
F.W. Murnau, *Shadow of the Vampire*

"All right, let's shoot this fucker."
Bela Lugosi, *Ed Wood*

The Blood-Soaked End of a Cheap Slasher Film

Annise knew something was wrong when Ulrich called *cut* early. He almost never did that, preferring instead to let the cameras roll, to keep the cast in the moment, to encourage the actors to iterate and improvise without ending the shot. It was a frustrating affectation inspired by a collective of '90s-era European digital film pioneers who had embraced the misguided sentimentality of *director-as-auteur* with the arrival of handheld digital cameras. Shooting like this was going to be hell on the editor, assuming *Herr Director* could rope anyone into the gig.

"What now?" Annise said, her words slipping out with the weight of frustration born from two weeks of behind-schedule shooting in mosquito-infested wilderness. She caught amused looks from the handful of other actors standing behind the cameras. Trying to keep this cut-rate horror film on schedule and on budget in the middle of the goddamn woods as both associate producer and lead actress had worn down her patience, and she was letting it show. During the interminable takes when she was not in front of the lens, she would often drift off, thinking of what her career had been like before the near-collapse of the industry during the pandemic—and her own inability to reclaim the quantity and quality of work since production schedules ramped back up. She longed for the opportunity to earn steady money on season-long TV shoots down in Georgia or up in Vancouver, or the monotonous but well-paying gigs filming car commercials in the Catskills and Adirondacks. Those jobs were never high art, but they were professional operations. Two weeks into the mess Ulrich had made of *Ripper Woods*, a destined-for-streaming blip in the cast and crew's various downward-spiraling careers, she would have sold her soul to sleep in a bed or use a real toilet.

"Did you hear that?" Ulrich whispered, lowering his camera. The usual forced confidence of his voice was gone and the color drained from his face. Of course they heard *that*. They had been hearing it for hours: inarticulate moans growing in proximity and volume as the sun retreated across the sky and the forest shadows grew bolder. When it started, Annise had chalked the sounds up to rabbits or foxes crying out in their predator-prey melodrama, a natural reflection of the synthetic horrors generated by their small production team. Director's delusions of artistic grandeur aside, the cast and crew were pros—or close enough—so they worked through the growing sense of unease that had settled over their campsite-turned-movie set, ignoring the cold and disquiet sticking to them like so much red-dyed corn syrup. They hit their marks and delivered their dogshit lines, even as the voices grew closer and were harder to dismiss as the errant cries of wildlife. Acknowledging the sounds directly felt like both a mistake and somehow inevitable, as if doing so might attract the attention of some preternatural force.

Stu, the stuntman playing the picture's masked jack-o'-lantern killer, emerged from behind the tree from which he had been popping out to menace Annise in take after take. He took off the mutated pumpkin-head to reveal his once-handsome face, now riddled with scars from years of hard labor and stunt work on second- and third-tier productions at home and abroad. He stepped forward into the dull glow of twin portable lights and

PROJECT VAMPIRE KILLER 3

scratched at the side of his head with the blade of his prop machete.

"That's a person," Stu said. "Or people."

"No way," said Jem, the screenwriter and producer. She operated the second camera. Everyone had an extra job or three on this no-budget production. Annise had gotten really good at getting the color and consistency *just right* for the fake blood. "That's gotta be an animal."

"Foxes and owls can sound like people," Annise said, recalling her childhood memories of strange sounds in the fog-shrouded nights on the family farm down in the Southern Tier.

"Sure," Stu said, pointing a large hand toward the quickening dark of the forest beyond. "This is different. Someone is out here with us."

"Let's take five," Ulrich said, his eyes on the whispering pine branches above them. The boom operator and the other actors stepped away to spark cigarettes or joints. The production didn't have money for trailers or hot catering this deep in the woods—they had been sleeping in tents and eating hot dogs and military surplus Meals Ready-to-Eat—but Ulrich and Jem had generously provided enough cigarettes, semi-legal cannabis, and bottom-shelf beer to keep the crew simmering on the peaceful side of mutiny. Any opportunity to dull the brain for a few moments was a welcome one, even if the vibes were bad.

Annise hugged her arms across her blood-spattered SUNY Canaltown hoodie. Her character was ten years her junior, a *literal* junior in college. She had bad associations with her own college days—untreated depression, anxiety, and alcoholism made her late teens and early twenties a self-imposed hell—so being in a horror film wherein college co-eds were getting slashed to pieces across desolate stretches of haunted forest held a mild cathartic charm. But now she searched the flat plain of trees and undergrowth spread out before them, looking for movement, for the distinct outline of an approaching human form, for something to give shape to the presence that had, whether acknowledged or not, haunted them since their arrival.

"Here." Jem appeared at her side, holding up a small joint, smoke rolling off its tip in heavy grey spokes. Annise accepted the offering and pressed it to her lips, inhaling slowly. The rush of the cannabis's touch was a pleasant, warm sensation that stretched from the top of her head to her toes and, as she exhaled the eye-stinging smoke, glimmers of faint, angelic light appeared in the branches of the gaunt pine trees above.

"You see that?" she asked as Jem took the joint back.

"Every night since we showed up," the screenwriter said. Annise turned back, suddenly aware of the alien stillness behind them.

The light rigs stood alone, bulbs harsh and bright, their cables stretching back to the quiet-running generator. Stu's pumpkin-head mask and machete sat next to Ulrich's camera on the ground, as if dropped suddenly and forgotten. The red power light on the camera blinked, signaling the need for a battery change.

Everyone was gone.

The generator rumbled to a halt, its soft purr fading into a silence that was somehow less than the absence of sound. The light rigs went dark, inviting the descending shadows to overtake the clearing. Wind moved through the creaking branches above. Leaves and pine needles whispered *shhhhhh*, calling for quiet on the set.

"When did it get so dark?" Jem asked, her voice swallowed up by the wind. Blue light from her wristwatch illuminated her face, revealing her confusion. "That can't be right. I thought we had some time before sunset, before…"

The moaning resumed, sorrowful and insistent. It came from above them, then echoed back from a copse of pines beyond the generators.

"Let me see that." Annise took the camera from Jem, then

pointed it up into the cluster of darkness of the branches above. She pressed the button for Night Mode.

The viewfinder revealed a stark, black-and-white image: human forms floating among the branches, arms outstretched, hands twisted into grasping claws. Their feet hung limp in the air, faces frozen in rictus grins. Two women, unfamiliar. They wore mud-spattered hiking clothes from some fashionable outfitter, now faded and torn. They floated downward, two dummies on a rope-and-pulley system in some community theater production limping toward a clumsy *deus ex machina*. Blood dribbled from their boots and outstretched hands, spattering against the fallen leaves and undergrowth of the forest floor.

Annise and Jem sidestepped, letting the bodies drift between them. Annise kept her focus on the viewfinder, a degree of separation allowing her to keep her composure. Jem groaned and bit into her fist. The corpses floated beyond the darkened light rigs, disappearing into a rising bank of fog and shadow.

Annise swung the camera over to Jem. She heaved in medium shot, hands pressed to her mouth to stifle the scream she so very desperately wanted to free.

"We have to go," Annise said, matter-of-fact.

"Back to the trucks," Jem said through sharp, short breaths.

"The trucks."

"I've got the keys."

In the viewfinder, Jem's eyes were white, lacking definition. Annise flicked Night Mode off. Jem become a shade staring out at her from the dark. Annise flipped Night Mode back on. Jem's eyes were eerie white orbs.

More eyes opened behind Jem.

Blinking, staring. Eyes above her, behind her, white-hot, emitting waves of smoky radiation. Terrible and unnatural, emerging from veins of shadow that flowed and pulsed in heartbeat rhythm. Eyes leering through the broken grey clouds of a carnivorous, yawning sky and perched along the skeletal arms of diseased tree branches.

Stark-white hands emerged, wrapping long fingers along Jem's shoulders and neck, like lovers embracing her from behind. Annise tried to warn her, tried to say something like *run*, but found that her voice had abandoned them both.

Where Jem had been, only swirling darkness remained.

Drip. Drip. Drip.

She looked up from the viewfinder. Above her floated Ulrich and Stu, their limp bodies bobbing in the air. Smiles spread along their slack faces. Grotesque affectations. Puppets on strings, made to make merry for grim humor.

Bats, screeching and moaning with human voices, erupted in a burst of wings and teeth and fur, the smell of damp caves and graveyard moss, of moldering tombs opened on the Day of Judgment.

Annise ran.

She tried to cry out for Jem, but all that came out was a choked moan, quickly swallowed by the crashing of branches and leaves throughout the forest—and the crying out of voices in baleful pursuit. Cries of *want*. Jem's screams of terror. The lustful moaning of imminent evil.

She kept the camera in front of her, hoping the slim view of the world through the flip-out viewfinder would be enough to keep her from tripping over a log or tumbling into a pit. A rush of red overtook the world, casting trees and earth alike in a crimson pallor. A pair of lustrous, gleaming eyes appeared in the dark sky, watching her flight with wicked amusement. Streaks of blood forked across sclera like lightning.

Annise offered a scream, topping her best performance of the production. It only served to draw those terrible eyes closer. They descended through the trees, unbothered by clawing branches. The voices on the air changed their tenor from desperate hunger to anticipatory rapture, their hymn one of worshipers whose petitions had been heard and acknowledged by their dark god.

The camera's digital sensor captured errant scraps of forest, of red light, of sky occupied by those terrible eyes. Its microphone recorded Annise's desperate, ragged breathing and the squeaking moans she managed between pained breaths. It caught the other voices, too, crying out in mockeries of fear and predatory lust.

She pushed through a painful, scratching wall of thin branches and sharp thorns. The trees beyond clustered around a shallow oval clearing, above which was a stretch of open sky. She pointed the camera behind her, hoping to capture a glimpse of the impossible horrors in pursuit. Red illumination passed over the trees, phantom slivers of light, before the forest fell into black darkness. The voices simmered back into silence, and she was left alone with her terror.

She panned the camera back and forth, sure that those terrible eyes would reemerge, carried toward her on the winds of Hell. She swung the camera around, across the clearing, the images captured heaving with each of her desperate breaths.

White hands rose up, followed by arms, then emaciated heads, by ruined bodies, and limp hanging legs. The corpses rose high, marionettes ascending, floating up from the tall grass of the clearing. Faces familiar, known to her, becoming recognizable as they closed the distance, frozen masks captured by an open lens, seen through a small screen by her own wide eyes, scraps of light and data rearranged into visions of terror by microchip and fear-charged brain tissue and neuro-chemical signals. The cast and crew reached for her, Stu and Ulrich and the boom girl and the others, too, bodies draped with wires and their clothes covered in leaves and dirt and fresh wounds, as if recently exhumed from shallow graves by ravenous ghouls. Hands emerged from the dark, falling on her shoulders, sliding down across her chest, securing her in a firm and familiar embrace.

Jem.

Annise was with the dead in the air.

The camera fell to the ground, its view of the sky blotted out by the flapping of countless wings, all hair and taut skin and a heaving, glowing red light emitted from great eyes. Those terrible, wicked eyes, occluding the sky, the trees, and the final moments of Annise's strange and ultimately disappointing life.

PRE-PRODUCTION

1

The world hummed with an undercurrent of pain. Hateful sunlight pressed through the closed blinds over the kitchen sink, seeding a migraine deep within Alan Kneale's throbbing head. A formation of empty tall-boy beer cans stood impassive on the kitchen table, silent totems to his lack of self-control. The air was humid and heavy with the unpleasant smell of wet grain and half-finished cigarettes. He didn't remember buying smokes.

Lukewarm tap water was acid in his throat. He needed to hydrate, to get something in his stomach, or he would end up spending the better part of the morning dry heaving over urine-spattered porcelain. A half pint of freezer-burned ice cream went down okay, soothing his stomach. He never wanted to see the sun again.

Retreating from the kitchen to the dark of the living room, Kneale found his cell phone on the end table near the sagging couch. The screen held a VOICEMAIL notification icon. New number, familiar area code. One part of him wanted to cocoon up, to let the pain of the hangover wash over him like the briny waves of the deep sea and to insulate himself from the cares of the world with bad movies and worse TV. He wanted to eat junk food and drink children's electrolyte formula until the poison released its nauseating grip. And then, just as the pain started to recede, he would crack another beer.

But another part of him knew that the voicemail was important. That the man who left it liked to move quickly. That there was always someone else who was just as desperate as he was—but with bags packed, boots clean. Hangover-free.

He collapsed into the sofa facing the dust-covered TV and thumbed at his phone. He didn't bother to listen to the voicemail. He knew who it was. Nobody else called him these days, save for telemarketers and political fundraisers, hoping to separate him from his ever-diminishing funds.

Rob picked up on the first ring.

"Hey, Kneale," he said, papers shuffling, voices nearby, muffled and indistinct. "Not every day I get to speak with the dead. How ya been?"

Kneale took a moment to respond, his throat dry, the words rattling out like a cough.

"Fine, good," he said, the lies about his well-being coming easier as the years rolled on. He glanced around the room, as if searching for some symbol of his personal growth or accomplishments to latch onto for the sake of conversation. He found only dust and regret, illuminated by thin slips of caustic light snaking in through closed blinds. "You got something for me?"

"Yeah, I'm glad you called me back." The clack of keyboard keys like teeth poured from an open palm. "Got something for *you*, specifically. This is a big one. You busy? Like, through-the-end-of-the-year busy?"

No, he definitely wasn't.

"Depends on the gig," Kneale lied. "If it pays well, I could clear my schedule."

"You do that," Rob said. "The producer says there's more work to come if this pans out."

"Producer."

"As in, 'movie producer.' Making the pictures. *Le cinema.* Gonna slap your handsome face on movie posters to get people back to the theaters. You tracking?"

Not really, no. "Yeah."

"Client is an outfit called New Camlough Studios," Rob said, not missing a beat. "Film production and distribution company. Headquartered in Rochester, but they have a couple of satellite offices scattered across the US and Canada, and a small holding in Northern Ireland."

"Never heard of them."

"You keep up with the Hollywood trades, do ya?" Rob asked. One of his many personal foibles and failings: he liked to know things you didn't. Made him good at his job, maybe, made him an asshole sometimes, definitely. "Don't worry, I did a little digging. I wouldn't want to send in my best operator blind."

Kneale closed his eyes and pinched the bridge of his nose, willing the headache away. *Pain is weakness leaving the body.* Something one of his drill sergeants used to say. Well, there was an awful lot of weakness on its way out of his body this morning.

"Their business license in New York State goes back about ten years. A spinoff/startup from a couple of former talent agency folks. Managers and agents who liked horror movies and wanted to produce their own, something like that. Low to mid-budget. Spend a few bucks on monster masks and fake blood, make enough to fund the next one. It's not superhero money, but it's a niche, and there's an audience for it. Their first major move was to buy up the intellectual property and distribution rights of old Gothic horror movies made in Europe, way back in the seventies. Bought the entire Camlough Studios—the *original* Camlough Studios—catalog, trademark, original negatives, the whole deal, from a degenerate Euro-freak aristocrat who had debts with some NATO-connected Operation Gladio gangster types. Looks like they're developing new horror films based on name recognition of that old stuff."

"I'm not really into horror movies," Kneale said. "What's this got to do with me?" His forehead went hot. Sweat beaded on pallid skin. So, it was going to be one of *those* hangovers. The ones that got worse as the day went on, no matter what he did. Maybe he could call up his EMT buddy and get a saline drip to take the edge off. Otherwise, he was going to be the living dead until seven, eight o'clock at night. Maybe longer. He was getting old. Maybe he should just start drinking immediately.

The line went quiet. The sharp metal-on-metal *tink* of a Zippo lighter followed by the crumpling paper sound of a newly lit, hand-rolled cigarette held too close to the receiver.

"You're not really into horror movies," Rob said as he exhaled fresh smoke. Kneale recognized the tone: patience wearing thin. "It's not like you need the work, right? I guess you could finally use your GI Bill, get a college degree. I think you need a master's to get an entry-level job at Target these days. Maybe you could sell coffee to wine moms."

Kneale scrunched his face up in frustration at himself. Years of disappointment weighed down on him. Somewhere along the way, his default operating mode had become *shithead*.

"Look, I'm trying to help you, man," Rob said, "because you need a rebound, and because I think you'd be good for this one. The production's someplace in upstate New York. Finger Lakes region. Three-, four-hour drive from your place. You'll be roughing it in the woods, babysitting some rich-kid film weirdos. You'll be one-hundred percent in charge of security. Full authority and autonomy. They just need someone to run point on-site, keep lost hikers from wandering on set and walking off with the cameras, that type of thing."

Kneale reached over the side of the sofa and fished for a notepad and pen from the end table. Brushing off cigarette ashes from the water-damaged paper, he jotted down notes.

"Okay," he said, focusing. "Sensitive item protection and site access control."

"Right. Lots of expensive A/V equipment they don't want disappearing, yeah. Shouldn't be much of an issue, considering they're in the middle of nowhere. An old castle in some state forest. But the studio wants to protect their investment, and the producer requested someone with a specific set of qualifications. Someone with experience, but who's flexible, organized, smart, willing to keep their mouth shut. They're trying to keep word of this production under wraps."

"Isn't that the opposite of how movie marketing works?" Kneale asked.

"So you're an expert now?" Rob said. More shuffling papers, a long drag on the cigarette. "The producer took a look at your résumé and gave the approval. I can't make this any easier. Take the job."

"I appreciate that," Kneale said. "But I haven't updated my file since Colorado. It's a little out of date." There was a long pause on the other end.

"I vouched for the gap in experience. You survived Colorado. You got to keep moving forward."

"I wouldn't call it surviving." Kneale closed his eyes, willing his boiling migraine to a low simmer.

"Whatever happened on that ranch wasn't your fault," Rob said. "I don't hold it against you. No one should. It's not like Malthus Aerospace was anxious to advertise that fuckup. Word around the campfire is *nil*. No rumors, no jokes, nothing. Nobody is talking about it. At all. It's just like none of it ever happened. And most of the operators involved aren't coming around the shop anymore."

"You shouldn't say the company name over the phone," Kneale said.

"Right, sorry," Rob said. "I don't know the details and I'm not asking. And neither is this producer. As far as she's concerned, you did your time with the Army and have been working security with private firms ever since. You still rate classified, and nobody from the Department of Defense or the company has come sniffing around trying to suss out what went down with the Observer/Experiencer program. You're reliable and you keep your mouth shut, which is what she's looking for."

Kneale's memory dredged up images of the mountains, dark and distant. Of headlights spilling over dirt roads. Of endless nights spent in the cab of an SUV, overlooking vast swaths of darkness. Of moments of stark terror puncturing the veneer of hard reality that he knew now to be a lie. Lights everywhere, and voices coming through the phones, the radios. Voices and metal in the sky.

He pushed those thoughts away.

"What's the cast and crew size?" he asked. "How many film students will I be babysitting?"

"Two, three dozen, max, will be on-site at any given time. It's a closed set, mostly. Compartmentalized production, like spook work. *Need to know*. It was implied that if the state film commission got a whiff of it, there might be some complications."

"I'm not managing security for some prick's snuff film."

"No, it's nothing like that," Rob said. "I checked. The devil worshippers at Langley are into that sort of thing, but I'm out of that network now. This is a horror movie, straight and simple. A vampire picture, I think. Maybe some boobs or bush or a dong or two, but nothing explicitly pornographic. All the blood's gonna be fake, all sex simulated."

"What else can you tell me?"

"I've got some photographs of the area, a rough map of the castle grounds they're shooting in," Rob said. "They have some security concerns about the integrity of the site."

"What's that mean? Squatters? Bears stealing picnic baskets?"

"Something like that," Rob said. "Okay, I've got it here. They're shooting in a state preserve, away from the normal recreational areas. Lotta untouched acreage in pockets out there. She cited poachers, vagrants, lost city-idiots, Phish fans wandering around on acid. Weird Burned Over District stuff."

"What?"

"You can do some of your own research. That's what you get paid to do. Evaluate, internalize, act."

"Right." Kneale scribbled down BURNED OVER DISTRICT. "Problem. I don't have my pistol permit for New York."

"Not a problem. Take an online course, which we set up, and New Camlough will reimburse all the fees and expedite the paperwork. Weaponry and materiel will be provided on-site. You can set up a range somewhere in the woods to get your zero."

"They're supplying the firearms? This sounds formal."

"Your end of the work is on-the-books, such as it is. And you passed muster. Wasn't much to vet. You've kept off social media, which helps, and your criminal record is clean."

"How'd they know that?"

"Private detective, probably. Letting me know that *they* know that *I* know. Their checks cleared, so we're good to hook. This is your chance to get back in the saddle. Lotta my regulars are tied up in this patriot-militia movement thing, or headed to Eastern Europe. Cold War's back, baby. Desert warriors like us need to adapt to the times."

Kneale's mind was already working on the logistics: going through his gear in the basement, getting the house cleaned up, his mail held. He'd have to put on his running shoes and start working out again, too.

No drinking for a couple of weeks.

"Everything's my call?"

"They don't go wandering off in the tree line to smoke weed without your OK. The prop master doesn't bring weapons or firearms on-set without you knowing about it. You keep the cast and crew safe, keep their equipment from getting stolen, and they'll defer to you."

"Do I need to bring a tent?"

"You get your own trailer, which doubles as weapons storage. You'll be there from pre-production scouting, filming, to post. Two to three months, maybe."

"What's 'post'?"

"Editing, sound mixing, color correction, special effects. It's cool stuff. I'm kind of jealous. It's a little weird they're doing it on-site, but hey."

"Lot of responsibility," Kneale said.

"Good opportunity to be useful again, Alan. To be an asset to someone."

"Haven't been useful in a while."

"Yeah," Rob said. "You'll need to scout out some locations with the crew and get the lay of the land. You need equipment or manpower, you go through the producer. I'm headhunter only, so logistics are through her for anything you need. I get a bonus if you don't step on your dick and if they rehire you for future productions. Renee Balcombe is the contact. Fiery redhead, take-no-shit kind of gal. Don't fuck with her, she won't fuck with you. I like her."

"I bet you do. Text me her number."

"I mailed the contract and contact info this morning. You should get it in a day or two."

"How'd you know I'd accept?"

"Call it a psychic premonition," Rob said. "You're to be boots-on-the-ground in two weeks. That should be enough time to dry yourself out, maybe do a few push-ups, yeah?"

Kneale looked down at his gut spilling out over his waist.

"A few laps around the block, maybe," Kneale said.

"Do good out there. Earn a follow-up job. Life's not over just because the war's finished. There's always something else out there for old soldiers willing to do the work."

"Right."

"Oh, there is one more stipulation. You can't fuck any of the on-screen talent."

"What?"

"If it's in front of the camera, don't stick your dick in it. Easy, right?"

"I'm a little past being a threat to any pretty young actresses," Kneale said.

"It's not *them* I'm worried about. Don't let any of those sultry vampires get their fangs into you, okay? You're too old to go falling in love with some Barbara Steele understudy."

"Who?"

"Give me a shout once you've signed and mailed the contract," Rob said. "Needs to be returned via certified mail. You should get directions shortly after I send the paperwork up the chain. Balcombe wants to move fast, so get your shit together. Buy a new toothbrush, wash your ass, clean your boots, get a neighbor to water your plants."

"Hey. Rob." Kneale paused, trying to find the right words. He settled for, "Thanks."

"Thank me when the movie's wrapped," Rob said. "I'm just glad I can—I can't ever *really* repay you, you know? But I'm glad I can help you out if you're in a tough spot."

"I'm in a tough spot."

"Most of us are," Rob said. "Those of us who're left, anyway."

Half-formed words fluttered in his mind: platitudes, clichés, things that had gone unsaid for so long that they weren't worth saying now. The line went dead, saving him the trouble.

He set the phone down and leaned forward, rubbing his temples. He had some time, but there was a lot of work to do. He would start by dumping out whatever beer was left in his fridge, which was already beginning to call his name. His throat tightened. His head pounded.

Exercise could wait one more day.

2

Kneale's cell phone alarm offered a series of shrill chirps, rudely snapping him back into the waking world. The grey-black cloud of long-term depression that usually dogged the edges of his thoughts in the early morning was noticeably absent. Instead of languishing under the covers and staring at his phone for thirty minutes, Kneale got up quickly. He had something to work toward.

The sun rose over the distant, low eastern hills. Lake Erie glimmered to the north, the water rising to meet the sky with a kiss of light. The late summer air was cold but refreshing. Several blocks into the run, Kneale's lungs burned and his leg muscles tightened up in protest. The pain was an old friend dropping by to land a few good-natured insults. He pushed through.

When he had gone five blocks, he doubled back. Smoke rose from the industrial side of town. A fire engine wailed its lonely song several streets over. The waters of Presque Isle Bay shone bright. He cursed himself for not doing this more often. How much better would he feel if he had just pushed himself to do a little PT from time to time?

How long have I been in this hole?

After the run, he descended into the basement, legs and lungs still hot, to push boxes and bags of old gear away from his workout bench and free weights. His arms welcomed the work. He remembered what it felt like to be alive.

Kneale pulled the olive drab and digital camo pattern duffle bags up from the basement and dropped them onto the kitchen floor. He slid the table back against the far side of the room to clear out space. The gear tumbled out of each bag with the familiar smell of sun-baked plastic and old, dry dirt. Small granules of sand fell to the floor.

He inventoried the canteens, the compass, the sleep system components, his cold- and wet-weather outer layer pants and jackets. He chose two pairs of tan combat boots with tread remaining. His silver multitool was a familiar, cold weight in his palm. The knives needed sharpening and the mechanisms needed some oil, but it would serve again.

He examined ballistic sunglasses and threw out the pairs with scratched lenses, saving only one. His scrawl filled up a green government-issue logbook with notations for items he'd need to grab. New gloves, cold-weather socks, a pillow. Chem lights, road flares, a couple kinds of rope. His favorite assault pack was faded from years in the sun and needed a wash, but otherwise it was in good shape.

The contract arrived. The manila envelope inside the shipping sleeve was slim, with only a dozen pages or so to review. Bright yellow highlighter marked the places where he should initial or sign.

A handwritten letter accompanied the packet, its elegant scrawl set under New Camlough Studios letterhead. The logo paired with the name of the studio was little more than a scrawled sigil: a coffin in perspective, its lid beginning to creak open, with a bat in profile hovering above.

> Dear Mr. Kneale,
>
> You come recommended by Robert Sangster, who assures me that you have the skills and experience necessary to provide security and protection for our cast, crew, and equipment during the production of our new film, *Hierarchies of Blood*.
>
> We need someone proactive, someone not afraid to take the initiative, to work long hours and troubleshoot issues as they may arise. We need someone reliable who is not prone to drinking or absences from work. The production schedule is unbelievably tight, especially considering our budget. Rest assured, this is a professional endeavor in all the ways that matter, and we are offering you this position because your record is one of professionalism and the utmost discretion on behalf of your clients.
>
> Upon acceptance of this offer, you are to arrive at our production location no later than September 25. I am including my cell phone number and email address with these materials, but there is little to no coverage on-site. We will be "in the field" for the duration, so please pack accordingly.

As head of security, you will have a small, dedicated trailer in which to store your personal items, sleep, shower, maintain a weapons locker, and conduct your planning, but we will be fairly deep in the woods. The production will provide food and hot water, but we will be otherwise roughing it. That should not be an issue for a man like you.

You will be leading a team of two: Carmen Alvira, formerly of Third Marines, and Josiah Pore, a squad designated marksman out of the 82nd Airborne Division. They are new to employment with New Camlough Studios, but we have screened and evaluated them thoroughly. Their continued service to our studio is at your discretion.

Directions from Erie are enclosed with this contract. Do not rely on a GPS or an app, because you will get lost. Follow my instructions exactly. I am told that soldiers are good at land navigation, so I expect you will manage. I would suggest that you top off your fuel tank before heading into the preserve. Bring food and water in your vehicle, too, just in case. This deep in the woods, people tend to get lost. The night comes on quickly.

Please sign and date the enclosed packet and place it within the provided shipping envelope, which can be dropped off at any FedShip facility or drop-off box. Failure to sign and postmark this contract within a week's time as of the date of this letter means we will move on to other candidates. Please notify Mr. Sangster when you have mailed the contract.

Do not follow any lights into the woods. Do not head into the tree line at any point during this production. Not after dark. You have less time than you think, and you will not find what you are looking for.

Renee Balcombe
Producer
New Camlough Studios

3

Kneale finished locking up the house before the sun rose. He tossed his last duffle bag into the back seat of his SUV, then secured the rear hatch. The air was cold. An early autumn cold front moved in from the west. Inside the cab, the air was even colder, his breath visible and fogging up the windshield.

As he turned the key, the engine hummed to life. Headlights splashed across the garage door and house. Kneale had a sudden sense that he would never see this place again. The old house in the dark and quiet neighborhood did not hold any sweet memories of friends or family. It had merely been a place, one where he drank himself to sleep in the wasted years since he fled from the terrors of the Observer/Experiencer program. If he never came back here—as irrational as that thought seemed—he would simply start over again somewhere else. He had done it before.

His route took him by Allegheny State Park and the ancient mountains of lower Western New York. Clusters of trees already showed spots of color emerging from the dark green hills that rolled like waves against the sky. As he approached Olean, he passed a billboard featuring a slightly overweight man wearing a cowboy hat, dark aviator sunglasses, and a camo fatigue jacket. A cigarette dangled from his lips and a shotgun perched on his wide shoulder, pointing up to a bold, red-emblazoned caption in a spooky Halloween-style typeface:

RE-ELECT CECIL KOTTO
CATTARAUGUS COUNTY SHERIFF

Kneale thought he saw a wreath of white garlic strung around the sheriff's neck. Soon the billboard was behind him, and his mind tried to convince him that what he saw simply could not be.

Flipping through the radio stations, he searched for music or human voices to break up the susurrus of tires on the highway. Some of the presets out of Erie still worked, but the dark, forested hills increasingly played havoc with the signal. A rock station out of Buffalo became garbled. Voices discussing the latest woes of the Buffalo Bills suddenly dropped out, as if they were caught talking in church. There were pop-country stations and apocalyptic evangelical religious programming aplenty, but he didn't need that kind of brain damage this early in the trip.

He kept the scan function hopping frequencies, stopping it when he heard faint, high-note piano progressions and something like bells in the static. A girl spoke, softly, persistently, her voice and intonation flat while the music meandered behind her in a simple, repeated progression. She spoke alphanumeric sequences on a flat, repeating loop, punctuated by the sharp high notes of a church organ. Something within him cried out in worried familiarity—something bubbling out of his memories of Colorado. The phrase *military and intelligence applications* floated through his mind.

He slapped the power button on the radio console. The girl's droning ceased, her ghost sealed behind a veil of silence.

On the far side of Canandaigua, Kneale stopped for a turkey sandwich and a Utica Club beer, breaking his dry spell to indulge in the local flavor and to reset his brain from the monotony of the road. After his quick lunch, he headed to the closest gas station. The lot was empty save for his vehicle and the decades-old pumps and overhang, no credit card reader in sight. The old world held on in the cracks and crevices of the new.

Inside, an old man in a plaid shirt stood bent over the counter, looking down through thick glasses at a copy of the *Finger Lakes Times*. Wiry, strong arms pushed him upright as Kneale walked in. The old face creased tenfold as he offered a polite smile.

Kneale held up his credit card.

"Can you run this? Gonna fill her up on two."

The man nodded and accepted the card, turning to the counter behind him to slide it into a reader.

"Where ya heading?" the man asked.

"Nature preserve, down the road a bit," Kneale said, looking around, eyes sliding right over the various sugary and salty snacks on display. He considered stocking up on energy drinks for late nights of work, but they had been playing hell with his stomach as of late. Heartburn was worse than ever. He was many years removed from being able to down Rip-It energy drinks before a combat patrol.

"Anyplace specific?"

"Yeah, but it's my first time in the area," Kneale said, deferring. An old operational security habit. He did not think that his new employer wanted him advertising the fact that they were shooting a film at an abandoned castle. "Still trying to learn the lay of the land."

The man grunted in neutral response, then turned around

with the reader and card in hand. He slipped a receipt out and set it before Kneale alongside a chewed-over pen.

"What're you folks doing up this way?"

Kneale pocketed his card and then paused, mid-signature.

"Folks?"

"Assuming you're meeting someone," the old man said. "Assuming you ain't going alone. Usually not a good idea, going alone."

"Why's that?"

The old man looked away, something catching his eye outside. The glint of sunlight on a passing tractor trailer cab. Shadows spawned by a cloud passing over the late-morning sun. His old arms wrapped around slim shoulders and he stood motionless. He had been in this place, standing that way, for an eternity.

"Camping and hiking alone, generally, isn't a smart move."

"Oh yeah?"

"Yeah. But you already knew that. Apologies, mister. Just a bored old man talking when silence would do. I spend a lot of hours here, forget not everyone is as open to talking to strangers as someone who spends most of his days doing just that."

Kneale slid the signed receipt and pen back to the cashier, one eyebrow raised. The old man pointed to a lapel pin on his shirt collar. Crossed red swords, set within a blue shield, a tab overhead reading in tiny letters: *MOUNTAIN*. Kneale knew guys who had been in the 10th Mountain Division who lamented garrison life in Watertown. Boring and cold that far up in northern New York.

"You got the look. It's either ex-con or ex-military."

"Maybe it's both." Kneale tried on a wicked smile for effect. It didn't stick.

"Well. Just keep an eye on each other up there. And on yourself."

"Sure thing." Kneale took a half-step back. He wanted to get back on the road, but something held him here. Words unspoken. A ritual yet to be completed.

"Were you aware that our National Park system has disproportionately high rates of missing persons?" the old man said as he handed over the customer receipt. "Individuals, small groups—even people staying to trails or designated camping areas—just up and vanish. Rangers and hikers end up finding their shoes and their clothes piled up neatly nearby. Cell phones pulled apart, radios stripped of their batteries. Don't make much sense, except to say that maybe they got a little lost." The old man pointed to his temple and spun his finger in a shallow circle. "But that doesn't seem like a satisfactory explanation to me. Sure, the whole country is going crazy, maybe has been since the first religious fanatics showed up and started killing Indians in the name of their warped version of God. But the mass psychosis of our present age is not sufficient an explanation as to the scale at which these disappearances occur, or why it happens to people who otherwise appear perfectly sane and healthy. Before they enter the forest, anyway." The old man looked back outside as a new-model SUV lumbered in off the road.

"Good thing I'm not going to a national park," Kneale said, again, trying it with a smile, as if he were in on the joke. He wasn't.

"No, you're likely going to a state forest," the old man said, swinging his gaze back over to Kneale, fixing him in place. "The official numbers of the missing and the dead in the national parks are woefully inadequate. Incomplete data sets due to federal under-staffing. Budget cuts and bureaucratic roadblocks can hide all sorts of errors and inadequacies for a nation in freefall. What do you think that would mean for a state-level system's statistics, especially considering they lack a federal ranger or forestry program? Or do you think they've decided that there is no problem, simply because they decided not to look for one?"

The door swung open on screeching hinges. A group of three college-aged kids, decked out in designer camping and hiking gear, stumbled into the station. One of them laughed with a high-pitched squeal at some joke that had hit its punchline just before they walked in. The crisp air rushed in with the burnt vegetation tang of fresh weed smoke. Kneale was at once disgusted with them—young men who could have been doing something productive with their lives, like he had—and jealous, as they represented a path of freedom that his own choices had closed off long ago. Mostly, however, he was thankful for the interruption. It broke whatever spell he had found himself under.

"Thanks for the gas," Kneale said, then took steps toward the door that was swinging shut. The stoned kids headed back toward the cooler.

"Maybe it's best you don't shine your flashlight at anything you see glimmering in the distance, or floating in the trees," the old man said. "Maybe you let all that alone."

"What?"

A *pop* and a fizzing sound from the back. The group shouted out expletives.

"Sorry, man, we'll pay for the beers we dropped, too," one of the kids said, looking at Kneale, as if this explanation were due to him. Kneale opened the door and stepped out, eager to be on his way.

4

Kneale headed east as the sun hid behind a curtain of grey clouds. Traffic thinned out. The trees grew tall and dark, occasionally broken up by inns for hikers and tourists visiting the Finger Lakes region. Old houses stood far off from the road, flanked by rusting pickups or hollowed-out cars. Faded signs for businesses long since closed advertised products and services for the dead. Soon even these relics were left behind and tall pine trees pressed in close to the road, thick and unrelenting.

The producer's directions to the castle were thorough, but Kneale missed the turn leading into the forest. He realized he had overshot it after reaching an intersection not mentioned in Renee's instructions several miles down the road. He found a lengthy driveway leading to an angular building that may have been an abandoned church hidden within a clutch of trees, then turned his vehicle around on a patch of muddy grass.

Kneale made the turn—or what he hoped was the turn—and left the relatively smooth grade of the road for a bumpy, dirt path not quite wide enough for two vehicles. There had been signs for trailheads and camping and fishing access for miles now, but none appeared here. He took it slow over the overgrown road, careful to avoid the deep ruts carved into old dirt and dried mud. It wouldn't do to puncture his oil pan—or worse.

As he drove deeper into the forest, the trees loomed close and heavy, obscuring every curve and switchback on the path ahead. Branches reached for him, tangling with one another, competing for space above the road until they sealed away the sky.

There was little in the way of landmarks to guide him, save the occasional fork in the trail or turn off to small clearings with stone fire pits or abandoned camping chairs and coolers nearby, moss and dirt and weeds throughout. Nature reclaimed and buried all, eventually.

Progress was slow. He considered each turn carefully, checking off Renee's instructions. But soon a sense of unease welled up within him. It was the same feeling he often got during long-range land navigation exercises. Writing down the directions and calculations back at the start of the course was one thing. Being several miles deep into a dark forest, alone and unsure, was another.

He had made one such turn when the feeling of *wrong direction* tickled the base of his skull, spreading down through his spine and turning his stomach cold. He braked and slipped the SUV into park, then killed the engine. He took a moment to look at the trail ahead of him through the windshield, then popped open the door and stepped outside.

The air was sharper now, and cold, trying to slip its fingers through his black jacket, his ears and face stinging with the sensation. The distant rushing of the highway was long gone, subsumed by the wind coming inland from Lake Ontario to crawl over old hills. Branches clattered together in applause, as if a curtain were about to rise on a stage play and he was its star. Trees moaned and cracked, holding firm against the rush of the world. Water flowed somewhere nearby.

Kneale walked a few steps forward and confirmed his suspicions. The path he was following was the wrong one, as it ended a few dozen meters ahead, coming to a stop just short of a great wall of bramble, countless thin branches coming together to form an impassable barrier. Scraps of plastic bags affixed to its thorns flapped in the wind. Beyond the obstacle was a great rock, tall and dark, a slick of moisture and heavy green moss hanging down its face. Something about the way the thin curtain of liquid lingered over those indents and scratches implied form and purpose, as if the rock were no mere hulk dredged up by the passing of ancient glaciers, but that it was an augur of great purpose, of ritual. Of worship.

A cairn.

A branch snapped, somewhere close behind him. Hairs on his neck went rigid, and the icy realization that he had not been paying attention to his surroundings compounded a sudden rush of fear. He turned, ready for anything, but found only his SUV on the trail behind him.

Something moved in his peripheral vision. A glimmer, a quick flash of light. A right-to-left movement of form and illumination, so fast that it could have been a hallucination, a phantasm of paranoia. But there were only the trees and the clouds, and the strange, great rock.

He had to keep moving.

5

The slim logging roads of the forest divided the trees into the walls of a labyrinth. Kneale carefully considered each turn and point of direction on Renee's instructions, trying to discern where he had gone wrong, not wanting to waste any more time. Daylight was already thinning out.

He got back on track when he noticed a half-hidden turn he had missed his first time through. The branching path was little more than a hiking trail, barely wide enough for his vehicle. He followed this road and the subsequent turns—all matching with Renee's directions—until a metal gate emerged from the undergrowth ahead. The crosshatch metal glinted in the shadows of the forest floor, catching the errant remains of sunlight.

A thin man in an olive-drab corded sweater emerged from behind a tall tree. His head was bald, the sides shaved, and his face was pockmarked with acne scars. His right hand drifted down to his right hip, where a pistol hung in its holster. Kneale pressed the brake, which gave up a slight squeal as the SUV rolled to a halt.

The man approached the descending driver's side window. Kneale held out a slip of paper and a laminated security access card.

"Kneale, Alan," he said, leading with his last name first, figuring this guy to be like him. Ex-military. Ex-*something*. "Miss Balcombe recruited me."

The man didn't respond. He spent some time studying the access card and paperwork.

"She's expecting me," Kneale said, fishing for a response.

"Yeah," the man said, voice flat. He handed the card and paper back to Kneale and made his way back toward the gate. Kneale perched his hands on the steering wheel, then pulled forward as the gate swung open. The guard shot him an exaggerated salute.

The castle presented itself slowly, carefully, in the same way a spider might unfurl its legs from a shadowy perch. The outer walls appeared first—ten to twelve feet high, white and grey stone crumbling and covered in moss. The trees pressed in close on all sides, an invading army kept at bay.

Ancient metal gates, tall and rusted bronze, parted to permit Kneale entry to the wide, central courtyard. Within the walls, the grounds were expansive. Group camping tents were set up around the southern and western edges of the courtyard near a handful of SUVs and pickups. Two full-sized metal shipping containers were on the backs of flatbed trucks in the center of the area, their back doors thrown open. Sparse crew carried equipment and storage boxes down rickety wooden stairs. Nearby, white pop-up tents with plastic sheet walls held equipment and computer monitors that blinked electronic light. A rental moving truck was directly ahead, its doors open to reveal decadent prop furniture, costume trunks, cases of bottled water, and gallon containers of corn syrup. A pair of camping trailers stood near the eastern wall.

Presiding over all of this was the great castle itself, covered in vines and blotchy patches of dark moss and stain. The stone forebuilding stood with its double doors open wide to permit the coming and going of cast and crew. The main keep rose up behind it, three or four stories tall, its rectangular body flanked by cylindrical towers terminating in cutaway squares of stone that would have provided excellent cover for archers. Old glass windows stared out from beneath the sloped, turreted roofs, some boarded over, others still intact and glowing with candlelight from within. Staircases and metal fence railings twisted around the castle's exterior; arches curved over doors, balconies stood tall and vacant. There was an impression of great space within and beyond. Even in its state of disrepair, the castle was one of the most impressive things Kneale had ever seen.

He parked clear of the looping road leading into and out of the courtyard and then killed the engine. No one greeted or challenged him as he walked toward the castle. To the east, a break in the wall revealed a stone archway and metal gate guarding rows of crooked headstones and a tall, gnarled oak whose leaves were at peak color. A cloistered graveyard, curiously full. Gargoyles leered and angels wept, both groups turning to watch him pass. Then he was beyond their sight, wall and parked vehicles obscuring that place of eternal peace amidst the present rush of vain human activity.

Moaning drew his attention. A pair of voices, rising and falling in pain and pleasure. He followed the sounds to the far side of the supply truck, discovering a pair of women in flowing, white nightgowns holding tight to a third figure, who lay helpless in their long arms, face slack and turned toward the grey sky.

The women sensed Kneale's presence and fell silent. They turned toward him, slowly, faces frozen in pale rictus grins. Blood smeared their cheeks and lips and dribbled down their chins. The one nearest to him smiled wickedly, the blood on her sharp features accented by her red hair and pale skin. Green eyes fixed him in place with a playful glint. The other woman was dark of complexion and hair, eyes shining and limitless, black hair cascading down her shoulders, strands held together in braids. Their nightgowns were low-cut and soaked through with blood, drawing his eye in, requiring a great force of will and professionalism to maintain eye contact.

The women let the body between them fall to the earth with a soft *plop*. They raised their hands toward Kneale, fingers stretching out like claws, their dresses flowing in a sudden breeze. Phantoms of desire, approaching in a dream.

"Come to us, love," the woman with dark hair and braids said, affecting a vaguely European accent. "We would embrace you, and give you our eternal kiss."

"Please, spend a moment with us, lover," the other said, her Irish lilt naturally lending itself to the siren song. "What a horrible night for a curse."

Kneale regained control of his senses and took a step back, heat flushing over his face and the rest of his body. There was something familiar and primal about their seductive advances.

That allure evaporated in a rush of laughter, the women leaning on one another like drunks sharing a good joke. When the body on the ground did not rise up to join in the fun, Kneale realized it was merely a dummy, dressed in nineteenth century-style formal wear, complete with a coat with tails and a white-breasted shirt. Its face was malformed plastic that gave the vague impression of features. Smeared red lipstick marked its neck.

The black-haired woman extended her hand to Kneale.

"Yvonne," she said, handshake firm and confident. "You new here, man?" Her continental affectation was gone, replaced instead by the lightly drawl-inflected Mid-Atlantic accent of a born and bred upstate New Yorker.

"Alan. Alan Kneale. Just arrived."

"What kind of surname is Kneale?" the other woman said, her Irish accent still present—more pronounced, in fact. Her face furrowed with suspicion. "Sounds *English*."

"You can call me Alan, if you'd prefer."

"I *would* prefer, Alan," she said, her displeasure gone in a fluttering, bright smile. She extended her hand and they shook. "My name is Andrea, and I won't hold your ancestry against you if you won't hold ours against us." She grabbed Yvonne—who let out a little squeal of surprise—and pulled her in close. "An Iroquois warrior woman and a free-spirited Irish lass are the Englishman's natural enemies," Andrea said. "Imagine our peoples arrayed together on a field of battle, marching toward your lines, ready to devour the ranks of your wholesome colonial soldiers. What tasty morsels those good boys would make!" They both smiled wide, parting their lips, revealing sharp vampire teeth, stained red.

"We shouldn't tease him so, darling," Yvonne said. She slipped back into her continental—French-taught English, maybe—accent. "He's much too dark a complexion to be a Briton, except, perhaps, by some poor circumstance of distant ancestry or an unfortunate cousin by marriage."

"Quite," Andrea said, playfully pushing Yvonne away. "Yes, yes, we all get along famously here, us creative types. Bram Stoker, born in Dublin, died in London, the world capital of *diversity* and imperial tolerance, and all that. Countess Blair Oscar Wilflame, author of *The Crypt of Blood* and lifelong revolutionary, who found common cause for Irish patriotism with sympathetic English society types. 'That the hand works for our glorious cause overrules its weight in blood,' or something like that. I do read, you know."

"It is 'storytelling that can unite peoples, even ancient enemies," Yvonne said, speaking to Kneale now, playing at translator for Andrea's rambling. "Here, on the land of my ancestors, our myriad cultures and traditions coalesce around a symbol so powerful, so terrifying, that grievances can be put aside in its service."

"In service of what?" Kneale asked, head feeling light. While part of him greatly enjoyed the attention of the actresses, part of him felt as if he were the butt of some private joke.

"A symbol that unites all cultures, all peoples in terror," Yvonne said, wiping a spot of fake blood from her lips and holding it out for his inspection. "The creature that stalks every lonely wood and abandoned house the world over. Death herself, made flesh, deadly and erotic. The dreaded *vampyr*."

The women's eyes were on him, as if expecting him to hit some mark, some line they had practiced together a dozen times. He was saved from his on-stage flub by another actor who emerged with a line of improv to move the scene forward.

"Do not let these two ghouls frighten you, my friend," the man said, his own accent strongly French-Canadian. A hand fell on Kneale's shoulder. Its owner stepped forward, as if to place himself between vampires and victim. He was a good foot taller than Kneale, with a middle-aged, handsome face and short-cropped brown hair with errant greys, not unlike his own. "These ones, they like to play with their food."

"We weren't going to eat him, Christopher," Andrea said, feigning a pout. "Not yet."

"We were just going to have a little *taste*," Yvonne said, giving a quick lick to her blood-stained finger.

Christopher put his back to the faux vampire-women and gave a polite bow by way of introduction. "*Je m'appelle* Christopher Belgravia," he said, standing back up to his full, regal height and extending his hand. "*Et toi?*"

"Kneale," he managed. "Alan." Christopher's eyes made a scattershot scan of him.

"You go by your last name by instinct, at least with me, and your stature and eyes tell me much about you. Where did you serve?"

"Afghanistan and Iraq," Kneale said. "You?"

"Afghanistan, several times. Shorter deployments in the Canadian Army than the American one, I understand. Where?"

"Logar and Paktika. Iraq before. Baghdad."

"Those are bad places, or were, depending on the year. So many years now, between the beginning and the end, and from the end until now."

"Too many," Kneale agreed, or thought he did. He was not sure he would ever get used to the casual melodrama of actors.

"I will spare you the details of my own deployments if you will spare me yours," Christopher said. "Suffice to say it was a mix of terror, boredom, and frustration in varying portions. But our military careers have ended, and yet somehow brought us together, *no?* Kindred spirits, arriving at this lovely patch of forest, with such lovely company." He gave a quick tilt of the head toward the young women, who were already growing bored waiting for the end of the exchange. "Although my primary role is of actor, like so many of us here, I have other responsibilities. You will be in charge of material security matters. I will be in charge of another angle of defense."

"I'm not sure I understand," Kneale said, not liking the sound of that. It wasn't like Rob to miss details like this. "All security matters are my responsibility."

Christopher offered a warm smile and held up an open hand.

"Of course, you need not worry about competition or disagreement," Christopher said. "We will make the rounds together. Later. Then you will see. I am a *consultant spécial*. My work will not interfere with yours. It will complement it."

"Then humor me."

"I am concerned with spiritual matters," Christopher said.

"I don't follow."

Christopher shrugged. Yvonne and Andrea made their way back over to one of the pop-up tents where the crew was busy setting up a small light and mirror set. Makeup station, maybe. Kneale would have to learn how this whole movie production thing worked, top to bottom.

"I need to speak with Ms. Balcombe," Kneale said. "Where can I find her?"

6

"No, to the *left*. *Your* left! Son of a bitch. I'm coming up there." The woman started up the ladder set against the crumbling stone wall, where a young production assistant struggled to reorient a spotlight.

"Kathleen, darling, have you seen Renee?" Christopher asked.

"No," the woman said, reaching the top of the wall. "But I'm going to have a word with her about these conditions. I asked for a very specific setup, and she gives me this." She gestured at the spotlight and the wall, as if that explained it. "How am'I supposed to work like this?" Her dark skin and bright eyes stood in contrast to the whitewashed stone wall. Her arms were toned and her white undershirt, poor defense against the fall cold, revealed her back and shoulders. Kneale gave an admiring look, wishing he'd had a few more weeks to get in better shape himself.

"Alan Kneale, this is our director of photography, Kathleen Collinson," Christopher said. "She's a riotous, violent drunk, but if you put a light bulb and camera lens in her hands, she can accomplish miracles. From flashlights and consumer-model DSLRs all the way up to professional rigs and 8K studio-quality cameras. We count ourselves lucky to have both her DP skills and her personal charms present on set."

"Nice to meet you," Kneale said, receiving only the subtlest of nods in acknowledgment. He leaned close to Christopher to whisper: "What's a director of photography?"

"Light and camera setup to capture the essence of the director's vision, or to correct it, as is the case."

"'Vision' is putting it strongly," Kathleen said. "This is my second picture with Mr. Primrose, and his *vision* is more focused on Andrea's and Yvonne's tits."

"I got it!" the production assistant on the wall said, just before a grind of metal and a spark heralded a hot, wide beam of light trained directly on Kneale and Christopher below. They covered their eyes.

"Great," Kathleen said. "Now turn it off."

The light disappeared with a heavy metallic *click*. Kneale blinked hard, the world returning to him from beneath burned-over slashes and blobs. When he could see again, Kathleen stood in front of him, hands on her hips.

"You're supposed to keep us safe?" she said. Kneale blinked harder.

"I'm mostly here to make sure the cameras don't walk off into the woods," he said.

"You stay out of my way with your army-man shit," Kathleen said, raising a finger to point at them. "Both of you. I can keep accountability of my gear. And I don't need some goddamn alpha-male drill sergeant ordering my crew around."

"It is the *production's* gear and crew, my friend," Christopher said.

"See how far the production gets without my help." Kathleen reached into her jeans pocket and produced a small flask. She took a quick sip, then offered it to Kneale.

"Not while I'm on duty."

"Then come find me when you're off-duty," she said. "I'm a better judge of character when I'm soused."

"I wouldn't mind a nip," Christopher said, accepting the silver flask.

"I think Renee's over yonder, arguing with our illustrious auteur," Kathleen said, nodding toward the castle. "Inside the manor. It's a goddamn labyrinth. Gonna be a nightmare to shoot in."

"That's why we hired you," Christopher said, returning the flask. "The best."

"You're goddamned right," Kathleen said, offering a flash of a smile.

"Let's find Renee," Christopher said.

"Nice to meet you, ma'am," Kneale said, following Christopher's lead.

They passed a pair of crew members carrying a black tough box between them, hand-rolled cigarettes dangling from their young faces, smoke curling up to disappear into the grey sky. Hand-rolled joints, Kneale realized, as the vegetable-skunk smell settled over him. Life in the movies was going to take some getting used to.

Renee stood at the entrance to the castle's forebuilding, her dark red hair put up into a ponytail. Her bright blue eyes were behind heavy glasses. She wore a red vest over a black turtleneck sweater and black exercise pants, an outfit that would not have been out of place in an Adirondack ski lodge. She held a large tablet in her hands, her forefinger tapping at an on-screen keyboard, face lit from below by the harsh light. A man shouted out to her from within the castle, his voice echoing off the stone walls and through the open, massive wooden door like the cries of a condemned spirit.

"Renee, if we may have a moment," Christopher said. "Mr. Alan Kneale, security contractor. As expected." The producer reluctantly pulled her eyes away from the document open on screen, then offered Kneale a professional smile as she extended her hand.

"Welcome, Mr. Kneale. How are you finding our Devil's Castle so far?" She tilted her head back toward the grim fortress.

"It's a good place to shoot a horror movie," Kneale said. "Not that I'm an expert."

"It would be, if we could figure out how to keep power running for more than ten minutes at a time." She gestured to a bundle of wires near her feet. "Try it again, Terence!" A muffled, angry shout was her only response. "Our director. I'll introduce you two at a more convenient time. How was your drive in?"

Kneale thought of the strange light and movement he thought he had seen in the woods earlier—and of the ominous warnings of the old man at the gas station.

"The drive was fine. I'm ready to get to work."

"Great." Renee pressed a button and the screen went dark. "Let's introduce you to the security team."

"I'd like to take them on a perimeter check and get a sense of the terrain." He pointed at the castle. "I want to see inside, too."

"It's a little crowded with the crew running lighting and power lines through its hallowed halls at the moment. As for your team, I can get a PA to watch the gate for a few hours. During the day, we just need someone up there to shoo away hikers and people coming through on ATVs, assuming anyone wanders this far down the trail, which rarely happens. At night, we can secure the gates to the castle grounds. I'd prefer to have you, personally, with the first unit on most nights. That's when the spooky stuff tends to happen."

"Spooky stuff?"

Renee offered a wicked smile.

"Why, these woods are haunted, Mr. Kneale. Haven't you noticed? You never know what's going to come crawling out after the sun goes down."

7

Renee led him back to the checkpoint on the road to the castle. The man from before now stood sentry with a second guard. They both wore a mishmash of current-generation military surplus gear. Both of them had rifles slung over their shoulders. The man turned to watch them approach with a half-smoked cigarette dangling from his thin lips. The other guard sized them up with wide, brown eyes. She was younger than her partner. Maybe she was someone who had joined up, had enough, and got out quickly, instead of lingering on for decades. One of the smart ones. Her eyes were no less weary.

"Carmen Alvira, Josiah Pore, this is Mr. Alan Kneale," Renee said when they reached the swinging gate. "Kneale will be in charge of security while we're on-site, from now through post-production. You report to him directly. You only come to me if you have a pay or admin issue. All security matters run through him."

Alvira offered her hand and Kneale took it, looking her in the eye. She returned the look, confident, professional.

"Good to meet you, Ms. Alvira."

He turned to Pore, who was already looking away, back down the road.

"Good to meet you, Mr. Pore."

The man responded by taking a quiet puff on a cigarette. Renee shuffled her feet. Alvira smirked.

"There a problem here?" Kneale asked, stepping forward.

Pore mumbled something.

"If that was a 'yes'—which I can't tell because you won't look me in the eye—I'll have you pack your gear and hit the road. I got an attitude from you when I arrived, which I assume you give to everyone and not just to me because I'm special. That shit stops now, or I'll boot you from this team and have Renee here hire somebody else. Lot of former soldiers are looking for work these days. I'm sure you'll land on your feet. Somewhere else."

"No, uh."

"We're professionals here, right?" Kneale said, his voice sliding into his non-commissioned officer cadence. *Always offer folks the opportunity to do the right thing.* "So, if we all act *professional*, we'll get along just fine."

"Whatever you say, man." Pore blew smoke out of the side of his mouth toward Kneale. Kneale stepped into him, arms outstretched, shoving him back. The cigarette flew from Pore's mouth and tumbled to the dirt.

"Hey!"

Kneale got a grip on Pore's collar, holding him upright as he was about to fall.

"Want to keep going?"

Pore put his hands on Kneale's wrists, but couldn't dislodge them. Kneale leaned forward, forcing the man to struggle to maintain his balance at an awkward angle.

"No, man," Pore said.

"Then cut the bullshit."

"I didn't do anything!"

"That's the problem," Kneale said. "Show me—and this nice producer lady who signs our checks—some respect."

"Come on, man," Pore said.

"What do you think, Alvira?" Kneale said. "You like working with this guy?"

"I think I might go take a smoke break elsewhere," she said.

"I need to know I can rely on you, and you on me," Kneale said to Pore. "Hey. *Hey.* Look at me. You're not a private at his first formation, and I'm not some twenty-two-year-old buck sergeant assigned to babysit you. If you don't take this seriously, I will send you packing. I need this job and my guess is, so do you. Do you need this job, Alvira?"

"Could use the paycheck, Mr. Kneale, not gonna lie," she said.

"Okay," Pore said. He stopped struggling and held up his hands. Kneale set him on his feet and released his grip on his jacket collar. "Sorry. It's just, like, this is a movie set, right? How serious do we gotta take it? This ain't the Army." Pore glanced at Renee. "No offense, ma'am."

"We need to count on each another to make sure this thing goes smoothly," Kneale said, voice softening. "If you're not willing to be a professional for a few months, then I suggest you find another line of work. I'm not the kind of leader who is in your face and riding your ass all day, unless you push me. I *am* the kind of leader who expects you to do your job, and not give me—or the cast and crew—any kinds of shit. You read me?"

"Yeah. Yes, sir."

"I was an NCO, not an officer. None of that 'sir' shit. 'Kneale' will do."

Alvira and Pore nodded.

"You got it, Kneale," Pore said.

Renee clapped her hands, a forced smile lighting up her face.

"Great!" she said. "You're all fast friends. I have to get back to the director. Let me know if you need anything." Renee stepped off, eager to be away from the confrontation.

"Alright then," Kneale said. "What's the situation here? I want professionalism from both of you, but I need honest assessments. Giving me bad news will not make me angry. Keeping important information from me, however, will. Alvira. Tell me something I likely don't know."

"We've been on-site a couple of days," Alvira said. "They've done some initial shooting of the forest and castle exteriors. Camera and lighting tests, I think. Principal photography starts tomorrow night, assuming they can unfuck the power situation."

"So I've seen. Okay. Pore, what have you seen? What concerns do you have?"

Pore spoke plainly, but kept his eyes wide and focused on Kneale, wary.

"They've had us at the gate, mostly, checking IDs and keeping a log of people coming in and out. Nothing special. Castle grounds are pretty big. Even with the wall, it's gonna be hard keeping all that secure with just the three of us. Someone could slip over the wall if they were determined. A short ladder or some rope is all it would take, really." He fished his fallen cigarette from the forest floor, returning the ember to life with a slow pull.

"You worked on a film set before?"

"Not with this production company, but yeah," Pore said. "Did security for big corporate superhero movies a couple of times. Mostly crowd control and foot-traffic management. Showed some extras how to hold a rifle. Nothing fancy."

"I did some location work for commercials in the city," Alvira said. "Different vibe here, for sure. They've got good equipment, but this is an indie production. Lot of young talent. Some money behind them, enough to get us out in the middle of the woods and keep us fed, but not much else."

"What did they tell you the security concerns were?" Kneale asked.

"Just that they're worried about squatters or people wandering in the woods, that type of thing," Pore said. "The rifles were a surprise."

"Speaking of," Kneale said, pointing at the weapon slung over Pore's shoulder. "Where can I get one of those?"

"The weapons locker is under double lock here," Alvira said, leading them up to one of the trailers set against the eastern wall, near the row of parked cars and trucks. "Renee gave me the key, but it's yours now."

A large, bronze-plated skeleton key, pockmarked with green rust, fell into Kneale's open palm. His wrapped his fingers around it, finding it pleasantly cool. The lock on the trailer door was custom-made: old, heavy, a slab of metal set into the otherwise flush plastic of the door. It could have been a movie prop. It was a perfect match for the ancient key.

The lock accepted the finger of bronze with a series of soft, metal-on-metal clicks. The key turned easily and the mechanism yielded the door. Kneale pulled it open and walked up the steps into the darkened trailer. Alvira and Pore followed close behind.

Alvira flipped the light switch, revealing the cramped interior: a kitchenette and small, square dining table to the right, the bathroom and bedroom to the left. She pointed toward that end of the trailer and Kneale went in, his footsteps creaking against the floorboards as if they had just stepped into a haunted house.

The weapons case was a large, hard-plastic tough box chained to the floor of the sleeping area.

"This'll be your pad," Alvira said, pointing to the bare mattress. "Fit for a king."

Pore poked his head into the narrow bathroom. "There's a shower in here. Think it works? Be nice to have some privacy instead of using the bathroom trailer with a couple dozen other people."

"What do you say, Six?" Alvira asked. "Showers for the troops always improve morale."

"I'll talk to Renee about water resupply," Kneale said, taking a knee to inspect the weapons case. The chains were fed through the handles and sawed-out sections of the floor. He pulled the chains and found they had little give. Where they crisscrossed, another archaic lock held them together, keeping the box secure. The key was a smooth fit once again, the mechanical releases giving way easily, well-maintained and oiled despite the mechanism's apparent age. With the lock released, he loosened the chains and lifted the heavy lid of the box.

Inside was hard plastic molding, custom-made for six rifles or guns. His rifle waited within, along with three twelve-gauge shotguns. Kneale ran his fingers over the black shotguns, a patina of light oil sticking to his fingers. He withdrew the rifle and popped the bolt back to inspect and clear the weapon. A compartment revealed dozens of fifteen-round magazines, boxes of shotgun shells and 5.56mm ammunition, and a brand-new carrying strap, still in the packaging.

"I'll need to inventory all of this," Kneale said. "Serial numbers for the weapons, ammo count, the whole deal. Don't draw anything from here without my permission. I'll set up a log."

"There's enough to keep a team in a firefight for a few minutes," Alvira said.

"Since we've got the extra ammo…" Kneale removed a pair of short magazines, the rectangles of thin, hollow metal in his hands welcome and familiar. "Either of you have anything else on the agenda today? Let's get one of those film students to watch the gate."

"I know a spot," Pore said, a genuine smile gracing his face for the first time since Kneale arrived.

8

The deep forest welcomed them with a kiss of cold air blown in from Lake Ontario, far to the north. A layer of fallen leaves marked their path away from the castle and its crumbling Gothic façades. The trail was flat for a time, but then rose by slow degrees until they were met by errant rock formations covered in glistening moisture. Branches sprouting in vibrant autumnal colors danced for them. Pore led them to a spot about fifty meters shy of a tangle of dead trees clutching heavy boulders, with a sheer face of grey and red-stained rock rising up into a wide hill.

"Left limit, that pile over there," Pore said, pointing northwest to a mess of brambles and dead vegetation. "Right limit, that old gal right there." He pointed to an eastern white pine, grown tall and proud.

"Not bad," Kneale said, catching his breath. Pore and Alvira could move fast and quiet in the woods. *Good.* He filed that away for later. "We should pop up that hill real quick, get a glance beyond."

"Nothing out here to worry about," Alvira said, face flushed red from the hike and the cold.

"We'll confirm that before the range goes hot," Kneale said. "Spend ten minutes to save a lifetime of regret."

Once atop the hill, the group followed the cliff's edge back toward the far side of their would-be firing range. Looking back, trees and the cut of the terrain hid the distant castle, but a pair of fingers of smoke rose high to signal its location.

They turned around and walked in the direction they would be shooting. Low pines grew out of black soil, bent toward the downward slope, which reached a flat expanse of old red spruce and yellow birch beyond. Hidden among them was a great slab of brown stone hovering above the soft earth, supported by pillars of crudely cut rock. The formation was overgrown with a bony net of brown vines and green nettles.

Pore whistled. They made their way down, pulled toward the stones by some irresistible attraction.

"That's weird, right?" Alvira said, eyes locked on the structure. She reached it first, laying a bare hand on the cold stone. She circled it, keeping her fingers sliding across the coarse, grey surface. "Looks like a stone cap, with supports set up, each one aligned to one of the cardinal directions."

"A dolmen," Kneale said, taking a step forward. He produced his compass—an Army-issue, olive-drab hunk of metal that some careless supply sergeant had let fall off the books. The needle danced as he walked around the formation. "You're right about the directions. How'd you know that?"

Alvira shrugged. "Felt right."

Kneale pocketed the compass and went down on his knees to peer beneath the lip of the stone cap, which floated a meter off the ground. The four grey and red support rocks were wide and heavy, glistening with clear bits of shining minerals.

"Did you know this was here?" Kneale asked.

Pore shook his head. "Hadn't bothered to climb up and go beyond the cliff before. This looks like an altar."

"Funny you should use that word," Kneale said, leaning forward to run his gloved hands along the edge of the stone cap. "No one's quite sure what dolmens were used for. Maybe they are altars. Burial chambers, territorial markers, shrines of spiritual importance, maybe, in places of great power. There aren't many in North America, and none in this neck of the woods. I didn't think there were, anyway."

"Who's to say it's not still in use, now?" Alvira said.

Kneale scanned the ground.

"I only see our boot prints. No garbage, no evidence of someone lighting a fire."

"How do you know what this is?" Pore asked. He turned toward the trees, eyes trained on the deep woods. His index finger tapped against the rifle's magazine receiver.

"My previous contract was for site security in a place I can't name, specifically," Kneale said, examining the stone. "One of the researchers was convinced there might be these rock formations—dolmens—where we'd set up shop. We were supposed to look for them. I never found any dolmens, but I did learn a little about them from a PowerPoint deck."

"This is something religious, then," Pore said. "For the Indians, maybe."

"A better word might be *occult*," Kneale said, the word burned into his memory. *Spooky-ass shit.* "I don't think the Iroquois built stuff like this. But it's possible."

"We could ask Yvonne about it," Alvira said.

"Maybe some neo-pagans with trust funds and lots of free time built it," Kneale said. "Or maybe it's part of this production, and we're supposed to find it, then spread the word about how this movie was shot on haunted ground. Let me ask you something. Has anyone been feeding you two bullshit about how the woods are haunted?"

"I've heard the crew talk about things they've seen in the woods, but I've also seen them smoking weed nonstop," Alvira said.

"The woods *are* haunted," Pore said. His rifle was in his hands now, and his attention remained on the trees. "Question is, by what."

"Where was it you said you were working?" Alvira asked Kneale. "What kind of security job has you looking for rocks that shouldn't exist?"

Kneale gave her a hard look. Maybe some word about Colorado had gotten out, after all. He had already said too much.

"We're running out of daylight," Pore said, finally turning from the woods to face them. "Let's get some rounds downrange, unless you're worried about shooting up the find of the century here."

"You alright, Josiah?" Alvira asked.

"Just getting cold standing here, is all. Let's shoot."

"Why are you holding your rifle?"

"No reason." He paused, waited. Relaxed a degree. "Saw something, I think. Maybe not."

"You saw something."

Pore hesitated.

"Like flashlight beams."

"Hikers with lights on? Reflective materials, headlamps?"

"No." Pore took a moment, then turned to Kneale. His eyes fell heavy on the dolmen, which had assumed a countenance of hard shadow. His voice became a whisper. "I thought I saw lights in the trees. Up high."

Kneale started to smile, sure Pore was putting them on, but the look of dead-seriousness on the man's face gave him pause. On his own journey through the woods, he had seen something, too.

A branch fell from a tree, smashing into the dirt and leaves. Somewhere close. Kneale and Alvira found their weapons in their hands, their eyes on the forest, their backs to the dolmen. Time passed in slow, steady drips. The wind was cold and impassive.

"There," Alvira said suddenly, pointing up. A popping sound, followed by the stale aroma of ozone flooding the area. Lights flickered above—small, shuddering pulses of blue, purple, and yellow. Distant fireworks, or the glimmering, mild hallucinations that heralded an oncoming migraine.

"That's what I seen," Pore hissed. "That's what I goddamn *seen*."

"I see it, too," Kneale said.

"They're too close to be flares or aircraft," Alvira said, discounting an explanation no one had suggested. The lights pulsed, slowly—half a dozen of them, descending through the canopy, then rushing back to the heights of the tallest trees, before drifting off to the north, deeper into the woods. Flying against the wind.

9

When the security team returned to the castle, the smell of gunpowder clung to their clothes. Alvira set up a folding table outside of Kneale's trailer while Pore grabbed some cleaning rags and oil. They cleaned their rifles as the sun set. They did not speak of the lights.

Christopher Belgravia and another man approached the group some time later, just as Alvira and Pore were reassembling their rifles.

"Mr. Kneale, do you have a moment?"

He nodded. "Sure thing. Alvira, you've got gate duty from 0900 to 1300; Pore, 1300 to 1700. I'm assuming I don't have to handhold you, right?" Pore and Alvira acknowledged his order and headed toward the cluster of tents set up on the west side of the courtyard.

When they were gone, Christopher pointed to his companion: a tall, heavy-set man dressed in a black, dirt-encrusted suit, as if he were just dug up from a graveyard.

"This is Daniel Taumata, who plays our master vampire in the film," Christopher said. "He would like to join us for this evening's security preparations."

Kneale stood up, slung his rifle, and shook the man's hand. Daniel offered him a toothy smile, the prosthetic vampire fangs still in place, which he popped off with a click of his tongue. An imposing figure, yes, but the eyes and smile were warm and welcoming.

"Good to meet you, sir," Daniel said. It took Kneale a moment to place the accent. Australian or New Zealander, maybe.

"Likewise, Mr. Taumata," Kneale said. "To be honest, I'm not sure I understand your role here, Chris, especially if you're not assigned to my team."

"All will become clear," Christopher said. "Daniel here wishes to become my understudy on these matters, so to speak."

"I thought you said he was playing the vampire."

"He is," Christopher said. "But he'd like to learn about the ways of *sorcellerie*. I may know a trick or two his Maori forebears neglected to pass down."

"Likely not," Daniel said. "But it's worth a few hours' time to find out."

"The prop truck holds my supplies," Christopher said. "Let us get to our work."

Christopher threw open the sliding door on the truck, revealing a wealth of boxes, bags, and supplies held within.

"What are the props for?" Kneale asked.

"They're not props, not in the sense of being used on-screen," Christopher said. "They will help us play our roles in a different type of drama."

"How many candles will we need?" Daniel asked.

"Bring a dozen," Christopher said. Daniel hefted a box up onto his shoulder, wax and paper rustling together. Christopher popped open a suitcase, releasing the aroma of earth and garlic, then snapped it shut. He slipped a long, white cylinder into the folds of his overcoat, then pointed to a brown bag of salt.

"You mind carrying that, Mr. Kneale?"

"Sure," Kneale said.

"Lift with your knees."

"Just like throwing on a rucksack."

After Christopher secured the truck's sliding door with a heavy lock, he led Kneale and Daniel across the courtyard to the main gate, held open by lengths of fraying rope. A flock of the production's young crew had gathered there, running wires and adjusting light stands. The men cut west, following a narrow footpath that wound around the wall in a loose perimeter. The trees loomed over them, clawing at the edges of the stone barricade.

At the southwest corner of the property a small clearing in the brush and trees held a number of flat, black rocks. The men clicked their headlamps on, deploying sharp beams of bright light to push back the encroaching dark. Christopher reached into his overcoat and produced the bone-white object he had taken from the truck: a length of thin, shaved tree branch that terminated in a wishbone fork. He placed his hands on the spokes and held the long part of the stick out before him. Kneale gave Daniel a puzzled look. The actor smiled back at him, his wide grin barely visible in the dark beneath the glow of his headlamp.

Christopher walked several paces ahead of them, then turned right, and right again, allowing the rod to lead him. When the wand dipped toward the center of the three black rocks, he halted.

"As I suspected," he said. "Here, please."

Daniel stepped forward and placed the box of candles on the ground.

"How many?"

"Three is a number of divine trinity, of the intrapersonal godhead," Christopher said. He returned the dowsing rod to his overcoat. "One candle for each rock. A synchronicity of essential symmetry."

Daniel produced three short, off-white candles. The smell of wax was familiar, calling to mind memories of the quiet peacefulness of a church in the early morning hours. He set one down on each rock. Christopher opened the suitcase and withdrew sets of rosary beads which he carefully arranged around each candle. The crucifixes faced upright so that each silver-plated Christ could face the heavens to cry out for the Father who had forsaken him in those dark, limitless moments during which all the sin and death of the world became his countenance. Christopher made the sign of the cross, then pointed to the candles. Daniel bent over to light them with long matches. Tips sparked and wicks burned to release a pleasing aroma.

Christopher whispered something in French, then made a slashing motion with his left hand from his left shoulder down to his right hip, then repeated the gesture from right to left, his hand remaining a flat blade. His lips moved and his eyes vibrated beneath closed lids until Kneale felt he was expected to say something, to complete some step in the ritual that he had yet to learn. Once more he felt as if he were an actor who had forgotten his lines. The bag of salt weighed heavy on his right shoulder. He considered lowering it to the ground when Christopher's eyes opened and he offered a disarming smile befitting a charismatic actor.

"We do this at three of the four corners of the castle walls," he said. "Each night, at sunset, we light candles." He approached Kneale and produced a thin, silver knife that flashed in the candlelight. He sliced open a tiny hole in the bag, which leaked a steady stream of salt.

"Let's go."

They walked on, rounding the corner and making their way north. Salt trailed out of the bag with each step Kneale took.

"You're using Christian symbols and prayers, but this looks more like witchcraft," Kneale said, shifting the bag to his other shoulder, salt spilling down.

"My practice does not discriminate," Christopher said, the

light from his headlamp dancing over the narrow trail before them. "If you need a specific taxonomy, just say I'm practicing French-Canadian *sorcellerie*. I dabble in a number of traditions. When I find a tool I like, I add it to my practice."

"You're not a Christian?" Kneale said, trying not to sound winded. The heavy bag on his shoulder put the truth to the lie that a couple of weeks of exercise were enough to get him back into fighting shape. "You don't believe in God? Is this something else?"

"This is something else, yes, but of course I believe in God." Christopher paused, halting their advance north. "We are all prisoners to God's mercy, to his conceptions of justice. We are bound to his tolerance of evil. Made victims by it. Made objects of wrath and grace and communion, sometimes in equal measure. What we understand as Christian practice in our present age is not reflective of its historic reality. Magic, clerical necromancy, and pagan superstition are key components of the common Christian experience. The orthodoxy-worshiping Calvinists and Prosperity Gospel heretics are the aberrations in Christendom—certainly not my folk magic."

The wind moved through the forest in a sudden rush. Tree branches rattled and reached for them.

"Sorry," Kneale said. "I didn't mean anything by it. This is new to me."

"I thought you'd be more put off by these occult shenanigans, to be honest, mate," Daniel said.

"This isn't the first…" Kneale trailed off. He remembered the wide, expansive view of an endless, terrible sky. He considered letting some details slip, to provide some cryptic answer. No. He could keep secrets. That had never been a problem for him, even if the people who demanded that secrecy had long ago moved on to other missions…or were long dead.

"Let's get moving."

Some time later, as the candles melted low and the flames grew tall and loathsome, a shadow moved through the air. It was heavy and long, a rectangular object constructed of old, marred wood. Dirt fell from its surface and thin metal chains hung loosely from its frame, clinking softly in the dark.

It rose and fell and moved from side to side, avoiding the trees and heavy branches in its path as it made its way unerringly toward the castle—more specifically, toward the points of light and heat and human musk that fouled these sacred woods.

This was an army of occupiers, quite unlike the small groups or individuals who ventured into the deep woods of the preserve in those endless and otherwise intolerable spring and summer months, those who made easy prey and whose disappearances did little to draw attention to the cloistered and secluded forest. No, these ones brought many loud machines, strange smells, and, worst of all, bright, terrifying lights that mimicked the damnable sun, overturning the shroud of night in favor of a synthetic and caustic forever-day.

The box floated up to the edge of the old castle's walls. It would take only a minor output of energy to lift the heavy casket over the barrier. Psychic fingers grasped through a flood of sensory inputs, encountering the first strains of repulsion. Augurs of power, formerly concealed by distance and the roiling energies of the ley lines abounding through and around the castle grounds, revealed themselves in a sudden, furious burst of sensation. The consciousness recoiled and the coffin with it, floating back a handful of feet. A pattern became suddenly apparent: three points of light spitting up like geysers, working together to form a wall of abominable energy that spun and whirled around the entirety of the grounds. Three points in holy configuration, representing the triune godhead and crucifixion and a dozen other holy and occult echoes now lost to humankind's atrophied racial memory, but remaining potent and powerful despite their ignorance.

The creature within seethed and clenched its teeth. Fangs drew pinpricks of black blood from chapped lips. Long, sickly fingers writhed, anxious to be wrapped around human throats. So. There were those among these swine who knew the arts. It stood to reason, then, that they understood the true and terrible import of the castle, its grounds, and the stones beyond. It also stood to reason that they might know or suspect that the vampire himself haunted these woods, that he would test their defenses. That he would come for them.

This thought produced a curious sensation in the creature's mind, one it had not felt in ages. It was not fear, not exactly, but its excitement at the possibility of feeding on so many people in so short a time was suddenly tempered by it.

Worry. Uncertainty. Hesitation.

The hunger remained. Anger grew. How *dare* they bring the art to his territory? How *dare* they lay siege to and cut off a piece of his haunting grounds?

As that fevered mind directed its coffin to slowly back away from the energies swirling around the castle, it began to think. To plan.

To prepare.

PRODUCTION

10

They returned to the castle grounds through a narrow gate on the northern wall. Its metal bars and fixtures were adorned with decorations that called to mind the frolicking of the festival, of figures emerging ghost-like from behind trees, of goat-legged satyrs playing flutes, of bright stars overhead, spilling out rays of delirious light. The detail committed to something so utilitarian as a gate in a place so remote inspired a strange longing in Kneale. In contrast, the products of his own age were disposable, mass-produced, of poor quality. Craftsmanship was for romantics and those who could afford the luxury of not having to rush to produce. This contempt for the times he lived in was rooted in a kind of holographic nostalgia for periods he had never experienced and only understood in shadowy, imperfect impressions. Perhaps the gate and the castle it guarded were dredging up latent memories of old Gothic horror movies, seen on TV when he was very young. That would explain this sudden and invasive sense of want, of melancholy. These were feelings—like so many others—that his life experiences had taught him to strangle.

After they passed inside, Christopher reset the gate's locks with a key, which he then handed to Kneale.

"Add this to your collection," Christopher said. "It's yours now, captain of the guard."

They walked through an overgrown garden. Vines and

branches stretched out from stone walls laden with flat, featureless faces. The air was heavy with a potent vegetable smell. Grass and weeds burst up through the old path. The great house was all stone and old, dark glass windows dancing with candlelight.

Christopher led them through the servants' entrance into the kitchen, where the inviting smell of cooked garlic and onions clung to the air. Piled pots and pans were evidence of someone at work, the modern cookware designs clashing with the interior's original stone and patchwork brick.

The dining room sat in darkness, the long table and its attendant chairs empty and cold, anxious for doomed guests to arrive. The air was cool and held a curious, mineral taste, like a basement on a hot summer day. Candelabras and chandeliers glimmered gold in the light of their candles' flames, cast about from the high walls. Tall portraits and wide landscapes adorned the walls, their stories lost to time, layers of paint covered in layers of dust.

They moved through a pair of rooms, doors laden with hand-carved tableaux of strange, winged creatures and naked women crowded around eldritch rocks in the forest. Kneale's sense of direction was challenged by the turns taken by their unerring guide. They emerged in the foyer, where footsteps and voices could be heard coming from deep inside the castle-labyrinth. Finally, they passed out through the main entryway back into the courtyard.

Christopher led them to the ramp of the prop truck to return their supplies. The arrival of night brought out the full cast and crew. Dark figures darted across the courtyard, carrying flashlights or wearing headlamps as they moved from trucks to trailers, to the great house and back to the main gate. Powerful lights clicked on, casting the harsh rays of a false sun. A woman shouted orders. Voices were raised in the cadence of a group working together on a timeline. Kneale closed his eyes and imagined himself back on an Army post, which never really slept.

When they returned their supplies to the truck, Christopher brushed his hands together.

"Daniel, would you take Mr. Kneale with you to makeup?" he asked. "I believe you're due in the chair imminently."

Daniel nodded and went down the ramp. Kneale made to follow.

"Before you go." Christopher held out a closed fist. "Keep this close."

Cold metal beads fell into Kneale's open palm. A rosary. Christ-in-miniature stared up at him with sorrowful eyes.

"Never been the religious type," Kneale said.

"You're adapting to the movie-making life," Christopher said. "Adapt to this."

Kneale slipped the rosary into one of his pants utility pockets, offered a nod in thanks, then followed Daniel to one of the nearby tents bustling with activity, lit from within by bright, warm lights.

"*The count has arrived*," Daniel said in a faux-Transylvanian accent, spreading his large arms wide. Two impatient-looking women from the makeup team went to work, removing his jacket and cleaning his face with a cloth. The producer, Renee, leaned against a three-pane mirror, the bright lights overhead occluding her features as she puffed on a roll that released sweet-smelling smoke.

"We are all set, madam," Daniel said. The makeup staff guided him into the chair set before the mirrors. "Christopher wants you to know that the castle grounds will remain unbothered by the spirits tonight."

"Thank you, master vampire," Renee said, stepping out of the way so the women could begin their transformation of Daniel. She took a hit and offered him the joint. He accepted with a wide grin. She made an offer to Kneale by widening her eyes and raising her eyebrows, but he shook his head. Daniel exhaled the smoke in a silent geyser and handed the spliff back. She took one last pull before opening the tent flap and flicking what remained into the dark.

"We haven't scared you away yet," she said. She crossed her arms and watched Daniel's transformation into a vampire, his skin going white, then grey, with etches of black and patches of light blue for contrast and highlight. The detail-heavy work fell to the woman with dark, golden-brown hair, her brown eyes wide and catching the light. She frowned in focus as she went to work on Daniel's lips with a detail brush. In the cannabis haze of the tent, his transition seemed less like the result of Hollywood craftsmanship and more like a phantom emerging from the gloom.

"Alan Kneale, meet Nike Monlaur," Renee said. "Head of our small but capable makeup department, and in charge of special makeup effects. She can give you a makeover, prepare your body for a wake, or create the best damn gore gags this side of a Troma film."

"Lloyd and I didn't end on good terms, so I'm free to say I'm the best on any side, period," Nike said, not once looking up from her work.

"Nike is from Colorado," Renee said. "Pueblo, was it?"

Nike nodded. "Born and raised, but my family was spread across most of the south-central and western parts of the state. Made a lot of DIY monster movies with my cousins and friends in the San Luis Valley. You spend much time in the Centennial State?"

"Just for a job," Kneale said, wanting to change the subject. "I'm impressed you can do this kind of work in the field—"

"Women understand blood better than men, of course," Nike said, cutting him short, which was fine by him. "Nice to meet you and all, Mr. Kneale, but I'd prefer if you would clear the tent so we can finish in time. If Daniel here hadn't been out playing ghostbuster with you and that Quebecois goblin, we wouldn't be under the gun. Or the stake, as it were."

"That's our cue," Renee said. "Good luck, dear."

"*Thank you*," Daniel and Nike said in unison. Renee led Kneale back out of the tent, then cut a straight line toward the main gate, where set lighting shined like a beacon in the dark.

Leaning against one of the gate's columns was a man in a black hoodie, also smoking a joint. The vapor was heavy and sweet, smelling not unlike the wild garden behind the castle. His black hair ran down to his shoulders, accented by small, grey streaks. The light from the joint's lit end reflected in his glasses. As they approached, he stood up straight and blew a jet of smoke away from them.

"Kneale, meet our auteur, Terence Primrose, director of no fewer than five direct-to-streaming horror films."

Terence smiled as they shook hands.

"The soldier, right? Heading up security. Welcome." He offered the joint to Kneale, who shook his head.

"Not while I'm on duty." This was growing wearisome, but Kneale kept his voice neutral. Renee took the offered joint instead, allowing herself a pair of quick pulls.

"This is a little bit different than what you're used to?" Terence asked, his accent Irish, his voice a smoker's. "I appreciate a professional, but this," he paused to take the joint back, "is part of being a professional, here."

"Terence finds being a horror film director intolerable," Renee said in a frog voice, blowing smoke from her nose.

"Quite the opposite, dear," he said. "I've worked in the public service, the restaurant industry, in education, in retail. Even been on the dole once or twice. This line of work allows me, in short, furtive moments, to express myself, to foster human connection through the performance of drama. And to smoke cannabis cigarettes with my handler. You'll have to join me sometime when you're off-duty, Mr. Kneale. This particular strain is quite simply out of this world. Our benefactor has provided a generous portion to help us complete our great work. I'm told it's from a private grow in Colorado. 'The King in Yellow.' Curious name for a cannabis strain, don't you think?" He took another pull.

Kneale's attention drifted beyond the open gate to the lights and the crew working to set up the shot beyond. A woman held a large digital camera on her shoulder and looked through the viewfinder at a production assistant who paced to and from the open gate. Christopher and another man Kneale didn't recognize appeared at the periphery of the light setup, wearing period costumes: long, brown coats over colorful, voluminous shirts, their hair hidden under white wigs that called to mind Colonial or Old European history. Andrea and Yvonne appeared in long, flowing white dresses, sharing their own joint, the light glinting off Andrea's eyes from the shadows as she caught Kneale looking at her.

"This feels like something out of time," Kneale said.

"A throwback to the Gothic horror movies of a more civilized era," Terence said, taking one last drag before pinching the joint out and slipping it into his coat pocket. "Are you familiar with the work of Jean Rollin or Jess Franco? Perhaps Amando de Ossorio or Mario Bava?"

"I'm not really into horror movies," Kneale said, reluctantly looking away from Andrea.

"We shall endeavor to convert you. With this picture, we're looking to capture the mood and atmosphere of the continental *vampyr* film, but with some of the panache, the color, and Pop Art appeal of Hammer, Amicus, and AIP's greatest hits."

"Hammer?" Kneale said, not following.

"Yes. Hammer. Cushing and Lee. You may notice a number of synchronicities among the names of our cast and crew regarding that storied studio."

"I know those actors," Kneale said. "They were in *Star Wars*."

Terence barked out a laugh.

"Where did you find this one? He's wonderful."

"Not many security experts specialize in horror cinema," Renee said. "His qualifications were otherwise impeccable."

"Are you willing to learn, sir?" Terence asked.

"What do you need me to know? Horror movies?"

"About horror *cinema*, yes," Terence said. "It's important that we are all of one mind on this picture."

"I'm here to work, but I'm open to whatever you think is important."

"A company man, through and through," Terence said, clapping his hands together. "Perfect. We are arranging some screenings, as it happens. Selections from the studio vault. Rare prints or fresh transfers thereof. It will be good for the neophytes like Mr. Kneale here, and good for morale among the cast and crew. It will help us soak in the Gothic frequencies so exquisitely provided by our wonderful historic set. We must commune with cinema's past in order to create its future. Yes, nostalgia is a trap, of course, and all that. We must not dwell on repetition of form for form's sake, but iteration and a healthy respect for what has come before is critical to chart the psychosphere of terror that defines our present moment. We shall use the signs and symbols of tradition to blaze new paths. The world demands a competent horror picture, Mr. Kneale. The world *needs* an expression of anxiety-ridden id, a reflection of its own sense of limitless menace and fear."

Kneale couldn't get a read on this guy. Creative types and film nerds always struck him as more than a little self-righteous. And annoying. There weren't that many in the military—they usually got rooted out after one term of enlistment. He had encountered exactly none in the private security services, unless you considered pornography high art, in which case there was no shortage of enthusiasts. His attention wandered back over to the actresses.

"This film is a weapon," Renee said. That caught Kneale's attention, but she declined to follow up.

"Our aesthetic is not quite as erotic as the continental vampyr exploitation and art films, to be clear," Terence said, following Kneale's gaze. "Sex is the elemental force beneath the cheap veneers of ghoulish makeup, as is its bedfellow violence, executed via stagecraft. Though lurid it will be, this picture will be in good taste, accessible to audiences who would prefer not to see some arthouse director's vainglorious sexual fantasies projected on screen, courtesy the permissiveness and desperation of attractive art school dropouts. We will have heaving bosoms and bare, masculine chests, oh yes. Sensual embraces, erotic blocking, some nudity, perhaps, but no lingering camerawork to replicate the male gaze. Prime the audience, turn them on, yes, of course. But much can be accomplished with a little restraint."

"Terence, do you have a scene to shoot?" Renee asked, recognizing that her director had lost his thread.

"Hmm." The three stood in awkward silence for a moment, until Terence suddenly stepped off through the gate, emerging into the splash of set lighting and the buzzing crowd of actors and crew.

"Miss Collinson, are you happy with the lighting?" he shouted.

"Ready to roll, if you can wrangle your actors," Kathleen said.

"Cat herding is my specialty," Terence said. "Peter! Christopher! You're up. Ladies, please stand by for your appearance. Prop master, do we have the torches ready?"

Shouted acknowledgments and a flurry of activity settled into a rhythm as the space before the open gate cleared. Renee and Kneale navigated the obstacles of lighting, wires, crates, and crew hurrying to get behind the two people wielding cameras on their shoulders. Sizable digital screens revealed what the cameras saw. Terence checked each between calling out commands.

The techs adjusted the rigs to splash light over the courtyard walls and gate in discrete, purposeful layers, revealing rich textures and creating dynamic shadows. Under the artful eye of Kathleen Collinson and her crew, the moldering gate and walls transformed from ancient relics to ethereal totems set before the great castle looming in the natural light of the moon beyond. It all looked more real than real, and yet dreamlike at the same time.

"Quiet on the set!" Renee shouted.

"Roll film, ready board!" Terence shouted. Yvonne—in full flowing white gown—stepped in front of the two actors positioned at the gate and beamed a smile brighter than any artificial light. She slapped the top of a clapboard down. On its face was the film's title:

HIERARCHIES OF BLOOD

She walked off, stage right, as Christopher and the other actor stepped up between the cameras. Christopher lit a long, wooden torch, then shared the flame with his partner's. They raised them high.

"*Action!*"

The actors took several steps forward, then paused to turn to speak to one another, revealing their faces in profile for the cameras' benefit.

"Acting with Christopher is Peter Kenley," Renee whispered to Kneale. "He plays Wolfsbane von Hayden, God's madman. Our vampire killer."

Kneale nodded, but kept silent, his attention focused on the scene. The actors spoke dialogue he couldn't quite catch, but the image itself was transfixing. He felt like he had seen this before—perhaps not this exact scene, but a similar setup. The composition and lighting lent the proceedings a familiar quality that evoked a warm, comforting feeling, like being inside on a rainy day, alone in the house with nothing else to do but watch movies airing through the late afternoon into the deep evening. Perhaps he did hold some latent fondness for the genre after all. Perhaps, being here, seeing the moment as it was captured in this dark and haunted wood, evoked the same phantom nostalgia that the old garden gate had. Or maybe all the cannabis smoke was giving him a contact buzz.

"This is how the spell is cast," Renee said, smiling as she recognized the rapture in his eyes. "This is how we remake the world."

It took them an hour to get one snippet of dialogue shot to Terence's satisfaction, with Christopher and Peter delivering their lines with subtle variations in tone and emphasis. Then it fell to others to take their turns: Yvonne and Andrea wandering through the gate in a trance, called to the edge of the wood to commune with Daniel's imposing vampire lord. Then a group of extras—crew in slapdash costumes, shot from a distance—crowded in around the gate and demanded entry, torches and pitchforks raised.

Out of sequence, it was hard to piece together the narrative, but Kneale gained a newfound appreciation for the cast and crew's commitment and professionalism as the night stretched on and the coffee grew bitter and cold. Take after take, setup after setup, with cast and crew having to jump from one part of the script to the next—progress was slow but meticulous.

They finished the night's shooting with Andrea in her flowing white dress, all heaving bosom and smeared mascara, taken up into the trees by the vampire master for an erotic embrace. They hovered together via a complex setup of invisible wires, harnesses, and pulleys as he held her from behind and sank his teeth into her bare throat, spilling a river of fake blood down across her ample cleavage and streaking across her conveniently exposed belly. They had one chance to get the blood effect right, and when the shot went just as planned, everyone's relief was palpable.

Kneale felt lucky to see all of this, even through its many moments of tedium and boredom. Because when the shot worked, he felt alive, connected to a process and these people in ways both intimate and holy.

11

The rising sun marked the end of the first night of shooting. Renee called for lighting breakdown after Terence's fifth attempt to capture an establishing shot of the castle through the barred gate *just so*. He argued with her, voice raised in tantrum, until Kathleen pointed out that it was quickly becoming too bright to continue, *you dumb prick*, and unceremoniously ordered the camera operators to stop filming and to turn in their memory cards at the editing suite inside the castle.

The time had flown by for Kneale, but fatigue and drowsiness were catching up with him. As the weary cast and crew broke down the lighting rigs and carried props and gear back to the trucks and trailers arrayed in the castle courtyard, he decided to try out the food.

The mess tent was military surplus, olive drab green, its steepled shape and texture emerging from the early morning gloom near the eastern wall like a ghost from his past. Weak sunlight caught the tent in a sheet of dew and a miasma of rising mist. Inside, the air was heavy with the smell of hot grease and industrial-strength coffee. He found actors in costume and crew in camping clothes instead of soldiers in uniform. The production team sat at metal folding chairs and tables lined up in the cramped space, keeping warm and eating eggs and toast from trays made of recycled cardboard. Kneale grabbed a tray set on the counter before the makeshift kitchen, where a pair of cooks toiled over portable stoves and shining metal prep tables. A generator whirred somewhere outside. The tin foil stretched over his plate read "GREEN PEPP. OMLT," and a sign over a brown plastic coffee container read "BEST JOE FOR 666 MILES." Kneale helped himself.

"Hey, Six, over here." Alvira waved him over to a table, where she and Pore were eating. Kneale took a seat and unwrapped his plate.

"Not bad, considering the circumstances," Pore said, taking a long sip of his coffee.

Kneale got to work on his omelet and toast. Pore was right. Not bad at all.

After they finished their meal, they went to the checkpoint outside the front gate. Kneale handed out the radios. Unencrypted handhelds with long antennae and good signal strength. They established a cache of water bottles behind a crumbling stone pillar.

"We're all on duty, twenty-four-seven," Kneale said. "Whether you're on the gate or not, you need to be ready-up, weapon in hand, boots on, at any time. There's a lot of marijuana and booze floating around here. None of that is for us, at least not until the production is complete."

"Roger," Pore said, eager to head back to the mess tent for more coffee. Movement in the woods caught his eye. "What do you think they're up to?"

Despite having worked through the night, Christopher and Daniel had not returned to their tents, but moved east along the wall, back toward the stones where they had set up their candles and crucifixes.

"Casting spells and repelling spirits," Kneale said, not sure if he was making light of it or not. "Candles and crucifixes to keep the goblins at bay."

"This job is weird, man," Pore said.

A ghostly voice called for Kneale through a wall of static, summoning him out of a deep, exhausted slumber. Kneale sat up on the lumpy bed in the trailer, his hands automatically going for his rifle, finding it propped up against the wall nearby. Sweat was a thin layer over his forehead. He would have to get a fan set up in here if he was going to get any sleep during the day.

"*Kneale. You there?*"

He grabbed the handheld radio. "This is Kneale."

"*It's Renee. I'd like you to come with us for a quick setup in the woods.*"

Kneale checked his watch. It was just after 1500. He had hoped to sleep for at least another hour.

Semper Gumby. Always flexible.

"Sure, yeah, let me get my gear together," he said, pulling the covers off his legs and swinging them out over the floor. "Where do you want to rally? Where are we headed?" He dug through his duffle for fresh socks and underwear.

"*We're staging in front of the keep entrance. I was hoping you could show us the dolmen.*"

"Say again?"

"*We heard you found a dolmen in the woods. Terence wants to know if it's worth checking out. Kathleen and I were going to get some footage of the site.*"

He hesitated.

"You didn't know about it before? I assumed that's one of the reasons you picked this place."

"The visuals would really add something to the film, don't you think? An authenticity."

"I wouldn't know," Kneale said, shaking off an odd feeling of unease. He tossed a fresh pair of socks onto the tangled blankets and sheets. "I'll be in front of the castle in ten mikes."

"Mikes?"

"Minutes. Sorry. Kneale out." He tossed the radio onto the bed. He realized, then, that he didn't want to take them to the dolmen. He didn't want to go anywhere near the damn thing.

12

Kneale led them into the woods, rifle slung across his shoulder. Renee carried her production binder, while Kathleen carried a digital video camera by the handle. What should have been a cold, crisp September afternoon was instead humid and hot, with a heavy mist rising from the moist soil. Deer flies dogged their steps and buzzed around their heads, inviting frustrated slaps that never connected.

When they reached the rise of hill and rock that served as the backstop for their makeshift rifle range, Kneale brought the group to a halt. He took a pull of water from the hose to his hydration pack. Kathleen and Renee had kept up without issue, but they were breathing heavily and the forest mist had condensed on their foreheads.

"Drink some water," Kneale said. "Official security recommendation." Kathleen gave him a wink and took a pull from a flask.

"This heat is out of nowhere," Renee said between gulps from her water bottle.

"We'll be begging for a day like this come November," Kathleen said. "How much further to the rock structure?"

Kneale tilted his head toward the great rise of rock and earth.

"Other side. One last push."

When they reached the dolmen, Kathleen offered a low whistle.

"It's beautiful," she said, snapping off the lens cover of her camera. "We have to shoot here. Tell Terence it's a condition of my employment."

Kneale was no less impressed with the structure seeing it for the second time.

"This must be old as hell," Renee said.

"Maybe older," Kathleen said, moving in to get a close-up of the capstone.

"How's that?"

"Depends on what you mean by *hell*, and which ancient civilization you're giving credit for the idea," she said. Renee arched an eyebrow at Kneale.

"It pays to know your theology if you're queer," Kathleen said, not missing a beat. "Good to know what kind of bullshit people are going to lob at you, so you can lob it right back." She fiddled with the settings on the viewfinder, then moved the camera in for a macro shot of the rock's surface. "Contemporary Biblical translations often combine 'Sheol,' 'Hades,' 'Gehenna,' and 'Tartarus' into 'Hell,' which surely would have confused first-century Christians. These are distinct places from various traditions and historical contexts."

"That might have surprised my Catholic grandmother," Kneale said.

"Catholicism is steeped in tradition, tradition being a living set of ideas and historic principles that emerged mostly from European schools of thought in the centuries after the birth of the church. You could ask a dozen priests about Hell and get a dozen answers. Is it a place, or a state of being? Or maybe both? Are some destined for it, existing completely outside of the possibility of grace, as the Calvinists insist? Or, do all of us end up in Heaven, in the presence of God, no matter what, like the universalists would have it?"

"That's all underpinned by a belief in capital-g *God* in the first place," Renee said. "Which I'm not buying."

"I'm not selling," Kathleen said, stepping under the rock platform. Her voice came to them with a slight, muffled echo from beneath the cap. "It all comes down to sin, really, and notions of justice. Christ himself said that there is an unforgivable sin. *Blasphemy against the Holy Spirit*. What do you suppose that really means?"

"I get the feeling you've got an answer lined up," Kneale said.

"I think if there is a God, they made me the way I am, and it would be awful cruel to punish me—or any of us—for that. Or for the compromised actions we take in a compromised world, especially in the name of survival and self-preservation, which are hard-coded into every thought we have, every action we take. Sin *has* to be something more, something truly terrible. Sin must be a total repudiation of the truth and the holy, not simply cultural differences, a lusty look at a beautiful body, or one too many drinks after a rough week at work. Jesus ate with the lowlifes and the whores, the tax collectors and the outcasts, the aliens and the rejects, and promised them a party at his Father's house. Then there were the wealthy, the authorities, and compulsive law-keepers, whom he condemned. In which group would a person like me belong?"

"Is everyone on your crew into this stuff?" Kneale asked Renee.

"Most of them, yes."

"It was a requirement of our employment," Kathleen said, emerging from the other side of the rock formation. "Page four of the contract: 'Do you now believe or would you be willing to consider the existence of spiritual, supernatural, paranormal, and/or psychic forces and phenomena?' I answered yes. I got the job."

"She's right," Renee said.

"You signed it, too," Kathleen said. "Don't you read the fine print, Army man? I figured a guy like you'd be pretty attentive to detail."

"I must have missed that one," Kneale said, feeling a sudden chill.

"My supernatural experiences didn't have the tenor of the divine," Kathleen said. She set her camera on the rock cover. "Poltergeist activity. One of my old apartments. I remember one night, I spent some time staring into the bathroom mirror. A crack ran down the glass, splitting my face in two. Someone whispered, *'Get out of here.'* Could have been a ghost. Could have been errant noise from the neighbor's television set upstairs. Could have been the sativa." She drained her flask then held it out, upside down, letting the last scant drops fall to the soil. "Renee has some fun stories, if you can get her to talk about herself."

The producer finished whatever notes she was taking and folded the binder shut. Kneale turned to scan the forest, remembering that his job was to keep these people safe, not listen to ghost stories and religious ramblings.

"Tell it again," Kathleen said. "Makes me feel better about what I've encountered."

"I don't want to," Renee said.

"Please," Kathleen said. "Maybe it will get this one to open up." She tilted her head at Kneale.

Renee hesitated. But after gathering her thoughts, she spoke.

"All my life, I've seen what different cultures might describe as 'little people' or fey folk," Renee said. "Small, humanoid creatures up to mischief in the back fields, disappearing behind telephone poles, strolling through the backyard, knocking on windows of houses built too close to the woods. Not exactly sinister. But definitely creepy."

Kneale's throat tightened up. He kept his eyes on the forest, where mist and shadow were suddenly full of menace.

"And?" Kathleen said.

"*And*, that's it," Renee said. "I just see weird little guys sometimes. They never talk to me, they never really acknowledge that I'm there. They're probably hallucinations, or imperfect memories. Maybe they're my brain coming apart at the seams, symptoms of an early onset neurological disorder. Or maybe they're nothing at all."

"You don't believe that," Kathleen said, her buzz opening up a playful smile. She turned to Kneale. "Your turn, Army man. Why are you here? What's your experience?"

Kneale thought of that last day in Colorado. Of the smashed-up pickup trucks, of the field reports and research notes scattered over dry earth and fluttering in the air between the trailers. He thought of the science staff and the other Observer/Experiencers who should have been there, but weren't. He thought of the utter quiet of the ranch compound. The nights leading up to that had been full of a deep sense of unease. Kneale and the others had reported bright objects skimming the property, falling out of the sky only to hover above them like harbingers of impending doom. The reports spoke of dark presences on the ground that kept pace with their vehicles. They saw red eyes staring back at them from the murk, and the smell of sulfur and animal-stink, everywhere. The CO was missing. Or maybe, he had found what he was looking for.

But Kneale survived. He survived by *not being there* when whatever had happened, happened, and the other Observer/Experiencers and project scientists on-site had just…vanished. Maybe they were taken. Maybe some, like him, arrived after and, finding nothing, fled.

"Nothing like that," Kneale said.

"You're a bad liar," Kathleen said. Kneale turned around to face her. She didn't blink or look away. He decided to change the subject.

"Are you going to be shooting here?" he asked. "I need to know when and for how long. Filming away from the castle poses some security challenges."

Kathleen frowned, disappointed with his non-answer.

"That depends on Renee and Terence, but yeah, I think so," she said. "I'd like to get a few more shots of the structure from a distance. Power and lighting are the big problems for something this remote."

Renee pressed her lips together in thought.

"Yeah. Okay. If we can talk Terence into it, we can add another night of shooting to the schedule."

Kathleen raised her fists high.

"*Hell* yeah."

"But no more than eight, maybe ten hours," Renee said. "We have a three-day contingency, but that includes re-shoots."

"You won't regret it. Let me grab a couple more long-distance shots and then we can head back."

"Don't you need a new script or something?" Kneale asked. "How can you just add in a new scene?"

"It's horror," Renee said. "The plot isn't important. Just atmosphere, tone, and color. Vibe over verisimilitude."

"Hey," Kathleen said, some distance away from them. "That's funny."

"What is?" Kneale said.

"It's dark all of a sudden." The three of them looked up into the sky.

"Sun's starting to set," Renee said.

"No," Kneale said. "It already has."

"That's impossible," Renee said. "Must be a cloud front moved in."

"It's not clouds, it looks like it's goddamn nighttime already," Kathleen said, her voice taking on the sharp edge of worry.

Kneale pressed a button on his wristwatch. The face lit up. "My watch stopped. Hold on." He reached into his pocket and produced his cell phone, which he kept off to save on battery life. When the screen lit up and the device finished its loading sequence, it displayed the time. "It's almost 1900 hours. Seven p.m."

"No goddamn way," Renee said. "What time did we leave the castle?"

"Just about three-thirty," Kathleen said.

"We lost over three hours," Kneale said.

"What do you mean, 'lost'?" Renee asked.

"You asked about my experiences," Kneale said. "Missing time was a part of what I—what we were looking into. It would happen periodically, at certain places, to certain people."

"We can't just lose three or four hours like that," Renee said. Her words echoed back to them from the trees, as if the forest was mocking her.

"You were running the camera, right?" Kneale asked Kathleen.

"It's off, now."

"Did you turn it off?"

"No, but it does have an automatic timer."

"So, it's possible you filmed something?"

"It's possible." She flipped out the viewscreen. The camera turned on with a friendly *beep*. "I have footage I can't account for," she said, like she was delivering bad news.

Wind rushed, cold and heavy, through aging leaves. Branches and trunks cracked and popped in the temperature shift.

"I'm not so sure we should watch it, now that I think of it," Kneale said.

Kathleen pinched the bridge of her nose.

"Soldier-boy here might be right," she said. Her usual confidence was gone from her voice. "Maybe it's best we leave some things alone. There's probably some other reason for this. We just got mixed up."

"We have to watch it," Renee said, her tone one of finality. "Show me. Show us."

For Kathleen and Kneale, caution and fear were crowded out by wonder. Maybe they *did* want to see, after all.

They all crowded around the screen, faces aglow in soft, blue light.

13

The footage opens with a shot of the dolmen from a dozen feet away. The image is stable and clear, as if the camera is set on a tripod. The capstone is rough and flat, illuminated by shimmering light filtered through the autumnal canopy. The timestamp is in garbled white text, but the footage appears to have been shot during the golden hour they could not recall. The camera pans from left to right, guided by the steady hand of an experienced operator. This pan reveals forms—bodies—lying down on the surface of the ancient structure.

Renee. Kathleen. Kneale.

Their eyes are closed but their chests move up and down, breathing rhythmically. Green and amber light pulses beneath the stone cap in soft waves of growing brightness. From moment to moment the light is solid, but then it flutters, like the sun reflecting on a pool of water. Something shifts beneath the rock, its shadow covering the light. Something that had been there the whole time, heaving in the negative spaces of the frame.

The world quivers with the vibration of an oncoming earthquake. Pebbles and dirt on the dolmen's surface rise into the air, suspended by some foul trick of gravity. They are joined by fallen branches and small stones likewise levitating in the foreground.

The bodies float, too. Their eyes remain closed, their hands folded over their chests. Renee's hair flutters around her face. Kathleen's lips move as if she is whispering. Kneale's hands and fingers twist into the gesture of a saint in medieval paintings, fingers pointing to heaven and to earth.

This image is lost to static for a handful of frames, returns, and then it is gone again, replaced by a leering visage so out of place that it cannot be immediately processed: a skull, huge and imposing in the frame, inhuman eyes set within its dark sockets, aflame in yellows and reds. But then it is gone, and it is an easy thing for the viewers to convince themselves that it had never appeared at all.

The bodies rotate, feet and heads following clockwise tracks in the air. The bodies descend back to the dolmen's cap. The levitating dirt, stones, and branches likewise are lowered, the magic spent, the spell broken.

Some moments later, Kneale is the first to rise. He shakes his head, then gets off the dolmen and walks past the camera. Renee follows, eyes closed, wandering somewhere off-screen. Kathleen is resurrected last, her eyes finding the camera lens, setting herself down to the forest floor and making a straight line for the device. Her hands carefully take the camera. Her face is the last thing recorded, looking down, flat and without emotion, into the lens.

Static streaks across the image. The recording ends at precisely the twenty-five-minute mark.

"Holy shit," Kathleen said, eyes wide, looking at Kneale and Renee for some sort of acknowledgment. Kneale said nothing. His insides had gone cold. Renee closed her eyes and rubbed a spot on her neck.

"I don't remember lying down on the rock," she said.

"I don't remember floating in the fucking air," Kathleen said. "I don't remember *any* of that."

Kneale walked up to the dolmen and placed his hand on the rock. Cool, but charged. A popping sensation crawled along his skin. A static field.

"Nice trick," he said, trying to sound like he meant it, like he believed that was the explanation. "Did you two cook that up in editing? Special effects software?"

"No," Kathleen said, voice on the edge of cracking.

"Are you trying to spook me? If you want me to do some viral marketing or whatever-the-fuck, just ask. I work for hire. Marketing is basically just psychological warfare operations, right? I can tell people whatever you want, for the right price. There's no need for all this theatrical bullshit."

"No," Renee said, voice low. "You know we didn't do that, Kneale. Look at me. Look at *me*." Kneale turned away from the charged stones, his fists balled and shoulders squared. Renee's eyes, wet and wide, told the truth of the matter. He unclenched his fists and looked away.

"Does any of this match your experience? From before. From your time in Colorado?"

Kneale should have recoiled at the mention of that state. She wasn't supposed to know. Maybe Rob had said something in passing, trying to impress her. They were making a horror movie, after all. Is that what got him this job? All this talk about Hell and God and the supernatural meant she was probably susceptible to bullshit. He knew he should ignore the question, beg off as he had already, earlier...three *hours* earlier.

I'll see you in Colorado.

A voice in his head. The voice of a man gone missing. A voice back from the dead. A phantom memory, a phrase that might mean something to someone else, but that haunted him instead.

"I don't know what it means," he said.

"It must mean something to you," Renee said, eyes on Kneale.

"Why?"

"Because it wasn't here before you showed up."

"What?"

"The weird rocks. *This*. The thing that you gave a name. You called it a dolmen. You did that."

"What's that supposed to mean?"

"It means you were the right man for the job. This revealed itself to you. Not to us. Not to our crew's scouts. Not to local hikers or the New York State Department of Environmental Conservation."

"You must have known it was here," Kneale said.

"No," Renee said, her voice falling into a reverent hush. "We've been over this ground a half-dozen times."

"I'm going to delete the footage," Kathleen said.

"No way," Renee said, putting her hand on the camera. "You can't. It's property of New Camlough. Everything shot on that camera is." Renee took the device. She found the memory card slot and popped the card out, slipping it into a chest pocket of her shirt.

"What it means is that we have to shoot a scene here," Renee said, fire in her eyes and excitement in her voice. Religious fervor, rising in her soul. "Kneale's dolmen has to be in the movie."

The production lost precious hours due to the short-term disappearance of its senior producer, director of photography, and head of security. Terence was incensed, his rehearsals with the actors on the night's schedule suddenly for naught. When Nike got word that the evening's scheduled shoots were pushed back a night, she stormed into the editing room within the castle, ready to shout at Renee about the hours she had wasted getting the actors into costume and makeup. But when she opened the creaking door, she found Terence, Kathleen, and Renee hunched over the screen bank, watching the footage captured during that stretch of missing time.

When she saw them floating above the rock, rotating in place, her jaw dropped.

"How can I help?" she asked.

The crew loaded up a pair of small trailers with lighting gear, mobile generators, and crates of supplies. The pickups hauled them through the front gate and made their way over a narrow and overgrown logging trail that skirted the castle grounds to the east, leading to the dolmen beyond. A train of crew and actors carried flashlights and prop lanterns through the garden gate, warm light splashing against the narrow pines guiding them deeper into the woods.

Kneale and Pore played good shepherds, getting a headcount and personnel roster from Renee just before the production started its dark march to the weird stones. Kneale felt like a platoon sergeant again, ensuring that no little stray soldiers got lost or twisted their ankles in the dark. Having something to do kept his mind off what the footage had shown them, and kept him from thinking about what else might have happened in that stretch of lost time.

Stone pillars appeared out of the autumnal gloom of a dream, spotlit by the headlights of the pickup trucks. Flashlight beams danced across the stones, making them shimmer. As the crew filed around the stones, a hushed awe overcame them. They were in the presence of the holy.

Given adequate time for reverence, the crew then went to work. The generators, wires, and light rigs went up first. Terence gathered the lead actors at the stones. Christopher and his partner Peter, Daniel-turned-vampire, and the two damsels in distress Andrea and Yvonne crowded together in the parchment-light of a lantern held aloft by their director. The generators came online with a purr of motors. Light rigs popped on, temporarily blinding those unlucky enough to be looking in the wrong direction. When the flare faded, the dolmen remained, larger than life, haunted by great shadows, backlit by strategically placed LED lanterns that spilled out subtle blue and purple lights. Kathleen and her lighting crew were as good as advertised.

Pore and Kneale each took a headcount as best as they could.

"No little lost lambs," Pore said. "What now?"

Kneale shrugged. "Watch the woods. Watch them film. Check in with me once an hour. I'll be wandering around."

"I gotta admit, I feel a little out of place carrying a goddamn rifle around all these Hollywood types," Pore said. "Feels like we're local guides in a third-world country, escorting them through guerrilla territory."

"Funny. That's the feeling I got, too."

Kneale found Renee standing behind the camera operators, production binder in hand, headlamp illuminating the notes she scratched into the margins of one of the sheets of paper. Kathleen was a ghost, floating between the light rigs set up before the stones, light meter in hand. Nike stood with the actors before the dolmen, applying last-minute touches to Daniel's fearsome vampire scowl.

"Will the audio be okay, with all the generator noise?"

"What we capture here will be for editing purposes. We'll record the dialogue later. Automated dialogue replacement—ADR. Standard practice for many European horror films made in the twentieth century. Some US audiences rejected the practice, but many viewers find that it lends films a charming, eerie effect."

Terence, standing between the two cameras, suddenly called *action*, and the actors went to work. They filmed take after take, shot after shot. Just a brief discussion beforehand, a consult with Kathleen, a question or two for Renee. If Kneale had not known otherwise, he never would have guessed they were shooting without a script.

Yvonne and Andrea, wearing torn, wispy, form-fitting Victorian dresses, danced and writhed over the stones, among them, under the cap, atop one another. Peter and Christopher stage-fought Daniel atop the structure, their footing slipping, their crucifixes and stakes raised high and casting great shadows on the trees beyond. The stones were the stars, dominating every frame, every take. The forest was alive with strange lights, swirling and phantasmal.

When it was the proper time, Kneale, Renee, and Kathleen lay down in their prescribed places. They floated on cue, just as they had rehearsed. A great, leering skull replaced the moon, breaking through the clouds, red and yellow eyes aflame, twin vampire fangs aglow with a terrible neon-green light, ready to drink the blood of the world.

14

The handful of rooms Kneale had passed through before were but a fraction of the castle's vast interior. Cobwebs hung from countless corners, home to great spiders. Hallway ceilings were adorned with bats, slumbering or resting, having come in from the long night as the sun threatened to rise. Vibrant stained glass windows showed saints and nobility alike in portraiture. The saved and the damned stared at one another from across shadow-filled rooms.

A set of great doors held closed the entrance to the dungeon. The classical wooden portals were carved with an intricate scene: gargoyles and sprites frolicked in sinful play amidst a lush forest, where trees had grinning faces and the earth was marked by strange, concentric circles. Wooden frieze paneling flanked the door, framing it with depictions of twisted, dead branches bound together in unseemly, erotic configurations.

The doors opened inwards, releasing a cloud of moist, earth-smell laden air, almost visible in its weight. The stairs were stone, wide and long, and descended into a darkness made navigable by the light of torches held in sconces the shape of inhuman hands. The stairs terminated at a wooden door held together by great strips of black metal. It opened into a larger space where grey and black columns held the weight of the castle. Multiple drafts competed to bring in fresh, cold air and carry away the sputtering smoke of burning candles. Ancient wine racks, holding in place glass bottles long-since gone dark and opaque, stood against the far walls. The smell of popcorn competed with the dank odor of the earth, carried around the chamber on unseen eddies.

Rows of metal folding chairs stood before a handcrafted altarpiece, which was home to a digital film projector atop its surface, pointed toward the whitewashed wall. A finger pressed a button and the room grew bright with grey light. Cords rustled and cheap plastic clicked together. A small metal disc pressed into place. Speakers popped. A face floated in the dark, revealed by the dead light of a laptop screen. The audience found their seats, rustling small paper bags of popcorn.

"I should have someone watching the entrance to the castle," Kneale whispered to Renee as they took their seats near the back of the dungeon-turned-theater.

"The sun will be rising soon," she said, as if that explained everything. "I want you and your team here, watching this. It's important that you understand what we're trying to accomplish." Kneale turned back to see Alvira and Pore in the last row of chairs, rifles slung over their chests and pointing downwards. It was too dark to see their expressions.

Terence took a seat on the other side of Renee. He rubbed his eyes in exhaustion.

"What a night," Terence said. He produced a matchbook from his sport coat pocket, then struck one. He brought the flame to the joint pressed between his lips. The cannabis smoke spread rapidly throughout the chamber, soon joined by the rolling fog of others. An earthy, metallic note underpinned the smoke. Terence handed the joint to Renee, who immediately took several quick drags, vapor spilling out of her nose in successive waves. She held in a cough, then offered the joint to Kneale.

"Why is everyone trying to get the head of security stoned?" he said, frustration plain in his voice.

"This will enhance your perceptions of the events to come,"

Terence said. "And of the film we are about to watch." Kneale didn't know what to make of that.

"I'm responsible for the security of this production," Kneale said. "Say there's an issue, an emergency, and I'm too gonked to do anything about it. That's grounds for dismissal. Not to mention, most security clearance jobs require a drug test as part of the intake process."

"What if I told you that 'being cool' was a condition of your employment here?" Renee said, more of a statement than a question. "What if I told you that this will sharpen your senses, and that the imminent rising sun will provide enough security to satisfy me as your employer? What if I told you that this cannabis strain is of a special provenance, grown in sacred Colorado soil touched by the crawling fingers of a god-king?" Renee leaned in close. "Your job and that of your team for what remains of this wicked night is to get high and watch this fucked-up horror movie with us."

Behind them, Pore and Alvira both waved off offered joints. Renee turned back and raised her voice, until it echoed across the dungeon.

"I'm the senior producer on this production. A condition of your continued employment here is to accept the hospitality we now offer you." She looked directly at Pore and Alvira. "There. Now you're all just following orders. You can follow orders, can't you?" The two contractors looked to Kneale. He threw his hands up in defeat.

"You heard the boss," he said. His team disappeared in a haze of smoke and pulses of golden light from the projector.

"So did you."

Light hands moved over his shoulders, giving him a quick squeeze. Lithe fingers took the joint from Renee, then brought it up to blood-red lips, vibrant in the gloom. Andrea knelt down to him, bringing their faces close. She pursed her lips, just inches away from his own.

Breathe in.

He did as he was told. Smoke flowed out. Kneale opened his mouth and let the intoxicating vapor pour in. The effect was immediate: the darkness encroached around his awareness, pressing it down to a narrow circle. Then it drew back, the world reclaimed from nothingness. Pleasant fingers of warmth cascaded down his body. The popcorn smell was textured and tempting. Andrea's smile was equal parts beauty and mischief. Renee grinned. Terence howled like a werewolf.

"Let the show begin!" he shouted, in the grips of transformation. "Awoo! *Awoo-awoooo!*"

The speakers popped and scratched with the initial rumblings of a creaky soundtrack, all theremin and synthesizer organ, rumbling bass and drums, overwrought horns and the faint squealing of animals.

Andrea pursed her lips playfully, then sat down next to Kneale. She draped an arm across his wide shoulders.

"Pass me the popcorn, sweetheart," she said. Kneale's eyes were glued to the screen, which was a pulsating portal to another, Gothic world. Renee handed him two bags of popcorn. Andrea plucked one from his quivering hands. Her skin was pale in the light of the screen, her eyes reflecting magic. She took another drag from the joint and, when she offered it to him, Kneale did not refuse.

"This film, and others like it, are foundational to our great work," Terence said, his voice little more than a whisper but perfectly clear and audible, despite the distance and the scratchy soundtrack emanating from the speakers. "These are more than movies. They are augurs of history. Movers of minds and mountains. *Cinéma goblin.*"

What?

"Films made in concert with forces occult and supernatural," Renee whispered, likewise perfectly audible. She put a handful of popcorn in her mouth. "There are few who have succeeded. Monty

Blackwood's *Camp Ghoul Mountain Part VI* is perhaps the most commercially successful example of the art, and that film is barely remembered."

What are you making here?

"What are *we* making, you mean," she said. "As a soldier, you understand the importance of psychological warfare. Now, consider the implications of the *spiritual* axis of conflict."

The assembled cast and crew, pressed together in the lower reaches of the ancient castle, sharing the communal experience of smoke, popcorn-smell, and moving light and sound, fell into reverent silence.

15

The title card appears with a fanfare of tinny horns and droning synthesizer notes, the words splashed over a lush matte painting of Colonial New England homes perched before a dark forest in the throes of late autumn. The houses are all stone or wood, with steep gable roofs and small, black windows, inadequate defenses against the cold to come. The typeface is lurid, dripping red, as if writ in fresh blood:

WITCH HELL
COPYRIGHT MCMLXVIII BY CAMLOUGH STUDIOS, INC.

    The horns cede ground to the synthesizer, which has gained channels, an increasing accompaniment of overwrought, reverb-laden notes creating an echoing, almost surround-sound effect, one that produces a sense of horror-movie unease, but also a calm, hypnotic sensation achieved through harmonic vibration that spreads from the base of the skull, warm and welcome, to the cannabis-primed nervous system beyond.

    The title card fades out to a series of establishing shots of Colonial New England-by-way-of-Northern Ireland production design. The music downshifts to aural ambiance, droning and vaguely sinister. Skinned deer hang off roofs and poles; a body of water churns and froths; brooding houses stand in silent judgment along narrow roads where actors in pre-Revolutionary period costume are seen from afar; trees loom impossibly tall and dark.

This staccato-style montage is repeated several times throughout the film. The landscape and setting-establishment shots grow darker and more menacing, with a greater frequency of shots depicting dead or decaying animals and fish. These recurring symbols of death are eventually replaced by human forms, represented by both actors in impressive makeup and by body props molded and detailed by ringer Italian special effects artists fresh off their work on that country's burgeoning giallo and supernatural horror movements. These setting and thematic montages bookend character scenes, and often begin and end in jarring moments of discontinuity. Characters are interrupted mid-scene by sudden cuts to grotesque imagery, their dialogue played over vile close-ups of decaying fish or a ravaged deer corpse (and later, the dead townsfolk) mid-conversation.

Witch Hell concerns itself with the paranoia and patriarchal horror of pre-Revolutionary American Satanic panic. A more contemporary, lesser film would have indulged the obvious interpretations and presented itself as a lazy morality play, inviting a compliant audience to nod in agreement with its milquetoast liberal messaging about the virtues of girl-boss capitalist femininity. But this is a film willing to indulge its feminism and revolutionary politics in a way that skirts a reactionary reading— one that takes the surface-level, center-left assumptions about its intentions and runs with them, laughing maniacally, hurtling toward the dark woods that beckon to us with promises of true freedom, and all the horror that implies.

The accused in *Witch Hell* are witches. That they cast spells and exercise power is seen as evil in the eyes of the prevailing socioreligious order. But can violence and self-expression ever truly be evil, if committed as acts in resistance to injustice? Why should revolutionaries be held to the moral standards of their oppressors, who never account for the mountain of corpses they amass by their own actions?

Women gather in the old wood. They dance, often naked, before the flames of a roaring pyre. They summon demons—or, in this case, contortionists in costumes designed to distract and confuse the eye, lending their rhythmic gyrations and thrusting movements a highly weird and disorienting quality. Their faces are many, their eyes aglow, and their bodies are a mixture of actual nudity and odd prostheses implying warped, angelic physiognomy. The lesbotronic copulation among witches and demons and witches and witches is matter-of-fact, shot at a distance or from above, absent the explicitly pornographic inserts one might expect.

The women who shed their clothes are comely enough to have appeared in the beer, liquor, and cigarette advertisements of their time, but the rhythmic, percussion-led music is overlain with an unpleasant synthesizer noise, just out of tune and off-key enough to counterbalance audience titillation with a nauseous unease. The close-ups we do get are of the performers in makeup and costume, who, as objects, are the antithesis of alluring, and the nudity of the conventionally attractive model-actresses that is present is half-obscured by shadows and tree branches writhing in ecstasy.

Certainly, a few cuts would be made to the American and United Kingdom releases, but in Europe and farther afield from censorious, repressed, Protestant-dominated film ratings boards, this scene would find appreciative (if not titillated) audiences. The version shown in the basement of a haunted castle in the Finger Lakes Region of upstate New York is the uncut version, its run time a full eight minutes longer than the official US DVD release of 2009. The extra minutes are due to a few lingering shots here, in other scenes, and the additional frames held on several unnerving gore effects whose technical and artistic qualities are appreciated all the more with the additional viewing time.

Thus, the actors writhe in inserts between longer and longer shots of the great pyre, the camera moving in, slow and confident.

A dark form rises, its great, muscular body backlit by orange light, its arms and head burning with a crown of orange fire. It raises its great ram's head, massive horns winding together in a Fibonacci sequence of keratinous growth. Black wings spread out on invisible wires, underlit by flame and spreading to occlude the diseased sky. The music winds up to a fervor pitch of electronic noise-wash, and the moaning, *oh*, the moaning—

In the village, a young couple goes about their daily labors: washing clothes in the river, tilling soil in the distant fields, stalking through the woods with muskets in hand. They return to their home, meager as it is, but so clearly full of youthful love and vibrancy. He is tall and handsome, his curly hair form-perfect around his unblemished actor's face; she is short and full-figured, filling out her corset and dress, her hair blond in a way that only an actress recruited from southern California in the late 1960s could be. For all their stumbling, ADR dialogue, they have real on-screen charisma and chemistry, likely due to the fact that both of them are very, very hot. The camera is not sparing when it comes to their frequent sexual unions, of course, which are often contrasted with the escalating occult horrors that soon overtake their world:

A sheep's head, mounted on a pole in the center of the village, near the well. The water within has turned red with blood, and buckets of the crimson wash are produced by screaming children and terrified old women, only to be poured out in the cobblestone street as the villagers cry out to God for mercy.

A great swarm of hand-painted bats, fluttering and floating over the village at all hours of the day and night. The settlement is rendered in detailed matte painting, complete with tiny villagers scrambling around the bottom of the frame in composite.

Children, caked in the grey makeup of the grave, found in corpse piles scattered throughout the village, set aflame by men in tricorn hats, hate and disapproval on their stern, hard faces. Their voices carry throughout the alleys of their village and the valleys of the wood, laden with words of wrath intoned from the grim Old

Testament. One such man spots our young female lead, his cold blue eyes finding hers. His severe face is stretched taut over his skull. But his advanced age and foul temper are no obstacles to his desire for the young lass, perched as he is at the head of a vanguard of religious fanatics. It is not mob rule, per se, that has fallen on the town as the unholy tragedies pile up. Rather, the pitchfork-kills, torches set to homes and bodies, and gruesome lynchings are the purest expressions of the cruelty and hate that has always burned at the heart of their community, and of ours. The murderous manias of the hamlet are simply outpourings of the id that was—and is—the roiling core of the ongoing American colonial project.

Indeed, it is this actor, hired for his passing similarity to Peter Cushing but whose acting prowess was sharpened on the vaunted Irish stage, who leads the others on successive marches through town, rounding up women suspected of conspiracy and deviltry.

These accusations may be accurate, but when they are not, the victims die anyway, failing at some arcane challenge of pain, blood, and flame. The lashing of whips and the burning of bodies at stakes are pronounced *justice* by the men who see themselves as God's Christian soldiers but who could not be further from sainthood.

While the audience knows, very early on, that a coven is indeed at work, the identities of its members remain a mystery. Scenes of torture and sadism play out between setpieces of occult horror conducted atop altars of branch and antler. Shadowy feminine forms take flight on broomsticks; familiar cats prowl and even murder; skeletons rise from the local graveyard and lay siege to the village under the light of a blood moon. This scene is notable for its multiple decapitations, delivered to a lusty audience by the specter of grinning Death himself, cloaked in black and wielding a magnificent scythe.

This is a war of faith and attrition: men with the power of the state and religious fervor, the coven with secrecy and sorcery. It is a carrion dance of escalating terrors, with the innocent townsfolk caught in the middle—including, eventually and inevitably, our two leads.

Houses burn, actresses scream, blood flies, demons dance, the young and old alike die, either at the hands of the coven's machinations or through the frustrated sexual violence of the puritanical enforcers. It is not clear if there is indeed conspiracy at every level, or if the villagers simply choose a side out of hopelessness. Or maybe this is something worse. Maybe this is an expression of directionless violence. Maybe this is anachronistic Manifest Destiny turned back in on itself.

The mob and the witches set buildings aflame. Families turn on one another, carrying out murder-work with dull knives and sickles meant for the fields and forest game. Fanatics confront women with accusations of impropriety and adultery, only to rip their bodices open and tear at their soft flesh with bloody nails. Seduction and murder happen behind closed doors. Technicolor-red blood arcs over bodies covered in occult runes and pentagrams. The stars turn green and alien, a swirling madness overhead that drives the witch hunters into a frenzy of final insanity, lost as they are in the burning remains of the village they swore to defend and then tore apart, piece by piece, house by house, bone by bone. Finally, the trees themselves uproot and, led by the demons from the orgy, march in to join the fray, their killing indiscriminate, the corpses piled up to the firmament of Heaven itself.

Following the conflagration, the severe-faced, blue-eyed man who led the inquisition finds the object of his desire. She flees with her wounded husband from the wreckage of the village, hoping to reach the river and follow it to the next town over. The witchhunter is overcome by rage and lust in equal measure, his desire to kill and rape one and the same, having formed of him a perfect instrument of death and desire—and desire for death. The husband, suffering from a wound still dripping with ichor, is no match for the madman's ultimate assault. He falls under the blows of a great maul, fingers and hands destroyed first, bones in his arms shattered next, his head caved in at last.

The heroine retreats in terror, unable to speak, unable to keep upright, tears streaking down her face.

You're the last witch, he says, holding the maul outward at waist level, emphasizing its phallic connotations. *One more whore of Satan must die, and this village will be pure.* He pauses his advance only to undo his belt. The bronze clasp sticks, holding fast, distracting him for a fleeting moment. It is enough. Our heroine grabs a tree branch and raises it defiantly. He sees her final act of resistance, is infuriated by it, and lunges for her, his pants falling down, finally, to tangle around his ankles. The maul head is aimed for her cleavage to hammer home the clumsy symbolism of the moment. She dodges right, then brings the branch down across his face. A small projection of the branch pokes into and pops his eye, releasing a flow of yellow goop and producing a scream of impotent rage. He stumbles, clutching his face. She strikes him again, his blood spurting onto her dress in erotic fashion, and he falls to one knee. He lashes out, swinging the maul in clumsy arcs.

Where are you, whore? Where are you, vile witch?

This pathetic mewling continues for a moment, but is interrupted, finally, as the synthesizer score drops out and we are left only with the sound of his labored breathing and the churning of the inferno that has consumed the village. There is a rush of air, and a burst of light, and, as the villain turns toward the camera, his face goes stark white in shock. Brilliant illumination overtakes him, and a golden sword swings forth, neatly severing his head from his quivering body.

16

Kneale dreamed of the dolmen, where the pinup girl sorceresses of *Witch Hell* conducted Black Mass. The stones reverberated with each chanted prayer, with each burst of flame spewed forth from cow and ram skulls set about the site. Fire and stone churned and twisted, becoming something else, their particles resonating with unseen magic and dancing to new psychosexual frequencies. Matter and time itself were reconfigured into the building blocks of an ancient, grey city. A city built into a spiral, above which floated unfamiliar stars whose orbits were a nauseating dance of color and radioactive light. The place beckoned him, this city was also a stage, an undergirding scaffold upon which the petty dramas of the human race played out, shuffled off, reconfigured, and were trotted out to perform again. A great castle loomed at the center of the spiraling streets and endless rows of primeval architecture. But when Kneale tried to angle his awareness toward it, all he could see and taste was lingering smoke and the tantalizing hints of fresh, buttered popcorn.

The sun slipped past the tops of the distant hills when the banging on the door to his trailer roused him. He sat up, eyes adjusting to the dark of the narrow bedroom, throat dry, ears ringing with the chiming of distant bells. He looked at his watch.

"I'm owed two more hours of sleep," he said.

The knocking continued. Kneale dragged himself out of bed. He unlocked the door to the trailer and swung it open.

"What?"

Christopher and Peter stared up at him from below.

"Sorry to bother you, Mr. Kneale," Peter said, his English accent somehow both charming and mildly condescending. "I'm not sure we've had the pleasure of being introduced. Peter." He held out his hand and Kneale accepted it with a brief, disinterested shake. "We'll be on together tonight."

"What?" Kneale said again, turning to Christopher for explanation.

"Nike needs you in the chair, ASAP, comrade," Christopher said.

"The chair."

"For special makeup applications," Peter said.

"Makeup."

"To go in front of the camera," Christopher said. "In two hours' time. We're down an extra today, and Terence said you've got the right build for it."

"The build for what? What is this?"

"You've been drafted, old soldier," Peter said, smiling. Kneale tried to shake the fog from his mind, but couldn't. That Colorado cannabis was powerful stuff.

"Let us make you a monster," Christopher said. He clapped his hands. "Get some clothes on you. You're on Hollywood time now."

"Keep your eyes closed," Nike said, turning on the lights framing the mirror in front of the makeup chair. "You can have a little water and coffee while we work. But try not to move too much."

One of the makeup assistants mercifully brought him a

steaming cup of black coffee, which tasted bitter when sipped through a straw. But coffee was coffee. And strong, too. The caffeine pulled his mind out of the fog. They made him skip breakfast—or, dinner, considering the late hour—but Nike had promised him a protein shake once she had applied the first layer of prosthetic skin and underlying features. He didn't ask any questions. That is what made him a good soldier.

The whole process took over an hour. When it was complete, Kneale saw a monster in the mirror.

"We're ready for you on the western wall," a PA said, leaning inside the tent. "If that's alright with you, Ms. Monlaur."

Nike nodded. "Our monster is ready for his close-up."

She helped him get to his feet and guided him out of the makeup tent and into the courtyard. The body suit and legs were cumbersome to move in, but he got the hang of it after a few dozen feet. The crew they passed on the way to the shoot all gave him wide, awed smiles. Pore was with the crew at the gate, and he gave an uncharacteristic thumbs up.

"Lookin' good, Six."

Kathleen and her team had prepared an array of lights and reflectors on the far side of the courtyard. They were angled upwards, illuminating the top of the stone wall and the bare branches that reached overhead. Terence and a handful of actors stood back from the glowing stone. Kathleen was speaking with one of the camera operators when she spotted Nike and Kneale approaching. She gave Kneale a nod of approval.

"You've outdone yourself, Nike," she said, between puffs of cannabis smoke. "Well done."

Andrea ran up to Kneale. Her flowing white dress was hidden beneath a cold-weather jacket to keep her warm between takes.

"More handsome than ever!" she teased. "I could give you a kiss!"

"Don't you dare," Nike said, shooing the girl away. "You'll smear the makeup."

"Let's get you on the wall," Terence said. "We have a stepladder here. There's a platform built onto the edge, just out of view. It's quite secure, I assure you."

"Okay," Kneale said, his voice muffled. It was hard to talk with the prosthetic fangs in his mouth.

"You're going to do great," Andrea said, barely holding back a laugh.

***

Terence ran through the stage directions. The director was remarkably patient, in contrast to his usual caustic tone with actors who couldn't quite hit their marks. Kneale repeated the strange dance several times, moving slowly, careful not to misstep and go plunging off the edge of the wall. The tape marks helped, and the short wooden platform set against the inner edge provided a small margin for error, but his costume was unwieldy and he lacked a significant portion of his peripheral vision.

Terence climbed back down the stepladder, then carried it back behind the two camera operators. He conferred with Kathleen while Kneale studied the castle from his vantage point on the wall. The castle was larger than he remembered. Its walls were wider, with greater depth and height. Its towers stretched high into the young night sky, and its stained glass windows were probing eyes, flickering with candlelight from within. Parts of its structure seemed new, as if Kneale had missed them before. Was that the servants' quarters, just near the derelict stables? Or was it a whole other wing of the great house, its dimensions previously hidden by shadow and perspective? Was it a part of the set, built by the crew?

Kneale fought against a sudden sensation of vertigo, as if the stones beneath his feet were shifting. The lights swelled and spun, and his already limited vision condensed in a diminishing iris of black. His head reeled and he stomped a clawed foot forward to keep himself from tumbling over the edge.

ACTION!

Kneale shook his head, the prosthetic applications of bat ears and high, molded brow held in place by dried putty. He risked a quick glance to his clawed feet, spotting the green neon tape nearby. His first mark. He hit it, then shuffled on to the next, then back again. His tongue ran along the backside of the prop fangs affixed to his teeth, finding them sharp and tasting of dried glue. The lights grew hotter, and others shifted and squirmed just beyond where he could see, but he kept his focus and shambled along the edge of the wall, just as Terence had instructed him.

When his humble dance was complete, Kneale stepped back carefully, feeling the heel of his claw-foot finding the edge of the wooden safety platform. He raised his long arms to the sky, wriggling his middle fingers to manipulate the fishing wire. His wings unfurled, emerging with a satisfying rustling of fabric. They stretched taut and opened to embrace the night. The wind picked up, threatening to lift him into the sky. Voices whispered to him from the trees, encouraging him to soar. He would have given anything for that power.

17

Now that he was one of them—having officially been cast in the film as Vampiric Horror #2, complete with a spot in the credits among the actors—Kneale increasingly felt more at ease, more comfortable among this selection of bohemian weirdos and artists. The woods, however, still held an abstract terror, an unease that emerged whenever he escorted the cast and crew out beyond the protection of the walls.

After that first, strange week, Kneale had to admit that, all told, this was a good gig. He had taken to walking the perimeter when he wasn't with the crew, sometimes accompanying Christopher and Daniel as they conducted their odd rituals. After his experience—or, rather, his lack of memory about the experience—at the dolmen, Kneale no longer found what they were doing so absurd.

Something else began to gnaw at the back of his mind. It was an insecurity, an anxiety that, no matter how ridiculous it was to think about directly, he simply could not shake: the castle was getting bigger.

It expanded in small bursts. New rooms and sections appeared in the outer wings. Rooftops widened to accommodate these new spaces. A tower rose on the north side, complete with great stained glass windows that slid down into existence from stone sheaths, aligned to catch the light of the setting sun in glamorous arrays of color. The perimeter walls grew, too, as evidenced by the closeness to the rocks upon which Christopher and Daniel set their candles and crucifixes, and the ultimate displacement of one such set by stacked stone. They had not made mention of it, choosing instead a new location for the totems. Kneale, unsure of how acknowledging this strange revelation might be taken by the others, kept quiet, too.

18

Within the woods, the brave vampire hunters [Peter Kenley and Christopher Belgravia in full period costume, complete with wreaths of garlic about their necks] confront their ancient enemy. The Master Vampire [Daniel Taumata, ghoulishly resplendent under the lights and makeup] looms tall, his massive shoulders home to a flowing black cape held tight before him like a shield. His pale face reflects ill-omened moonlight, his sharp nose and pointed ears lending his countenance a fearful, predatory symmetry. A vulpine smile breaks along his lips, emphasizing fangs already bloodied by the evening's murderous delights.

"I bid you welcome," he says, his words not quite matching the movement of his lips. His accent is vaguely European, its tone and cadence implying an aristocratic lineage. Shorthand for noble breeding and a landed, comfortable existence that stands in contrast to the simple, working-class lives of his many victims thus far [various members of the cast and crew filling out the remaining roles]. He is, like all classic vampires, a predator of privilege.

The great cloak takes on a life of its own, sweeping open to reveal the vampire's double-breasted suit, a lurid red velvet slash set across his breast in contrast to the dark greens and ominous greys of the haunted forest beyond. The cloak expands, a black and purple-fringed cloud that forms into great wings. The vampire hunters pause in their advance, their faces cut into masks of grim determination.

"We must not look it in the eye," says one [Kenley, God's Madman], streaks of grey hair just above his ears marking him as the senior of the two. "Nor must we comprehend his words should he speak further, as his voice will make a terrifying sort of sense to us, and ultimately place us under the direction of his will. Fill your mind with images of holiness and piety or, failing that, romantic thoughts of your beloved."

"Yes, yes, of course," his companion [Belgravia, playing the Betrothed in search of his missing lover] says, clutching a wooden stake tight to his chest.

"It has been many a year since I faced men who would be vampire killers," the fiend says, his hands moving in a strange, rhythmic pattern before him. Wicked lights appear about his fingers: green, gold, and blue orbs, orbiting like planets, drawing in the eye as his smooth voice washes over them. "I do not recall their names, nor their faces. Only the taste of their blood, and that of their families."

"Do not listen," God's Madman says. "He means to ensorcell us."

"Then we have but one choice," Betrothed says, rushing forward. "Die, fiend!"

"No—!"

As Betrothed closes the distance, stake raised high, the vampire snaps at his great cloak. It contracts, then collapses together in a flurry of bats' wings and black fabric. The cape pulls itself back apart, and in its place stands a beautiful young woman [Yvonne Munro, playing the Maiden]. She wears a flowing white nightgown that practically glows in the dreadful illumination of the moon [Kathleen Collinson's custom-built light rigs, perched just out of frame]. Her dark hair flows freely over her shoulders, which she uncovers by pushing the straps of her gown down her arms. Her eyes flash red and yellow, and the Betrothed stumbles to a halt just before her, stake held to his chest.

"My love?" he whispers. "What...what has this foul creature done to you?"

"He's made me *more*, my dear," the Maiden says, taking a slow step forward, her dark skin radiant, her eyes locked on his, her lips a subtle shade of red. Her voice is soft and inviting, silk and fine paper, and her beauty is overwhelming. "Come, my darling, and let me make *you* more, too." The Maiden holds her arms out, inviting her lover forward. His eyes drop from her lips to her breasts, and he offers a moan of despair, shuffling toward her, into her arms, into death itself.

"No! Back, you foul devils!"

God's Madman leaps forward, an ornate silver crucifix bared to catch a flash of moonlight [a stunning if brief shot in insert]. The reflection of Christ shines a violent slash over the Maiden's suddenly pale face, her too-wide mouth and viperous tongue [courtesy Nike Monlaur] lanced by a sudden burst of holy flame.

She cries out and covers her face; the Master Vampire snarls and swirls his cape about them both. The black and purple fabric is suddenly alive with lines of corpse-blue energy, and these lines coalesce into the shape of bats, bats that come bursting forth, made once of cloth and light, but now of coarser stuff, carrying within their material bodies the incorporeal spirits of the vampires. They retreat in a swirling vortex of wing and fang, funneled off toward the castle, which looms over the forest, stretching high into the sky itself, one of its towers touching the red crescent moon [rendered on a matte painting via composite].

"To the castle, to commit holy and just violence upon the master," God's Madman says as the shot lingers on the ancient fortress. "Perhaps we can save your beloved yet."

"*Cut!*" Terence shouted, clapping his hands together for emphasis. "Excellent work, everyone. Especially you, Yvonne. You could seduce the snake in the garden himself."

"It's all in the fangs," she said, popping them from her teeth with some effort. Nike came forward to collect them and to run a brush over Yvonne's face.

"Reset for the next shot in ten," Terence said. "Kathleen, I wonder if we can't use rig number two, rather than setting up a whole new set for…" His voice blended in with the others and with the flurry of cast and crew activity as they rushed to prepare for the next setup. The production had hit its stride, even jumping ahead of schedule despite their impromptu scene at the dolmen. Kneale had worked with dysfunctional teams before, with bad leadership and confused mission objectives. This production did not suffer those problems. Even Terence's occasional *auteur-*attitude did not slow things down—in fact, the actors responded to his demanding approach to shooting multiple takes with varying levels of expression and intensity. He was getting good results, at least to Kneale's layman eye.

So focused were the cast and crew in preparing for the next shot of the evening that none of them noticed the lights. But Kneale did. It was his job to notice.

They were the same odd flecks of illumination that had haunted him since his first journey to the castle when he had gotten turned around on the forest road. Those lights had been ephemeral, disappearing just as quickly as they made themselves known. These lingered, tracing burning afterimage arcs in his vision, leading him away from the commotion of the production and the castle with its physical barriers of stone and its spiritual barriers of crucifix and salt.

Streaks of intermittent blue illumination descended to the forest floor, dancing among the bushes, thorns, and weeds that choked the earth, but never straying far from clear patches of dirt that allowed Kneale to follow them easily, even in the dark. He followed as the streaks coalesced into vibrant azure orbs, glowing bright, leading him deeper into the woods.

The will-o'-wisps gathered in a small clearing, glowing in a magnificent display that brought to mind the spiral arm of the Milky Way galaxy. Then they were gone and Kneale was alone in the dark. This realization gave him a nervous flutter in his core, but he was used to being by himself in the wilderness, and he knew that he was not far from the castle. He had been walking roughly southwest and the night sky was still clear and dark. He went to check his watch but then remembered that it had resisted all attempts to repair it. That gave him a proper chill.

The lights had disappeared just ahead of him, so he walked to that spot as he clicked on his headlamp. He swept the beam across the space, finding the trees to be less crowded together and the ground to be relatively clear. He surprised himself by thinking it would be a good spot to film a scene for their horror movie.

As if in response to that idle thought, equipment appeared in the gloom. Two box lights, unattended and dark, stood before him like great snakes rising to threaten him, hoods open. He approached the nearest one, finding its canvas covering to be wet with condensation but still intact. The plastic frame and metal pole upon which it was held had no noticeable defects, despite being derelict. The other light was in a similarly good condition. Kneale followed their power cords through a series of rail-thin young trees and discovered a field generator, the scent of gasoline still hanging in the air, a half-full can nearby.

Sweeping the headlamp's beam across the area, Kneale discovered more: a cooler, half-full of beer cans and bagged sandwiches; folding camping chairs, some still standing, others fallen into the dirt and low grasses; scraps of paper and empty energy drink cans scattered around the moist earth. On one sheet was a title, smeared and crumpled, but readable: "RIPPER WOODS."

Hitting their mark with perfect timing, a rush of bats descended from the tree branches above, swooping low to screech and swarm above his head, churning the air. Something heavy tumbled down after them, landing next to Kneale with a threatening *thump*. As the screeching horde fluttered off into the forest, Kneale bent down to see what offering the night had made.

19

Inside the castle, the stone and old earth smell was complemented by the subtle aroma of brewing coffee. The editing room had once been a guest bedroom, as evidenced by the old frame and canopy, sans mattress, pressed against the outer wall alongside a dust-laden vanity. Renee perched over an old-wood desk in the center of the room, twin computer monitors aglow and casting her face in an awful blue pallor. She was absorbed by the spectacle on screen, reviewing the early dailies and backing up the footage on portable hard drives.

"Can we watch this in here?" Kneale asked, holding up a pair of small digital format tapes.

She turned back to him, annoyed at the interruption. On the screens in front of her, Yvonne, playing the Maiden-turned-vampire seductress, embraced her Betrothed in a violent, erotic kiss of death in take after take, an endless loop of lust and blood.

"What is it?" she asked.

"I don't know," Kneale said, setting the cartridges on the table as he took a seat next to her. "The lights led me into the woods and the bats dropped these."

Renee cast him a sidelong glance, then reached over to the ashtray. She lit a joint and took a puff, offering Kneale a hit. He waved it off, but she kept toking, filling the room with pungent white smoke. The haze gave the images on screen a languorous, dreamlike quality.

Kneale pointed at the monitor.

"I know we're shooting out of order, but I'm having a hard time following the plot of the movie." Renee blew out more smoke.

"Remember: this is more about atmosphere and vibe, with sexy and gory setpieces," she said.

"Won't some people have a hard time with that?"

Renee shrugged. "That's their problem. This is for people who appreciate what we're trying to do—an extended mood piece punctuated by thrilling, decadent explosions of color, fog, practical effects, and blood. *Plot* is for brain-dead YouTube film critics pointing out logical inconsistencies in works that operate beyond logic. We're creating an experience, one driven by the idiosyncratic tastes and output of the creatives involved, including us." She picked up one of the tape cases. "We're not using this cassette format on this shoot. I wasn't sure why I felt compelled to bring the converter, but now I have my answer."

She reached behind the main monitor and pulled out a plastic deck trailing wires. She set it down between them, hit the POWER button, and popped open the case. The cassette slid perfectly into the receiver, which she snapped shut. A few mouse clicks later, and Yvonne and Christopher's erotic embrace was replaced by a black window. Then the tape's footage began to roll.

It opened with a series of brief shots of country roads: signs riddled with bullet holes, rusting cars set before dilapidated trailers, endless fields and distant forests cast in gold by the rays of the setting sun. Shots of a campsite. Brightly colored tents and coolers arrayed around a stone fire pit. Six or seven people in their twenties and thirties slapping at mosquitoes and deer flies, beers in hand. Several of them stood before a light box. A man gave blocking instructions to a woman in a SUNY Canaltown hoodie and a man wearing a suit of tattered fabric and a grotesque jack-o'-lantern mask.

"That's a good design," Renee said, pointing at the mask between coughs of thick smoke. "Lots of detail, but not, like, *over*-designed. Simple, iconic. Like a hockey mask, or a green and red sweater."

"What is this?" Kneale asked as the shot cut to a clapboard with the name *RIPPER WOODS* scrawled across it in black marker. There was a series of repeated takes, all captured in a single, unbroken shot: the woman in the hoodie hiding or moving among the trees; the lumbering slasher-killer in pursuit.

"Someone was making a movie," Renee said. "Slasher film. Low-budget, from the looks of it. Someone with a rich dentist uncle, maybe."

"Did you hear that?" a voice asked from behind the camera.

"That's a person," someone else said. *"Or people."*

"No way." Another woman, revealed by an errant swing of the camera. She held the second camera. *"That's gotta be an animal."*

"Foxes and owls can sound like people," the woman in the hoodie—presumably the final girl—said. The next few shots were a jumble. The director must have been nervously hitting the record button off and on, as there were only snippets of movement, half-said words, worried faces, and shots of the branches above. Streaks of light and static marked the end of the tape.

As the screen went to a blur of electronic wash, Renee leaned back in her seat.

"That's it?"

"One more." Kneale held up the second tape.

"Where did you say you found these?"

"A swarm of bats dropped them off, just south of the castle. Play it."

"I'm just high enough to accept that explanation," Renee said.

On the second tape, there was more of the same—landscape shots, candids of the cast and crew, and some inspired gore effects: limbs split by an axe, a dummy's rib cage popped open by a chainsaw, geysers of pink blood flowing from corpses. Then, familiar setups: the killer chasing the final girl; the conversation from before, captured from another angle.

"Let me see that." An exchange of the camera from one set of hands to another. It pointed up into the cluster of darkness of the branches above. The recording mode shifted into a black and white, low-light capture setting.

Bodies floated in the air, reaching, grinning, grasping. Drifting toward the camera, dripping blood. The operator had the good sense to move out of the way. More confused shots of corpses floating away. A medium-shot of a woman struggling to keep a scream from escaping, her hands pressed to her mouth.

"We have to go."

"We have to get back to the trucks."

"The trucks."

"I've got the keys."

Eyes appeared among the trees and the digital artifacts, trailing heat and smoke. More leering corpses, more gnarled trees, all reaching for the woman in the center of the frame. They wrapped around her shoulders, covered her face. They pulled her into the dark.

Blood dripped down from ruined human forms unbound by gravity. The audio track snapped and hissed. The panicked breathing of the woman holding the camera. A crimson shroud fell over the wood. A shot of the sky, out of which emerged something impossible: the luminous, bloodshot eyes of the devil. The images captured by the handheld were red, red, *red*, the trees and bodies alike grasping as a chorus of the damned sang a song of despair.

"This is all one take," Renee said. "Or, they're really good at hiding the cuts. Those bodies are practical, not CGI…" She trailed off, lost in the parade of beautiful horrors. She gave up trying to convince herself that the footage was anything other than what it was. That it wasn't real.

"Turn it off," Kneale said, looking away. Renee didn't respond.

After a few moments, the howling madness on screen came to an end. Renee exhaled, long and slow.

"It's over, I think." Renee put out what remained of her joint in the ashtray. Kneale reached for the tape deck when Renee pointed to the screen.

The forest floor. Night. The lens was obscured by fallen leaves. The camera moved up, dirt and leaves tumbling down during its slow ascent. Higher, *higher*, until the camera passed through the branches and the foliage. A form-perfect crane or drone shot, revealing the full scope of the forest and the hills beyond. The moon was a great red slash of a crescent, so low you could prick your finger and draw blood. The camera rushed over the treetops, smooth and steady.

"What is this?" Kneale asked. "What the *hell* is this?"

"Must be drone footage. Very stable. Good platform."

"A drone?"

"Good one, too. The wind is barely affecting it."

The camera altered course, revealing stone towers in profile, set against the glorious night sky. The castle. The camera rushed toward it, the fluttering wind redlining the microphone. Then it decelerated until it came to a static position, floating high enough to see most of the grounds. Trucks and cars were parked in the courtyard. A grey, inhuman figure danced along one stretch of wall, lit from below, a crowd gathered around to watch from the dark.

"This is the pickup for Vampiric Horror Number Two." She pointed at the screen, her face pale and in awe. "That's *you*, Kneale."

The strange character danced its strange dance. An inch of moving pixels, of shadow and light. An impossible record of his debut performance.

"We're being surveilled," Kneale said. "They want us to know that." His hands balled up tight into fists. He wanted to punch through the computer monitor. He wanted to punch through the image of himself. "You need to tell me if you have any idea what this means."

"You said bats gave this to you," Renee said, voice low and careful, eyes on his fists. "What the fuck am I supposed to do with that?"

"The lights led me to it. And bats dropped it out of the sky."

Renee leaned back and crossed her arms over her chest.

"I think you're right about the tapes," she said. "They do want us to know that they've been watching us. If they were here when we were shooting your scene, that means they've probably been here other times. But from the looks of the footage, I'd say Daniel and Christopher's defenses kept them out of the castle grounds proper."

"The salt, candles, and crucifixes deal," Kneale said.

"Yes. The precautions are working."

"And the others on the tapes—they didn't take the proper precautions? Do you know who those people were?"

"Not specifically, no," she said. "But we're not the only ones interested in *cinéma goblin*. There are other...parties." She searched for the right word. "Other factions."

"Am I part of your marketing scheme? Is that it? Hire some burnout vet, get him to smoke your space weed, then show him ghosts and goblins on videocassette, convince him the woods are haunted?"

"I don't think I need to convince you of anything," Renee said. "Everyone here knows the woods are haunted. With cameras, a crew, and a few tricks, I can make monsters come to life. On *film*. I'm not capable of engineering what you're describing. Something else led you to those tapes."

Kneale was willing to entertain her reasoning for a moment.

"Who, then? Or what?"

"We chose these woods for a number of reasons," Renee said. "Proximity to certain forces can...*alter* things. Reality itself can become more pliable. Magic—real magic—becomes easier to perform. Filmmakers are masters of manipulating light, sound, and shadow. Imagine what kind of movie we could make if we could go beyond the simple tools we've been using for a hundred years. *Cinéma goblin* is that idea. An evolution of the art by harnessing forces that predate the Lumiere brothers, that predate modernity."

On-screen, Kneale danced and gesticulated wildly. He crowed like a great beast. He felt a deep, painful longing to perform again, to find that spirit of playful chaos and ride its coattails into rapture. It was as if a piece of himself had been unlocked, revealing desires that resonated with possibilities that went beyond the mundane drudgery of his life as a soldier and security contractor. The word *performer* appeared in his mind and, with it, a dozen competing images of possible outcomes: wearing that costume, wearing others; following this production on to its next film, and the next, Renee and Terence finding him new roles, new work; finding camaraderie among these strange people who had so readily accepted him as one of their own, despite his background.

A hard cut. The camera was in flight over water. Shallow and dark. Then the tape ran out, and the screen went blue.

"Roll that back," Kneale said. "To when the water first appears. Can you slow that down?"

Renee did as he asked. The playback progressed frame by frame, blurring the image, obfuscating details.

"There. Pause."

The tape deck held fast with a sharp *click*.

"Buildings," Kneale said.

"Cabins," Renee clarified.

"Where is that?"

"Not sure," she said. "There's a lot of unsurveyed sites out here."

"But not too many lakes, right?"

"We might be able to narrow it down, assuming that stretch of footage was captured nearby."

A knock came at the half-open door. Yvonne, sans vampire makeup and wearing a hunting camouflage hoodie and cap, leaned inside the room.

"I'm sorry to interrupt, Renee, but—have you seen Andrea?"

Renee leaned over to the computer monitor, pressing the power button and sending it into darkness.

"No. Sorry. What's going on?"

"I haven't seen her since makeup."

"Did you check her tent?"

"And I asked everyone I've found in the castle, yeah," Yvonne said.

"Is she missing?" Kneale asked.

Yvonne gave him a worried look.

"No one seems to know where she is."

"Maybe she went on walkabout with Christopher and Daniel," Renee said. "Or one of your team, Alan."

"I'm on it," Kneale said, getting to his feet.

20

Renee gathered the cast and crew in the courtyard directly in front of the castle's main entrance. Its imposing stone façade was impossibly tall in the early morning hours, cast in fleeting illumination by the flashlights of the assembled.

Kneale went over a list of names on his clipboard. "We need to confirm that everyone is here. Read their name, hear their voice, touch them on the shoulder. Put a little check by their name. No one can vouch for anyone else. You have to *touch* them, do you understand? And no one is to leave the castle grounds. Anything beyond the walls is officially off limits until I give the all-clear."

"I need everyone gathered here, in neat little rows," Renee shouted, her voice echoing off the castle. "No one is to leave the courtyard until my say-so." She took the clipboard from Kneale and proceeded to work through the roster, moving among the uneven rows of persons huddling close in the early morning cold. When she was finished, she returned to Kneale, worry etched in shadow across her face.

"That's all accounted for, save Andrea," she said. Kneale addressed the crew.

"When was the last time you saw Andrea? Anyone?"

Yvonne stepped forward.

"I saw her at the makeup tent. Nike was there. We were there for about thirty minutes."

Nike nodded in agreement. "We had her there until just after 7 p.m.," she said. "I haven't seen her since."

"Did anyone see her after that?" Kneale asked.

"We had four or five shots with her, first thing," Terence said. "Interiors. The main bedroom." He nodded toward the great castle looming behind Kneale. "We wrapped that location around 10, 10:30."

"Anyone else?"

No one else came forward.

"We start with the castle," Kneale said. "Alvira, Pore, you're with me. Chris and Dan, if you don't mind. I need five more volunteers to help search inside." The castle behind him loomed tall. It was larger than he remembered. "Make that ten volunteers. The rest of you, search the trucks, the vehicles, the tents. Search the graveyard. No one goes beyond the walls. Gates stay closed. Meet back at this location in thirty minutes for another headcount. Do not go to sleep, don't hit the shower trailer, don't get chow, don't go smoke a damn cigarette without checking back in here. Chances are Andrea is still here, or very close nearby. Let's move out."

Ten volunteers and the security team were not enough. The castle absorbed them as little more than rats scurrying along the floors of a labyrinthine dungeon. The halls stretched on endlessly, with doors leading to a multitude of derelict and dust-covered rooms and staircases that led down into darkness or up to floors that, when reached, seemed larger and more expansive than possible. Outside, the crew shined flashlight beams and cell phone app lights into tents, cars, trucks, and storage containers. Neither party found Andrea.

As the sun rose, Kneale dismissed the exhausted cast and crew but gathered Alvira, Pore, Renee, Christopher, and Daniel at the door of his trailer.

"We have to expand the search," Kneale said. "With the sun coming up, our chances of finding her increase, but only for a short while. Alvira, Pore, get some gear together for a trip into the woods. Pack food, water, and kit for overnight ops. We'll start with a spiral pattern around the castle, work our way outwards." Kneale pointed to Christopher and Daniel. "I need you two to reinforce our defenses here," he said. "We have reason to believe that whatever it is that you've been doing has had some effect. But with Andrea missing, it's possible you missed something."

"No," Christopher said, somber and assured. "We did not. Andrea must have ventured beyond the protection of the salt."

"Then confirm that," Kneale said. "There's a video I want you two to watch. Renee will show you."

The producer spoke up.

"If you're going beyond the castle, I recommend that you return before nightfall," she said.

"Why?"

Renee ran a palm over her cheek, searching for the right words.

"If it took one, it will take more," she said. "Search during the day. Return at night."

"If you're aware of a specific threat, you need to tell me," Kneale said, frustration creeping into his voice. "Andrea is missing. I'm assuming this isn't some boneheaded publicity stunt conducted at my expense, because if it was, we would have a serious problem."

Renee's face flashed surprise.

"No, of course not. We would never."

"I'll take your word for it. Now, be honest with me: is she in some sort of danger? Are *we* in danger?"

"Yes. All the time. This is the reason we hired you. But I'm afraid of what might happen to you and your team if you search for Andrea after dark. There's a lot riding on this production. It's important in ways that go beyond recouping an investment."

"Then fill me in."

"I can't do that. No more than you could betray the confidence of an employer. Or a former employer."

"We're a relatively short drive back to the public road," Kneale said. "If you don't want me out in the woods, then let's call this in. File a missing person report. I was hoping to confirm she wasn't just taking a stroll through the enchanted forest before we took that step, but I get the feeling we're moving beyond that as a possibility."

Renee's eyes drifted over to the sun rising from behind the great hills. Her lips trembled, as if working through what she should say next.

"I have a satellite phone. But I don't think it'll work."

"Why not?"

"Find out for yourself." From her messenger bag she produced a bulky slab of plastic with a large silver antenna. Kneale accepted it, along with a small card bearing a handful of scrawled numbers. "The number second from the bottom is the nearest state police barracks." The phone was not unlike the ones they occasionally got access to downrange. He suspected the connection would be just as bad, with a significant delay as signals bounced up to the satellites and back again.

"Dial zero-three-two-two before the area code," Renee said.

Kneale followed her directions, punching in the number. The others waited, eyes on him, unsure of what this was about. He put the phone to his ear and waited for the linkup.

A series of odd beeps and subtle waves of static preceded the warbling, deeply unpleasant ringing, like a songbird being strangled by someone who was not quite up to the task. The noise ceased and a voice floated to him over waves of distortion.

"Troop E, Sergeant Joe Johnston speaking," the voice said, tinged with static and echoing from across the atmosphere.

"Hello, officer," Kneale said, speaking slowly and carefully to account for the delay. "My name is Alan Kneale and I'm head of security for a—" Kneale's voice came back to him, a duplicate, as if he were speaking to an echo. He paused to let it pass, then continued. "New Camlough Studios. We're on location at a castle in the nature preserve off of Route—"

A wash of static interrupted him.

"Say again? Who is calling?"

"Alan Kneale, head of security for New Camlough Studios."

"Alan... Camlough... Alan..." The words were clipped by static and interference.

"I told you," Renee said.

"We need to report a missing person," Kneale said. The interference suddenly stopped and the line went quiet. "Hello?" When he spoke again, there was no echo, no static, no response. Until there was.

"We didn't expect to talk again, Alan Kneale. We are so rarely surprised these days."

Kneale's heart sank. Renee saw something change in his face.

"Hang up," she said.

"No, stay on the line, Alan. Let's catch up. How long has it been since Colorado? How long since you and we had a nice little chat? Do you still have the checklist? The rules? Are you allowed to talk to us now, or do your masters still compel you to only listen? To observe and experience?" The cacophony spoke with the gleeful familiarity of a longtime bully finding their favorite victim scared and alone.

"I'm hanging up. Now," Kneale said, as much to himself as to Renee.

"What's going on?" Alvira asked. "You alright, boss?"

"You've been busy since Colorado," the voices said. *"Well, busy drinking yourself into an early grave. But who can blame you for that? After all you've seen. After all you've dooooooooonne."*

That last word stretched out to impossible lengths, oscillating between high, screeching bursts of sound and low, sonorous reverberations. Kneale's brain sent a command to his arm to pull the phone away from his ear. The voices overrode the electrochemical signal.

"How many times do you think you've been to the haunted rocks?" they asked, whispering now in endless echoes. "How many more times than you remember, we mean. How much time have you spent there, and lost? How much time have you spent lying upon them as a corpse, or dancing with the goblins of the deep wood?"

Kneale's face went pale. He closed his eyes. Renee stepped toward him, just a few paces away but impossibly far.

"Maybe you have been coming out to the dolmen for longer than you remember, Alan Kneale. Maybe you are still there now. With us."

He opened his eyes. He saw tree branches and grey sky above. He felt the cold of the rocks against his back.

Renee tore the phone from his hand and slid open the back casing. She clawed at the batteries, sending them tumbling into the dirt. Kneale's hand remained near his ear, his fingers twitching, his breathing erratic. He stood upright. He was nowhere near the dolmen. He was nowhere near the dolmen. He was no where—

"Like I told you," Renee said. "Won't work." She tilted her head at his expression. "Did you recognize the voice? Did it mean anything to you?"

The spell broken, Kneale ran a hand over his face.

"No." He allowed himself a moment to gather his thoughts. He hoped his voice would not crack. "The road is what, thirty minutes out? Faster with someone who knows the way, right? And if the phones don't work there either, I'll drive all the way to the state trooper barracks myself."

"It'll be too late for her by then," Daniel said.

"Do you know something I don't?" Kneale asked. "Would any

of you like to share with the rest of the group? With me, the guy you paid to run things if they went bad?"

"We're this far along, and you haven't figured it out?" said Daniel, tapping his finger against a knife strapped to his hip. Its handle was made of intricately carved bone, its blade held by a decorative leather sheath.

"He won't allow himself to consider the possibility," Christopher said. He lifted a large bundle, wrapped in a rough fabric cloak procured from the costume department. "Here. For you and your team. Two for each of you. Just in case."

Wood rattled beneath the folds of the robe. Kneale accepted it, then pulled back the covering layers to reveal foot-long, freshly sharpened handles of wood. The points were fine enough to draw blood. They smelled faintly of rosewater.

"Daniel and Chris will watch the castle grounds today," Renee said. "I'll assign some of the others to the watch, too. But you three will be on your own."

"The creature will be satisfied for a time, with one so young and vibrant as she," Christopher said. "We have consulted, and believe that there is only one. Maybe two, if she is turned. If there are others, they have remained hidden, and are yet to be revealed."

"One *what*?" Kneale said, exhausted by this game, his head still reeling from what the voices had done to him. "What the fuck are you talking about?"

"*Le vampire*," Christopher said, all of his backwoods French-Canadian accent emerging as flourish. "*Nosferatu*."

"The undead," Renee said.

Pore barked out a laugh and turned away. He lit a cigarette out of nervous habit, mumbling to himself. Alvira said nothing at first, but then stepped forward to pick out two of the stakes for herself.

"You anticipated this," she said, to no one in particular.

"Of course," Renee said. "That's why we recruited you three."

"What about them?" Kneale nodded toward Daniel and Christopher. "They seem eager to play Ghostbuster."

"Our knowledge lies in preventative measures and defensive sorcery," Christopher said. "Although I was a soldier, and I'm sure Daniel and his *wahaika parāoa* are formidable, we are actors, and therefore a little out of practice. You and your team are the combat experts."

"We're expendable," Alvira said.

"Soldiers always are," Pore said, blowing out a plume of smoke.

"That's right," Renee said. "If that puts it in terms that help you accept what we're asking of you. Yes. You're expendable." Her eyes flicked back to Kneale. "We recruited you for this contingency."

"You hired us because you thought there might be a vampire in the woods?" Kneale said.

"Is it really so hard to believe?" Renee said. "Based on your experiences, Alan, I should think that you would be open to the possibility of the existence of supernatural beings. What's happening now is just one of several possible paths this project was expected to take. This location was selected for its connection to…otherworldly forces. It was inevitable that we would awaken something. When the dolmen appeared, I recognized it as the first step in a process that is now well underway."

"And the people on those tapes that dropped into my lap," Kneale said. "Did a vampire kill them, too? Is that what you're saying?"

"I think so."

"Bullshit."

"Fine. I'm full of shit. We're all full of shit. But Andrea needs your help. She's still out in the woods."

"I'm not buying this spook business, but I *am* going to find your actress."

"I have no doubt of that. But before you go." Renee nodded to Christopher, who held up a small wooden box. The top flipped open to reveal four palm-sized glass bottles with black cross stoppers.

"The stakes are courtesy Nike's production team," he said.

"They are very sharp, and will pierce a rib cage when applied with sufficient force. These, however, are a touch more fragile, by design." The water sloshing within caught the first rays of the morning sun and glittered with a holy light. "Keep them in pouches along your belt, wrapped in fabric. They will shatter on impact. Useful for close-quarters combat, or they can be thrown against the ground to create impassable terrain for the one you must face. Should you find an empty coffin, pour this water inside, and offer a prayer to cleanse it of evil. It will deny the enemy his place of rest, which is most effective. Or so I'm told."

Kneale hefted the stakes to his left hip, then accepted a glass bottle. He held it up to examine it in the quickening light. Alvira took two; Pore reluctantly accepted the final one.

"You should keep a few things in mind," Daniel said. "Firearms have some efficacy, perhaps up to the point of incapacitation, but only for a short while. There are variations in cultural traditions, but we believe that a wooden stake through the heart, followed by decapitation and incineration, will end the threat. That is pretty much universal."

"Andrea will be undergoing the transformation," Renee said. "But if you slay the master, there's a chance she will return to us. It may take a few days for the change to become permanent, but destroying the one that made her while she is still young with the vampire's kiss may give her hope of regaining her humanity."

"It affects everyone differently," Christopher said. "It depends on the blood, you see." He had one more gift to give. From the folds of his coat he produced wreaths of garlic, fresh and white as snow. "Compliments of the kitchen staff. Wear them around your necks."

"And pray often, if you are so inclined," Daniel said. "What you might understand as the power of God—the lifegiving, benevolent, cosmically conscious force of creative energy at the heart of all existence—provides us protection against the dark powers. They are beholden to the creator's will, as are we all."

"Use the Force," Alvira said.

"It is not the objects, nor the words of the prayers, but one's faith that serves as a conduit to the holy powers beyond," Christopher said. "Not *your* power, but the power of God. Do you understand?"

"No," Kneale said.

Josiah tossed his cigarette into the mud, then chambered a round into his rifle.

"I know where *my* faith lies," he said. "If we're done telling campfire stories, I'd like to go find that girl before a psycho has her cuts her up into a million pieces. Or worse."

"The discovery of the dolmen and of the tapes confirms that our caution was warranted," Renee said. "It also confirms that this is the right place to make this film. The only thing left to discover is if you three are up to the task before you."

"I've heard enough," Pore said. "I'm gonna pack my gear. When are we stepping off?"

Kneale thought for a moment, rubbing his thumb along the glass vial of holy water.

"Thirty mikes," he said.

"You got it," Pore said. He and Alvira made their way back to the tents.

"I'll call in a radio check every two hours or so," Kneale said. "If I miss a couple—"

"The radios won't work," Renee said. "I mean, they will, but you heard the voice."

"The *voices*," Kneale said. "Out of many, one."

Renee's eyes flickered with excitement.

"You *are* the right man for the job," she said. "Now, go save my actress."

21

They started at the dolmen.

Even in the light of sunrise, the site had an ominous atmosphere. The shadows and negative space that pressed around the stones churned with movement. The limbs of a vaporous mass of the dead flowed within those dark spaces, a cohesion of ghosts pressing through an aperture held open by rites enacted long ago. Kneale felt spectral eyes on his team, as if they were trespassers caught on the castle grounds by alert watchmen waiting in ambush. As the sun spread across the stones, scraps of white fabric were left behind by retreating spirits.

"From her dress," Alvira said, grabbing a slip. "Blood on the rocks, too. Or maybe corn syrup and red food coloring."

"Let's assume the worst," Kneale said.

"You two see all this?" Pore called over to them from the far side of the formation. They joined him among the thin trees.

"This wasn't here before," Kneale said.

"We'd remember something like this," Alvira said.

Before them was a wide column of tall, many-limbed green plants scattered across the forest floor. They grew over great chunks of stone that were the cast-off remains of the raw materials used to carve and assemble the crude altar-tomb. Their leaves grew in five points and their stalks were overburdened with heavy flowers of glistening gold and silver, as if the plants were mining precious metals from the soil to display them in the sunlight.

"I haven't seen that much weed since Afghanistan," Alvira said. She sniffed the air. Metallic skunk-smell. "I can't believe the crew didn't find this."

"Is this what they had us smoke?" Pore said, stepping into a clutch of tall stalks and long, five-pointed leaves. He rubbed his fingers along a bud shining with strange yellows and blues made resplendent in a slash of morning light. "I've never seen anything like this." The air shimmered around each plant, bending the light, reflecting the ghosts of rainbows.

"Colorado strain," Alvira whispered in reverence.

"What?"

"It's from Colorado," she said. "I heard some of the crew talking about the soil they shipped in. They talked about a 'gardening project' like it was some big joke. I figured it was a term of art I didn't understand. Not, like, *literally* gardening in the woods. To grow the biggest goddamn cannabis plants you've ever seen."

"They must have brought in whole plants," Pore said. "Ballsy to move this much across state lines, even if it is legal in New York. That smell. Potent."

"It got me pretty damn stoned," Kneale said.

"I was hallucinating," Alvira said. "I didn't think weed was supposed to do that."

"I can see them glittering for dozens of meters ahead," Pore said. "They would've had to fill a tractor-trailer to get all these plants here. When did they find the time to do this since we've been out here?"

A crawling sensation lanced up Kneale's spine. The fingers of a ghost, affecting an act of intimacy.

"They're growing along a ley line," he said.

"A what?" Pore said.

"Think of it as a terrain feature that you can't see," Kneale said.

He pointed at the cannabis plants leading deeper into the forest. "But they can."

When the team walked beyond the last of the plants, they emerged onto a great platform of red rock overhanging a precipitous drop-off. A wide and endless valley stretched out before them. The tips of conifers poked up from below.

"Where to now?" Alvira asked, admiring the view.

Kneale took a knee and set down his rifle. He took off his assault pack and produced a forest map from the main pouch, spreading it out before them. Pore and Alvira knelt down.

"We've been traveling roughly north from the castle, here," he said, pointing to a spot on the map where he had penciled in a circle. He moved his finger over to where the dolmen would be and to a stretch of tight-knit topographical lines, representing the cliff they found themselves standing on.

"What made you want to start the search here?" Alvira asked.

"Instinct," Kneale said. "You ever get a bad feeling on a mission? Or a sudden urge to do something, and it turned out to be the right thing? That."

In the valley below, a small body of water shimmered in the broadening sunlight. Trees and hills pressed in around it, jealous of its beauty. Alvira lifted a set of binoculars to her eyes. "Looks like buildings down there. Campsite, maybe."

A mass of cold unfurled in Kneale's guts. The footage—a flight over water, with cabins in the near distance—fluttered up from his memory.

"That's what, four, five miles distant?" Pore said. "We could make it there before noon. What do you think?"

"I think I've got that feeling Kneale was talking about," Alvira said, lowering her binos. "We'll find Andrea down there."

22

Branch and bramble parted on their own. Paths revealed themselves in glittering sunlight that fell on dew-kissed grass. The ground was dry and sure. The birds remained silent.

The journey down the cliff was easy walking, but the curve of the deer trail they followed led them west. When they reached level ground with the ridge behind them, Kneale produced the map to reorient the group for the movement to the cabins.

"They're not on the map, which means they're recent," Alvira said.

"Or much older," Kneale said.

He produced a handheld GPS from his assault pack. The MALTHUS DEFENSE APPLICATIONS logo appeared as black text over a light-green background. The device established a satellite connection, represented on-screen by a series of wire frame doors opening in a tunnel, something out of an early-generation 3D dungeon crawler. The USGS coordinates displayed in a pair of long, alphanumeric strings. Kneale scribbled them down on a notepad, then pointed to the map. Alvira ran her fingers along the grid lines, finding their location.

"Right about where we thought we'd be," she said. "Not bad for some washed-up vets who haven't seen a land nav course in a few years."

"See if you can set the coordinates for the lake," Pore said. "Make this real easy."

They kept their rifles at the ready, scanning the forest ahead. Kneale walked point, keeping his pace count. Alvira took the left flank, watching for movement to the side. Pore, a dozen meters back and to the right, turned his whole body around at regular intervals to keep an eye behind them. Their tactical movement was familiar—comforting even—a small sense of control exerted over a strange situation. Like slipping on an old pair of dependable combat boots.

Kneale led the team to a short hill overlooking the lake and found a break in the trees that allowed for an expansive view of the area below. The lake was home not to a forgotten summer campground but the scattered ruins of log cabins built in the early decades of the previous century and left to the whims of the forest soon thereafter. Most of the roofs were collapsed and walls were bowed. Stone foundations disintegrated under the press of time. Trees stood around on all sides like invaders ransacking an isolated settlement. Many of them had shed their leaves early.

"There," Alvira said, pointing to the shore riddled with fallen pines on the far side of the lake. "That one is in better condition than the rest."

Kneale raised his binos. Indeed, one of the cabins stood strong against the encroachment of time and forest. Its black-pitched logs blended in with the shadows, but its roof and walls held strong. The grasses that grew up around it were lower than the others, indicating that something had been moving over them.

"Good eye," Kneale said. "I'd say that's our target location."

"We still don't know if we've just blown right past Andrea," Pore said. "She could be anywhere."

"Not anywhere," Alvira said, lowering her binos to nod at the half-hidden building. "There."

Kneale nodded, then looked to the sky. Grey clouds muted the sun. Daylight would slip away from them if they were not careful.

"You've got five mikes to prep yourself for a movement to contact," Kneale said. "Take a piss, eat a granola bar, hydrate up. No cigarettes, no fires, no noise. Go."

23

Someone had been making patchwork repairs on the old cabin. Wood panels covered the smashed-out windows, beams held up sections of bowed wall, and a sun-bleached tarp lay over a section of roof.

Kneale brought the team to the rear of the building, hoping for a back door from which they could make their assault. But the forest was subsuming the structure, growing up to and beyond its eastern elevation, its overgrowth a tangled mass of impenetrable branches and twisted, malformed trunks that created a natural barrier. They would have to enter from the front door.

"No tire tracks or ruts in the ground that I can see," Pore whispered as they reached the narrow porch. "Whoever is keeping this thing standing is a scavenger."

"Or smart enough to hide their vehicle somewhere off-site," Kneale said.

"There aren't any roads this far into the preserve," Alvira said, keeping her voice low.

Kneale tested the rickety stairs with the toe of his right combat boot and found it sure. He kept the barrel of his rifle pointed at the door, which hung misaligned on rusted-out hinges.

"Alvira, cover the windows," he said. No light emerged from within. "Pore, you got our six. No surprises."

"Roger."

Kneale stepped up onto the porch and approached the front door. He scanned it for wires that would indicate explosives. An old habit. Nothing. Just a door, barely hanging on. He was overthinking this.

"On me," he said. "Stack up." With the speed and surefootedness of a practiced fire team, Alvira stepped behind him, her right boot against his, her shoulder to the wall, and Pore took up the rear position. He leaned forward, bumping Alvira. She sent the *ready* signal to Kneale with a tap from her boot to his. Kneale grabbed the handle and pulled. Unlocked. He swung the heavy door open and stepped into the darkness, rifle raised, scanning for targets.

The cabin's interior was an open layout, with scattered chairs and bookshelves marking the living room. A metal tub built into a handmade wooden shelf stood as a marker for the kitchenette. At the far end of the cabin was a wooden partition with a pair of doors, presumably leading to the bedrooms or storage. Headlamp beams probed the dust-ridden air, piles of abandoned dishes, derelict towers of moldering books, and cobwebs cluttering the ceiling. Kneale shined his light on the floor, following a trail of fresh dirt.

He moved further in, slowing to check the dark spaces behind deteriorating chairs and an overturned table. When he reached the partition, he pushed the left door open. It revealed a dark bedroom, the windows covered with planks of rotting wood nailed haphazardly to the walls. The bed was a collapsing, wet pile of torn fabric, with an organic mush that may have once been a large animal. The smell repulsed Kneale, pushing him back out of the room. The other door was covered with a set of crimson swaths, splashed haphazardly in roughly vertical lines. The impression they formed was of teeth, bared in warning. The door opened with a groan.

It revealed a stone hall, one that stretched well past the limits of the cabin's walls, upending any notion of spatial relations or sane architectural dynamics. The air was cold and moist, the draft pulled up from the depths of the earth.

Kneale pointed his rifle down the hallway. The beams of their headlamps only reached so far into the dark.

"How far does it go?" Pore asked.

"Far," Kneale said.

"This should be the end of the cabin," Alvira said. "The hall is made out of stone. We would have seen this."

"We missed it," Kneale said, hoping that by saying it, he might actually believe it.

Lingering would do them no good. He stepped into the impossible. His boots made soft footfalls on the moist stone floor, the echoes blending in with an ever-present dripping of water. Once they were all through the door, he held up his hand for a quick halt.

"We should don ear protection," he said. "If we have to shoot in here, I don't want to go deaf." He held out a small plastic case of orange cone plugs. The team slipped them in.

"How's that sound?"

"Good," Alvira said, her voice muted but clear. Pore gave a thumbs up.

They moved on. The tunnel narrowed. The air cooled. The darkness stretched on forever.

"My pace count is seventy steps per hundred meters, and we just hit that," Alvira said.

"Feels further than that," Pore said.

"Stay focused," Kneale said.

"What's that?" Alvira said, nodding ahead. "On the wall. To the right."

On the right-hand side of the hall were confused splashes of line and curve writ in wide swaths of red, of interconnected shapes forming patterns that called to mind fleeting associations with a half-remembered nightmare. Transfixed by the patterns, Kneale followed the great crimson slashes with his palm, tracing a bloody path along the stones.

"What are you doing?" Alvira said, trying to keep her voice low. The hall conspired against her, echoing her words back with peculiar modifications of warbling tone and length.

The stones shimmered. Kneale pulled his hand back from the wall. Ripples appeared along its surface like droplets falling into a polluted puddle. A deep, ghostly blue pulsed along the outer layers of stone. Something pressed out, warping the wall like a thin membrane. Alvira threw her arm across Kneale's chest and pulled him back as hands of stone burst out of the plane, grasping for him.

The wall's proper dimensions and properties snapped back in place, as if reminded of the rules of physics. The blue light glowed from within, soft and pleasant, spilling out from minute cracks in the stacked stones and through fissures in mortar.

The ground rumbled. A section of wall ten feet across shook in place, then slid back, dislodging chunks of stone and a spray of moist dirt. It drew back at a slow, steady rate, operated by unseen mechanisms. It disappeared into the far darkness, leaving only the impression of vast, empty space before them.

Kneale risked running his hands over the air where the wall had once been, finding only a deep, tragic draft of cold. His breath was visible in white geysers.

A pale hand emerged from the darkness, propelled forward at incredible speed. It opened desiccated fingers, nails razor sharp and encrusted with the dirt of the grave, its skin a sickly blue pallor, clinging in ruined curtains over bones blackened and pockmarked with mold.

Alvira and Pore shoved him out of the way, then jumped back as the giant's hand entered the hallway and grasped the space where Kneale had stood just a half-moment before. The great fingers curled back like scorpions' tails, then lanced out again. Kneale scrambled back, tripping over his own ankles as a pair of fingers struck the ground between his legs, nails cracking with the effort and carving wounds into the stone floor.

Alvira produced her combat knife—a brown USMC KA-BAR, a gift from her grandfather who worked at the factory in Olean a lifetime ago—and buried the blade in the oversized thumb. The flesh split easily. Shifting the hilt to both hands, she dragged it down the length of the member, spilling out a noxious wash of black blood. The smell made her want to vomit, but she kept her balance and split the digit from nail to joint. Pore joined in with his machete, hacking away with less precision but no less effect, sloughing off clumps of dried meat with every strike, black effluvium peppering their faces. No cry of pain or outrage came to their ears, but the tunnel shook with the fury of the unseen giant. Kneale scrambled to his feet, aimed the barrel of his rifle at the meat-dripping wrist, and fired. The flash was a sharp crack of light in the near-dark. Kneale stepped back and fired again, angling his shots away from the other members of his team and toward the arm and the darkness beyond the limits of the wall.

The great hand slashed out with its razor nails once more, tearing across Kneale's tactical vest and puncturing the fabric. Alvira and Pore continued their attack, but the hand receded into darkness and beyond the reach of their blades, disappearing into a haze of incorporeal vapor. The wall rushed back to take its post in the hall, slowing at the last moment to slide forward with a rough *click*. It was as if nothing had been out of place at all. The team moved further down the hall all the same.

"Okay, okay, okay," Pore said, catching his breath. Alvira wiped muck from her KA-BAR along her pant leg, then slid the knife back into its sheath at her hip.

"You okay, Kneale?"

The team leader set his firing selector switch back to *safe*, then examined his chest. Several of the pouches along his vest had torn open, revealing a layer of ripped shirt and bloodied skin beneath.

He explored the damage with a naked finger, finding a little blood and the sharp pain of recently broken skin.

"Nothing too serious," he said.

"Take off your gear," Alvira said. She swung her assault pack off as she took a knee. Kneale did as she instructed, staring at the blood on his fingertips. With his shirt off and Pore's headlamp beam trained on his chest, Alvira assessed his wounds.

"This is gonna hurt," she said. "A lot."

She wiped at the lines of torn skin with an alcohol pad. She was not exaggerating. Kneale managed not to scream, but a few involuntary whimpers escaped to echo back to him from the tunnel. The stones found great amusement in his pain. Alvira finished by wiping up what remained of his blood and wrapped his chest with several layers of gauze.

"You're lucky it didn't go any deeper," she said.

"What was that goddamn thing?" Pore asked, rifle trained on the spot of wall behind them. The red markings remained in place, inviting another touch.

"A trap," Kneale said. "I wasn't careful." He pulled his torn shirt and vest back on.

"I wanted to touch it, too," Alvira admitted. "I felt like something wonderful might happen."

"It did."

"Hey." Pore pointed his headlamp beam down the hall. "Was that door there before?"

Their beams joined Pore's to splash against the portal that marked the end of the hall, now only a dozen meters away.

"It must have been," Alvira said.

"It wasn't," Kneale said.

The door stood tall and proud, a great slab of wood carved from a mighty tree harvested from a primeval forest. Its outer layers had been carved and etched away to reveal intricate reliefs of dancing skeletons, leering skulls, elaborate coffins, flying bats, and weaponry writ in miniature: axes, daggers, swords, and whips. The dead and their bat familiars stood in contrast to the martial icons arrayed against them, conveying opposition. The metal doorknob was no less ornate. It was a screeching bat's skull, sharp fangs extended, eye sockets empty.

Kneale approached the door, the others close behind. He hesitated before trying the handle. There was nowhere to go but through. Andrea needed them.

Unseen mechanisms clicked and clambered. The door swung open.

24

Once they were inside the next room, the door groaned shut on its own.

If I were to try to open that door, I would find it locked, and all of us trapped inside.

Their headlamp beams revealed the room in swaths of uneven light. Kneale tried to work out the spatial relationships for the tunnel and this new chamber, but his thoughts kept slipping, like gears failing to catch. Like the hallway before it, this chamber was built of stone. Its ceiling was low, but built as a concave dome, held in place by mortar that had stood the test of time against ages of shifting earth and creeping water. The air was dry and laden with soft notes of burning candles. Along each side of the room were bookshelves built with the same masterful craftsmanship as the door, complete with inlaid memento mori. The shelves held oversized tomes of curious provenance. Three long tables bisected the room, likewise carved with a sure and artistic hand. High-backed chairs were thrones at the head of each, home to slumped forms wrapped in the disintegrating purple robes of scholars from an age long forgotten. Their hands were devoid of flesh, yet still clung covetously to black grimoires.

The books' pages fluttered as a low and terrible moan reverberated throughout the chamber. Twin candles on metal stands alighted on the far side of the room, revealing another ornate door through which they might continue their journey into darkness.

Kneale approached the nearest table. The corpse there was propped over the splayed-open book, its skull barely hidden behind its drawn hood, which had become its funeral shroud. The tome's pages were filled with elaborate woodcut images, including a simple illustration depicting three armored soldiers who carried swords and shields in a dungeon chamber where they were confronted by three skull-faced figures of death.

The skeleton's hand grabbed Kneale's wrist, wrenching it into a awkward position. It was as if two great bricks of frozen stone pressed together, eliciting a gasp and paralyzing his arm with sharp pain. The skeleton sat up straight, turning its death's head to offer Kneale a fiendish grin. Blue light fluttered up within the depths of its skull.

Kneale put a combat boot on the table and kicked himself back. The desperate forced a release of the death grip. Kneale landed on his back, his arm shuddering in pain.

Pale blue light radiated from the empty eye sockets and between the chattering teeth of the other skeletons. Robed arms raised as hand and finger bones picked over by time and vermin pointed in accusation at Alvira and Pore, who backpedaled in shock. Bones clacked and rattled in arrhythmic percussion for the march of the dead.

The skeleton nearest to Kneale stood up and shambled toward him. It lunged, jaw snapping and bare-bone fingers grasping. Kneale rolled away. Its skull smacked against the cold stone floor, the impact capitalizing on the ravages of bastard time to spread fissures through old bone plates. Kneale scrambled back, knocking over a stack of books that coughed up plumes of dust. The skeleton's hand grasped his left leg, its grip a vice of below-zero cold. It turned its fractured skull to face him, the blue light from within casting weird shadows. Kneale found his leg frozen in place, the flesh crying out in nerve-shattering pain. The revenant

PROJECT VAMPIRE KILLER

had him pinned as it pulled itself forward, eager for its snapping jaw to find purchase in man-flesh.

Kneale swung his rifle around, the barrel just inches from the creature's empty nose cavity. Muscle memory slid thumb along firing selector switch and squeezed forefinger against an eager trigger.

The room exploded in light and flame. A spent round casing landed on the stone floor, the metal producing chiming notes. Kneale fired again and again, the barrel poking through the collapsing frontispiece of monstrous skull until the target was shattered and gone, leaving only a shallow crown of broken shards on top of a mold-encrusted spinal column. The blue light fled, its vessel destroyed, and rose up to phase through the domed ceiling, leaving a residue of noxious ectoplasm in its wake.

The skeleton released its grip and Kneale regained control of his leg. It pulsed with the pain of frostburn but it accepted orders again, so he put it to work. Struggling to his feet, he stood up just in time to see one of the other skeletons reach a blue, flame-engulfed hand through Pore's open, screaming mouth, and emerge from the back of the man's throat like a worm bursting through rotten soil. Blood and fleshy matter slopped out onto the floor. Pore's eyes registered shock as his legs collapsed. The skeleton struck its other hand out to pierce Pore's abdomen, letting gravity pull the body down through the searing blue fire. What remained of Pore was his body from the waist down, as his torso, neck, shoulder, and head had disintegrated into a grotesque pool spreading across the stones in wanton offering.

Pore's killer turned toward Kneale, hand extended, glowing with blue fire, fingers slathering chunks of wet meat between them.

He aimed for center mass and fired. The bullets entered the fluttering robes of the horror and ferried eruptions of bone and black gore out of its back. But the damned scholar advanced undaunted, that fiery blue hand held out like a chainsaw bound for the bark of an old tree.

Kneale raised his rifle sights from dark robes to skull. Two out of three rounds he fired found the target, blasting out shards of bone and jets of blue spirit fire. The creature stopped, as if reconsidering, then slumped forward onto bent knees absent much of its cartilage and flesh. It collapsed into a pile of dust and torn fabric. The blue flames along its hand became wisps of vapor, soon snuffed out by the gloom.

Alvira screamed—fear and anger mixed into a battle cry. She held her KA-BAR knife at the third and final skeleton's throat—or where its throat should have been—sawing away at its ancient spinal column with clumsy thrusts of blade. Blue fire was a halo around its death's head, eating away the tatters of its robe. It placed a burning hand on her right arm, sending it into a fit of paralysis. The knife fell from her unclenched hand. She screamed again, marshaling all of her strength and fury, and lodged her right boot against the wall, kicking out to send them both tumbling to the ground.

Kneale rushed over to help, nearly tripping over Alvira's rifle. He found her pinning the skeleton down, her legs pressing on both sides of its hollow rib cage. She retrieved the knife and went to work smashing through its front skull plate with precise thrusts. Geysers of blue light erupted from dark holes carved out by her determined blade.

As the revenant went still and silent beneath her, she dropped her knife and rubbed at her right arm, still numb.

"Pore?" she managed between harried breaths.

Kneale shook his head.

"Let me see," she said, rising to her feet.

"You shouldn't."

She ignored him and made her way to the body and its attendant pool of gore.

They stood in the cold silence of the library for a time, neither of them speaking. A new and terrible light emerged through the cracks in the door on the room's far side. Something clicked, and a great weight shifted in the air. Their headlamps blinked out, leaving them in the near-dark with only spectral light to guide them forward.

Alvira pulled her headlamp off and popped the back casing open.

"These were brand-new batteries," she said, prying them out. The set of triple-As tumbled down to the stones. She produced a new set from a pouch on her tactical vest, slipping them into the compartment. A furious clicking echoed throughout the room as she struggled to activate the device. "These are dead, too."

"So are mine," Kneale said. "Something drained them."

"What's that mean?" she asked.

"On my last job, we learned about things like this," he said. "Electronics are susceptible to certain forces."

"What, you mean like an EMP?"

"No," he said. "Like spirits. Or energy fields that we don't quite understand."

Kneale reached down to retrieve an item from one of Pore's pockets. He felt a flash of shame, as if he were a resurrection man in a black-and-white movie stealing from the dead, bound for his dramatic comeuppance. But the puddle of gore that was Pore's neck and head offered no protest. He found the vial of holy water stashed in one of the blood-soaked tactical vest's pouches, then transferred it to one of his own. Kneale slung the dead man's rifle over his shoulder, then took the magazines and lighter.

"What should we do with the…remains?" Alvira asked.

"Our mission is the same," Kneale said, handing her one of Pore's magazines. "Andrea might still be alive. Pore is not. Cover that door."

"You mean the glowing rectangle to Hell? I should pay attention to that while you scuttle around in the dark?"

"Roger," he said. Kneale grabbed one of the nearby chairs, testing its durability in his hands. It was surprisingly lightweight, and one of its legs snapped off with little effort. Then he tore a strip of fabric from one of the skeletons' robes. He wrapped it around the chair leg, then sparked Pore's lighter. The makeshift torch erupted in a burst of light and heat, casting the room in a hazy, orange glow. Kneale switched the torch to his off-hand and held up his rifle against his right shoulder with the other. It was an uncomfortable position, but the barrel was pointed forward, toward the unknown, and they could see again. That was all that mattered.

25

The shadows in the next hall frolicked in the orange light of the torch. The survivors' footsteps echoed off the narrow walls and low ceiling, accompanied by the persistent dripping of water keeping metronomic time. The hall led them on an almost imperceptible downward slope. The earth and the void pressed in around them, threatening to break through ancient barriers of stone and black soil.

The hall ended at a low archway of jawless skulls mortared in place. Kneale raised the torch to illuminate their empty eye sockets.

Kneale led Alvira through the ossuary archway. Inside the next chamber, the darkness was reluctant to give way to torchlight. The air was foul and still. The taste of dust and iron was on their tongues. In the far corner was a small table and wooden chair, upon which more tomes were piled high and a broken mirror stood its shattered watch. Heaps of clothes, rows of boots, and stacks of hiking backpacks lined the floor against the walls, covetously held by the dark.

At the far end of the room were coffins. One was larger and higher than the other, held as it was on a raised platform. Elaborate, hand-carved decorations adorned its surface, rendered smooth by the touch of countless hands across time. Scratches marred much of it, but the wood retained a dark, reflective crimson sheen that hungrily absorbed the light from the torch. Chains hung from its sides, broken and loose, their utility ended long ago by some terrific force.

The coffin's mate was smaller, but no less remarkable in its form and craftsmanship, a vessel cut smooth from some great, ancient tree, and black as night.

"What time is it?" Kneale asked. "Check your watch."

Alvira raised her wrist. The glow splashed against her face.

"Just after twenty-hundred hours," she said. "Well past sunset. That can't be right."

"We've lost time."

"Huh?"

"Another phenomenon I have some experience with. Not the first time on this job, either. Certain places and things can warp time. Twist it around, and you with it. You walk into a place, and it feels like ten minutes, and when you walk out, you discover it's been an hour. Or sometimes you're just missing patches of memory. You don't remember certain events."

"Wait. This has happened before? Here?"

"At the dolmen," he said, his voice barely a whisper.

"I don't understand," Alvira said, adrenaline and fear making her voice quiver. Kneale moved to the smaller coffin, following a pull of instinct.

"Help me with this."

The two of them worked the lid open. The casket released a stench of moist earth and fresh blood. Inside was Andrea, half-buried in dark soil that writhed with movement. Her face was pale white, but her lips were bright red. Her hair was almost translucent in the torchlight. The white dress she wore was torn and spattered with blood—whether authentic or corn syrup, Kneale couldn't tell—but her hands, placed across her chest, rose and fell in a steady, peaceful rhythm.

"She's alive," Kneale said, setting the torch upright in the dirt near her feet. "Help me."

They lifted her out of the coffin, eliciting moans of discomfort. Her eyes remained closed as they set her feet down on the cold stone floor. Alvira produced a small packet from her tactical vest and held it under Andrea's nose. The smelling salts did their trick, and the actress's eyes fluttered open, bloodshot and confused. Her gaze fell on the garlic wreathed around Kneale's neck. She held her nose and turned away.

"No," she said. "I want to go back to sleep."

"We have to go, Andrea," Kneale said. "We're in danger here."

"No danger," she mumbled. Kneale and Alvira coaxed her away from the open coffin. She staggered forward as if sleepwalking, but allowed him to lead her. "Not anymore. Never again."

"What about the other one?" Alvira asked, grabbing the torch.

Andrea doubled over, vomiting onto the stones and Kneale's dirt-encrusted combat boots. He helped her keep her balance as she wretched. He couldn't ignore the iron smell. She was vomiting blood.

Alvira approached the larger coffin. The torch's flames grew, fed air from a fresh draft. The cover had two handles carved out, perfect for lifting. They were made to resemble bones, with skulls carved from the wood on either side, leering in warning. She slung her rifle and wrapped her hands around one and lifted, then slid the cover back.

Inside the coffin was more dirt—old, dried out. Nothing wormed its way within, and nothing lay atop it. No body, no victim. No vampire.

Something fell on Alvira's shoulder. Something wet that stuck to her fingers. More drops followed, pooling and soaking through her long-sleeve shirt. Stepping back, she raised the torch to look up.

The darkness peeled away. Stone texture and shadow became disjointed, ill-fitting. She squinted, focusing on a blurry shape that resisted the clarity of the light. A pale hand reached for her, followed closely behind by a grey face that was home to a pair of blood-red eyes and dripping, neon-green fangs.

Alvira shouted and fell backwards, dropping the torch and aiming her rifle at the horror emerging from that foul trick of shadow. She fired three rounds in succession, releasing a burst of black-red blood and dislodging small chunks of flesh. The dark roared in fury.

Kneale put Andrea behind him and raised his rifle. With the torch on the floor, he could barely see Alvira and the nearby coffin, let alone what she was shooting at.

"Right above me!" she shouted. "On the ceiling!"

Kneale aimed above her and fired a single round. In the muzzle flash he saw it—a wretched, pale human form clinging to the stones, scrambling toward the far corner of the room.

Kneale rushed over to Alvira to help her to her feet. She grabbed the torch and waved it around the room. The dark pressed in around them from all angles. They pointed their rifles into that murk, unable to cover every avenue of approach at once.

"I'll cover our six," Kneale shouted. "Get to Andrea. Get down that hallway. Now."

"Roger." She rushed back to the actress, then pulled her forward by the wrist. Andrea stumbled but followed, her bare feet slapping against moist stones. Alvira's rifle bumped against the magazines in her tactical vest, metal-on-metal.

Kneale kept his weapon trained on the far side of the room, but the darkness closed in around him, teasing death from all sides. He backpedaled toward the archway. His headlamp flickered back to life, illuminating the chamber for the briefest of moments. The creature was on the far side of the room, naked, arms raised, hands out like claws, face pale and mouth open to reveal green fangs dripping with red blood. Andrea's blood.

Kneale aimed and fired twice, hoping an unlucky ricochet wouldn't catch him and make this place his tomb. He turned and ran after Alvira and Andrea, who were already well down the hallway. It was remarkable the actress was on her feet at all, let alone able to flee. She was half out of her mind, eyes wide and mumbling incoherently about *sleep* and *dirt* and *the master*. Her words became howls, echoed back by the hallway, which was longer and darker than ever. Perhaps the failing torchlight altered their perception. Perhaps the architecture itself conspired against their escape.

A section of wall fell away in a wash of blue, spectral light, and the giant skeleton's hand emerged from the dark to terrorize them once more. Its massive fingers curled around a still-coherent stretch of wall, sharp nails digging into solid stone, pulling itself into material reality.

Alvira let go of Andrea and sprinted forward. She fought against the cold fatigue in her arm to raise the rifle, aim, and fire. Chunks of wall and bone splintered off where rounds impacted. The hall shook and the hand reached in further. The palm opened, fingers rising high, great lengths of bone-arm rushing into the tunnel. Alvira roared a furious battle cry borne of despair, of the soldier seeing her death and finding, in her last moments, courage and resolve. The rifle's magazine ran dry as the great hand reached her. She swung the torch up, its dying flames finding fresh fuel. Fire spread across the bullet-riddled hand. The fingers recoiled, writhing in pain, and the member withdrew beyond the portal of static and radiating energy from which it emerged, leaving a solid wall in place once again.

Kneale came running up from behind, firing sporadically back down the hall to keep the encroaching shadow-horror at bay. In that jumble of cursed darkness, the hall stretched on forever.

"It won't let us *leave*," Alvira shouted, gasping for breath.

"It's a trick," Andrea said, voice calm and matter-of-fact. "Don't despair. The end is just ahead." Alvira grabbed Andrea's hand and pulled her forward. The library was somewhere in the hazy darkness, the vague impression of the great door revealing itself to them as they approached. They kept moving, even as the pursuing presence closed the distance, growing bolder as Kneale's clumsy shots grew less frequent.

Their faith was rewarded. Alvira slammed into the ornate door, her shoulder smacking against the ancient wood. She shook off the blow and found the handle, swinging the door open. She waved Andrea through.

"Let's go!" she shouted back into the hall, which had become a tunnel of inky darkness that hung like smoke. Kneale seemed so far away, his muzzle flashes faded and distant. Hadn't he been right behind them? And suddenly he was, as if slipping through a hole in time and space to appear in a miasma of brimstone and rifle fire. Then he was through the door, too, and Alvira followed close behind. Once inside, she slammed it shut.

"Barricade," she said through ragged breaths. "Tables, chairs, whatever."

Kneale dragged the nearest table back to the door. Alvira helped him slide it into place. They dragged another over, and together lifted it onto the first, top down. The third and final table they overturned and set against the stack. Kneale tossed a chair onto the pile for good measure.

"Grab Andrea," he said. "Keep moving."

The actress stood in the center of the library, casting glances at the grimoires arrayed on those strange shelves and at the skeletons' remains scattered along the floor. When she saw what remained of Pore, she cocked her head like a curious animal.

Alvira knelt down at Pore's body and untied his boots. They came off with a few tugs. She presented them to Andrea, who stared at her in blank-faced confusion.

"Put them on."

Andrea did as she was told, her small feet a clumsy fit in the dead man's boots. Alvira helped her tie them as tight as she could, then led the actress through the next door, her uneven footsteps echoing.

Kneale trained his rifle on the barricaded door behind them, backstepping slowly out of the library chamber. Pore's body remained otherwise unattended, just another prop in this house of horrors.

26

The moon hid behind heavy clouds. Their headlamps, free of the vampiric drain of the underhalls, summoned scraps of energy to sputter on, providing intermittent, hazy light for their retreat through the forest.

When they had put the lake well behind them, Kneale paused to survey the terrain. He saw no movement beyond the wind passing through branches and brush. He had no sense of pursuit or imminent threat. Maybe something prevented the creature from following them. Maybe they would make it after all.

A chorus of howls, yips, and barks emerged from the near dark. A coyote pack, close and agitated, their cries melancholy and desperate. Then came the infant-like cries of foxes from the near side of the water. Their alert was taken up by a mass fluttering of wings, a flock of unseen creatures taking flight, the tree branches shaking with their sudden departure. An owl hooted directly above Kneale. It stared down at him, eyes a sickly, bloodshot red, and eerily familiar.

Kneale got to moving. He followed the flashes of light from Alvira's headlamp. His heart jumped when a pale, naked form appeared in a pulse of grey light, only to disappear the moment his mind registered it. He shook it off, dismissing it as some phantasm conjured by his adrenaline-addled brain, an errant reflection off dewy leaves manipulated into a human form by combat stress.

But it appeared again. Closer now, features more defined: eyes alight, ears pointed, head bald, skin deathly pale. Kneale's core went cold. The apparition disappeared in a flash of light and a churning of shadow as Kneale barreled forward, trying to close the distance between himself and the others.

Just as Kneale was about to reach Andrea, the form appeared directly ahead of him, all sharp teeth and glowing red eyes—the eyes of the owl, which had been no owl at all. But when Kneale raised his rifle to fire, the vision was gone. The wind was a whisper of ill words, half-spoken in the darkness of a haunted forest.

Something swooped in low from the branches above. Kneale dropped to a knee. Above him were branches tumbling in the wind. Leaves shook loose. Headlamp beam splashed from branch to branch, dead tree to dead tree.

The familiar *pop-pop-pop* of 5.56-millimeter rounds drew his attention uphill. The intermittent muzzle flash of Alvira's rifle was all the beacon he needed. The night chorus of beasts resumed, rising to a fever pitch. Something or someone screamed.

"Friendly coming through!" Kneale shouted, scrambling over a fallen pine. He paused to sweep his light over the terrain ahead. A specter of white drifted from tree to tree.

"Andrea! It's Kneale! Alvira?"

A pop and sharp *hiss* came from his right. Alvira stood under the glow of a red orb of light, holding high a flare that sputtered and shed sparks. Her face was a ghastly red, her mouth hanging open to catch her breath.

"There was a man in the trees," she said. "I don't think I hit him. Moved too goddamn fast."

"I saw Andrea ahead. Come on."

Howls dogged their steps. The call of strange beasts echoed across the hill. They crossed over into a primordial night-world, an inverse of the idyllic forest they had passed through before. The world hungered and the terrain made them pay for each step. They ignored the branches and barbs scratching at their faces and catching on their sleeves and pant legs. They clung to their rifles and Alvira held onto the flare like an anchor for her own sanity. Andrea would appear ahead in a flash of white, only to step behind a thin tree and be snatched away by the dark.

Kneale had lost all sense of direction, so he was deeply relieved to recognize the vertical stretch of rock and earth leading up to the cliff above, beyond which was the dolmen and the castle. A part of his mind protested against the convenience of this happy discovery, despite their route being a haphazard flight through the dark. That part of him spoke of *being led back* and *ambush*, but relief overrode logic, spurred on by exhaustion.

Andrea stood up from a clutch of shadows. Kneale and Alvira froze. There was another flash of white flesh, an implication of bodies aligned, of neck bared in presentation, of flashing teeth and the carnal release of dark red blood. But then it was gone, and Andrea slumped forward, catching herself on an emaciated tree trunk.

"He told me to wait for you here," she slurred, as if that explained everything. Alvira ran up to grab her. Kneale shook his head, clearing it of an unease that fluttered around the back of his brain, of a sense of confused memories scattered like puzzle pieces on the floor. The weight of his rifle grounded him in the *now*, so he pressed the buttstock to his shoulder and looked down the sights, sweeping the branches above them for the pale phantom.

"Are you alright?" Alvira asked.

"Fine," Andrea said, shrugging like a drunk confused by the question. "He's been taking care of me. He loves me. I am his now, and he is mine."

The coyote pack's howls rose up behind them, closer than ever. Alvira raised her flare high.

"We have to keep moving," she said.

They began their slow climb out of the valley.

27

Christopher and Daniel waited for them at the dolmen, their necks strung with garlic, crucifixes, and other adornments of strange and occult provenance. Their torches burned brightly against the dark and they stood firmly within wide circles of salt spread at their feet. An orange-red glow appeared in the distant trees, one spooklight among many on this horrible night. They braced themselves for whatever horrors may come, refusing to abandon their post. The light revealed itself as the burning glow of a flare, held aloft by Alvira, against whom leaned their fellow star, Andrea. Kneale followed not far behind, lingering only to turn back and aim his rifle into the deep dark, wary of pursuit.

Christopher reached them first, torch held high and a large, six-shot revolver in his left hand.

"Andrea. Oh, Andrea. Thank God you've returned." He offered his co-star an embrace that she accepted. Daniel approached next, face a scowl, a glimmering blade in his right hand.

"There should be four of you," he said.

Kneale shook his head. "Pore didn't make it."

"But you did."

"I think it let us go," Kneale said.

"Of course he did," Andrea said. "We're playing a little game together." She emitted a fluttering laugh that the woods echoed back to them tenfold. A chill came over Christopher, and he pulled away from her. He held the torch up to inspect her neck. Bloody gouges revealed themselves in the wild light, white skin rendered red.

"She's been bitten." He put his gloved hand to her chin and roughly turned her face to his. She offered him a pretty smile. "There's blood on her lips. He fed her some of his blood. You were too late. This is bad."

"What do you mean, 'bad?'" Alvira said between breaths.

"We may be able to help," Daniel said, helping Christopher keep Andrea on her feet. The woman's head slumped forward and she nearly collapsed, her preternatural endurance exhausted at last. "We have to get back to the castle."

"Why would it let us go?" Kneale asked. The idea that they covered all that ground for nothing suddenly ate at him, driving a spiraling anxiety that fed on his exhaustion and fear. The only reply he received was a gunshot fired from Christopher's six-shooter into the darkness from whence they came. It burned the air itself, turning it acrid. Blue-purple light glowed along the hunk of metal.

"We must withdraw!" Christopher shouted. Daniel pulled Andrea's arm over his shoulder and hurried her back toward the castle, her feet dragging, the tips of Pore's boots clawing at the mud. Kneale waved Alvira after them. He raised his rifle in the direction Christopher had fired his antique pistol and scanned the darkness for targets.

A terrible fog emerged from the deep night, crawling over tree roots, disturbed soil littered with boot prints, and the magnificent stone structure. No night birds called, no coyotes howled. Kneale made for the castle faster than he thought his tired legs could manage.

Lines of fresh salt protected the garden gate, itself secured by a length of chain and decorated with wreaths of garlic. Kneale allowed his conscious thoughts to drift to the question of how he and Alvira had managed to survive, then remembered the garlic around their own necks. A crew member removed a length of chain and opened the gate, permitting them entry into the fallow garden. The castle stood large and illuminated before them, windows casting out the bright glow of candelabra light. The smell of frying butter emanated from the open door to the kitchen nearby.

Christopher and Daniel rushed Andrea inside. Kneale and Alvira collapsed against the outer wall, sliding down to sit on the cold earth. The crew member secured the gate once more, then stood in silence, wielding a blazing torch that illuminated his determined face.

Kneale watched him, wondering what the kid was thinking—wondering if he had been briefed on there being a goddamn vampire in the woods. His fists and teeth clenched as he thought of their movement into the valley, of how easy it had all seemed. How the lake and the cabin presented themselves as logical targets, and the doors so easily permitted entry to that impossible hallway and the horrors within. Pore, brave to the end, died doing his job. For all of his failings, he at least had that to his credit.

And now he's dead. On my watch.

It was not the first time a soldier under Kneale's command had died. But this was different—it wasn't in war, where it was expected, inevitable. This was stateside, on some would-be cake security contract, babysitting theater kids and art weirdos playing at *Dracula*. The idea of what this job was supposed to be was a taunt of a memory, an arrogant misconception that had led him here. Kneale ran through all the things he *should* have done: taken a few hours each day to run the team through close-combat drills, mandatory time at the rifle range, organized physical training, daily safety briefs and homework assignments…Things he might have done with his platoon or company in the Army, or with his team at a long-term job. Hell, even at the ranch in Colorado, there had been biannual rifle and pistol qualifications, plus the weekly classes the eggheads put on regarding theoretical physics and occult history. But here he had allowed the schedule and the routine to bypass his discipline. And a man was dead for it.

"This isn't your fault," Alvira said. "I know you're thinking it."

Kneale didn't reply.

"The strong-silent-leader bullshit isn't helpful to me," she said, an edge to her voice. "This isn't the Army or the Marines."

"No," Kneale said, his mind flashing fangs and living skeletons. "It's not."

"You need to shake off Pore. It's unfortunate. It's a fucking tragedy. But there was no way to prepare for what that was."

"We survived."

"We got lucky," she said. "We were all a bad dice roll away from getting our throats or guts torn out. You can Monday-morning-quarterback what went wrong for the rest of your life, but it won't bring him back."

Pore's neck splitting open. His jaw, cheeks, skull—

"You're right. We need to prepare for what's coming. We can mourn him later." He stood up and held out a hand to help Alvira to her feet.

"He was kind of an asshole," she said. Kneale laughed. She held out her hand and he pulled her up. "My legs are smoked. I haven't covered that much terrain on foot since Mojave Viper. I'm starting to think Pore was the lucky one."

Kneale laughed at that, too, and they made for the kitchen door.

28

"And you believe it let you go," Renee said, arms crossed over her corded sweater. Her blue eyes were hidden under the lenses of her glasses, reflecting light from the many candles spread around the dungeon-theater. Most of the cast and crew had gathered here, seemingly unconcerned with the terror looming over them and the entire forest. "Why would it do that?"

"Maybe the garlic necklaces and the stakes in our tactical vests spooked it," Kneale said. "Or maybe it wanted to follow us back here."

"But it already knows we're here."

"Probably. But it's just as likely it didn't want a direct engagement with us. We can hurt it, or at least keep it at bay. We managed to kill three of its guardians. Maybe it wanted to see what we were capable of, first, before another confrontation."

"You brought Andrea back to us. It would seem that you're capable of a lot."

"We lost Pore."

"I see that."

"You're very nonchalant about losing a member of your crew."

Renee tilted her head away from him, as if considering her next words carefully.

"There were…certain contingencies planned for," she said. "I argued for a larger security team, truth be told, but I was overruled. The conditions had to be *just so* for this project. Three against one seemed to be the right ratio."

"Now it's two against one."

"Assuming there's only one, yes."

"I think it's time we spoke plainly," Kneale said.

"I agree," Renee said. "But would you have listened before? Would you have taken me seriously, when all you've seen thus far are spirit lights, strange rocks, and found-footage special effects? Would any world-shattering revelations of the darkness that creeps behind the veil of the world have stuck with you, or would you have simply laughed them off while you took New Camlough's money?"

More people filed into the makeshift theater below the castle. At the front of the room, Terence stood up and projected his voice over the murmuring.

"The film is prepared. Everyone to their seats, please."

Renee turned away from Kneale, but he put a hand on her arm.

"We need people manning the gates," he said. "I think there's a counterattack coming. We have to be prepared."

"And we will be," Renee said, sliding her own hand over his and lightly brushing it away. "It won't spend the energy necessary to try our defenses so close to sunrise. Our two remaining soldiers are exhausted from a successful mission; your enemy likely needs rest as well. His powers are not unlimited, and are greatly diminished in the light of the day."

"We should prepare now," Kneale said.

"You're exhausted," Renee said.

"Combat operations don't stop because you need a nap."

"We will give the cast and crew a few hours of sleep and personal time, then muster by mid-morning." She shot him a clumsy British-style salute, her palm upraised. "You can give us our marching orders then."

"I'll give my orders *now*," Kneale insisted, raising his voice. "You're not taking this seriously. What I saw out there—"

"...was some variation of what I expected you to encounter," Renee said. "You're not listening. We planned for this. For *you*. You have met my expectations thus far. And if you would like to continue to meet those expectations, you will defer to me in this matter. We must prepare the minds of our cast and crew for the coming battle. We must prepare your mind."

"What the hell does that mean?" Kneale asked, trying to keep his voice down as the others shot concerned looks in their direction. He wanted to collapse, to crawl into a corner of that dark basement and shut his eyes. He wanted to sleep for days. He wanted all of this to be over.

Yvonne appeared next to him, the smell of perfume competing with the sugary-sweet scent of the corn syrup splattered on her chest and neck, running down from her lips. She lifted a rolled joint in offering.

"No way," Kneale said. "I need to be clearheaded about this."

"Your mind is a weapon," Yvonne said. "It can be yours to wield, or the vampire's." She offered him the cannabis. "This, when made to resonate with tonight's film, will steel your mind against his dark powers."

"It will not try for us tonight," Renee said, putting a hand on Kneale's shoulder. "But it will come tomorrow, when the sun sets. This is the only way we can prepare now."

Kneale, his mind at odds with itself, his body shaking with post-adrenaline exhaustion, accepted the joint. Yvonne gave him a glowing smile as he inhaled, accepting the gift of that strange smoke. It rolled over his mind like a comforting, warm summer rain, cleaning away the detritus of his anxiety, his worry, his sense of self. Yvonne's beautiful smile floated in place beneath her bright coffee-colored eyes, fixing him in place. The walls of the dungeon-theater slid back into darkness. The projector's bright glow grew large and vibrant.

More, Yvonne said, without saying it.

A flash, then, of a memory that couldn't be—of Kneale, atop the cap of the dolmen, his naked back against the rough stone, the wind blowing through his close-cropped hair, the sky above him a swirl of strange stars. Yvonne atop him, smiling down, gyrating, riding him, her face twisting into others': Renee's, Andrea's; Andrea's eyes turning red, her embrace suddenly grown cold, his body spiking with a flood of pleasurable chemicals, her fangs at his throat, piercing his neck, drawing him into her in every way imaginable. From the swirl of stars overhead emerged the dead city, its ancient paths and streets twisted into a self-reflexive spiral, wound tight in on itself. A necropolis of causality, reaching out from beyond the veil obscuring what had always been there, from which the movie—the vampire movie, now—always distracted him. It floated among the great soundstage machina of time and space, of the world underpinning the world, the mechanisms behind the movie magic of all things.

He—his body, which held some anchor over his adrift mind—sat in a folding metal chair, Renee and Alvira next to him, Terence in front. The director spoke to him from within the glow of the projector's light.

"I don't suppose you've seen this film, either?" he asked, taking a long drag from a joint. His words afterwards came out as smoke. "One of the greatest of the period and of the form, certainly. Everyone likes to focus on the 1980s as the golden age of horror cinema, but the 1970s were an embarrassment of riches, with its Gothic movements in Europe, its postmodern awakenings in exploitation and drive-in splatter films, its perfection of the zombie, its post-*giallo* and proto-slasher miasma. One foot in the Gothic past, one stepping forward into a blood-soaked future."

Kneale listened despite his exhaustion, which at present had receded to a dull thrumming in the background of awareness. Curious that he didn't find Terence's ramblings pretentious. Curiouser still that he felt the presence of a familiar form nearby, a presence that invited him to glance behind him to the far back row of chairs. There he was, seated among the other production personnel, one more body among many: Pore's headless and throatless corpse, a bucket of popcorn in its lap. Bloody hands ferried popcorn to where his mouth should be, tossing morsels into the air, only to have them fall into the bloody mess at the top of his torso, or tumble down from his shoulders.

"Watch the movie," Yvonne said, guiding his attention back toward the screen.

The rectangle of light grew to enormous size and scope, stretching across the entirety of the far wall. It clawed onto the ceiling, onto the floor. The film covered everything, defining and re-configuring all, a sorcerer's spell cast to undo and remake the world.

29

High-pitched strings and horns precede the appearance of a spectral castle slouching over a crumbling seaside cliff. Great sheets of rain slam against the battlements. Lightning spreads across the painted sky, illuminating the fortress and its many spires. The title's typeface glows and shimmers green like ectoplasm appearing from the ether:

DR. ORLOCK'S CASTLE OF TERROR
COPYRIGHT MCMLXXI BY CAMLOUGH STUDIOS, INC.

The castle dissolves to an interior laboratory. Stone pillars hold up a high ceiling. Tables and shelves full of alchemical glassware, taxidermied animals of strange physiological composition, and stacks of great books brimming with the secrets of the prophetic insane occupy the room. Candles are set in elaborate holders of ornate bronze, or burn and melt atop human skulls stacked in obscene columns.

At the room's center is a tall figure in a flowing purple robe adorned with runic slashes of gold. The figure removes its hood to reveal a scowling face with a great, well-kept beard and shining blue eyes. The sorcerer sneers, right on cue, as lightning crashes outside and illuminates the laboratory chamber through a great stained glass window, whose dark red and black panes form Baphomet in geometric abstract.

The sorcerer tosses explosive powder about the room. Geysers of colorful smoke erupt. He intones insults against God and creation, and calls forth the shades, the goblins and hobgoblins, the demons, the devils, the lackeys of evil, the witches and warlocks, the werewolves and vampires, the Deep Ones and the ghouls.

The candles flicker as darkness flows into the laboratory. The rain battering the castle slows to a trickle. The night grows still, and even a great clock *tick-tick-ticking* within the laboratory falls silent. Light erupts from five stones arrayed in pentagram on the floor, with the blasphemer at its center. Black light transforms the wide eyes and beaming smile of the sorcerer into a Cheshire Cat's wicked visage.

"Well? What are you waiting for?" he demands of the shadows. He whirls around, searching the darkened corners of his chamber for evidence of evil, for eager partners in perdition, for Beelzebub about his business. "Are you here, or not? Will you reward my persistence, my loyalty, my worship? Or should I go back to tithing to the church and caring for the poor? Out with it, then, be my destiny penance or damnation."

His demand is met by laughter. Soft at first, feminine, and rising, loud, louder, until the sorcerer must cover his ears, the room (the camera) spinning, inverting, the cackle drowning out everything, even the sorcerer's own thoughts.

And then it stops.

"You are beyond penance, Orlock," a woman's voice says. "But not beyond me."

Orlock removes his hands from his ears, his shoulders adopting a suspicious slouch. He turns toward the sound of the voice, away from the camera. A shadow moves—a shadow that we thought merely part of the scenery, out of focus in the background, just stage-left to the sorcerer. It rushes toward him, all black, a dancer in a form-fitting bodysuit, an impression of a woman's shadow obscured into hazy incorporeality by gel on the lens and soft lighting set in fractured rays.

"There you are, my love," Orlock says. "I feared you would not join me, and that my practice was for naught."

The shadow approaches, hips and shoulders swaying in a strange rhythm. It wraps elongated limbs about him, holding him in place.

"I would never abandon you to your own pleasure," it says, the sensual ADR performance practically dripping.

"Have I done it, then, finally? Is the ultimate ritual complete?"

"Not the final one, no. That comes later. Much later. After you."

Orlock slouches, his head hanging low.

"I have failed, after all."

The shade moves to his side, around him, holding him from behind, the lens hazy, the soundtrack a mix of quiet distortion and distant, reverb-laden strings.

"Failed? No, my darling. You simply cannot see the full scope of your work, how it will be fulfilled beyond this short life of yours. Your accomplishments resound across time itself." She pauses, running a shadow of a hand over his neck. "Have you spirited away your wife?"

"Yes. She suspects nothing."

"And you are sure she is pregnant?"

"The doctor confirmed it this morning."

"And the child is yours?"

"By your command, my love, though it felt wrong to lie with another."

The shade titters.

"Ahh, Orlock, my pet. She may share your bed, but with me, you share your *soul*."

The shade leans in for an abominable kiss. The sorcerer relaxes in her grip, accepting her embrace. Their kiss stretches on. The candles burn low. There is the shuffling of figures in the dark, the moaning. The light slaps of flesh-on-flesh.

Coverage of the lab takes us through the following:

The books, in close-up or medium shot, with ominous names in Latin or Greek; a table of ceremonial knives, blades stained red, set along a crimson cloth; a live owl in a cage, its great, black eyes searching, its head turning toward the camera; stairs, leading down to a landing where several doors are barricaded shut, where out from their small, barred windows strange digits probe the dark. It is over this shot that Orlock screams.

The female voice moans, rising in sexual ecstasy. The shot shifts suddenly to the stones in pentagram, aglow with neon purple, between which the conspirators writhe. The feminine moan grows louder, overpowering the wet-mouthed grunting of the sorcerer. He screams again, and the soundtrack's horns blast out an ominous, warbling crescendo, joining him in pain and terror, shielding our ears from the finer details of the sensual violence occurring at the center of that dread formation, between body and shadow.

Orlock's pale, terrified face is shown in close-up, held by hands covered in dull scales and with nails as sharp as knives. The actor earns his paycheck, contorting his face in a variety of painful poses, eyes practically spinning, mouth twisting, blood dripping from teeth he sheds like autumn leaves.

From the shadows of the lab emerge inhuman freaks with long noses and ears, with third eyes and sewn-shut mouths, with cloven hooves for hands and fur slick with blood. They watch and bray in satisfaction as the man is pulled apart, his lover removing one limb—one member—at a time.

The sorcerer's blood runs from his now-limp (in more ways than one!) body, draining over the floor and among the glowing stones to accrue in the mortar canals that lead to the walls of the laboratory. The walls accept this gift, his blood absorbed into the stones of the castle itself, shown once more in glorious matte painting exterior. The shade's orgasmic fervor is replaced by her laughter, which is soon joined by Orlock's, his liberated spirit finding humor in his body's grisly demise.

A slow tracking shot runs through the castle's main hall, lit by a cadre of low candles. The camera tilts up as it climbs the grand crimson staircase. Two more candles alight below the great portrait on the landing above. Its gold-plated frame is alive with fire, liquid in its vibrancy. The portrait itself is of the sorcerer, Orlock, resplendent in his alchemical robes, a black cat familiar perched on his left shoulder, a crooked sneer spread across his thin lips, his blue eyes tracking the camera—tracking you—on the approach.

Time passes, as it always does in such stories, with the decades tumbling into a century or more, communicated by the candles blowing out, the house going dark, and a layer of dust rising over the set in transitional jumps. The line of the castle's masters has fled elsewhere, and there is no one left to direct the stonemasons or the servants to keep it in good repair. The great tower sheds stones; the walls crumble; vegetation climbs and spreads across the castle-become-corpse. All throughout, a cold, lonely wind blows, as if passing through a tomb.

The castle disappears into a fade to black…and then returns with the rising sun, and the sound of horses' hooves on the road leading up to the main gate.

A young man—with blue eyes and bearing a striking resemblance to the older actor who portrayed Orlock in the opening scene—calls for the driver of the great, black carriage to halt. He steps out first, then quickly moves to the other door, which he opens for his lady. Her beauty is radiant, her blonde hair long and perfect, her figure stunning even and especially in the modest, dark dress she has worn for travel. The actress, played by Clouta Smithwick, is unfamiliar to most of the viewers in the dungeon, but for those who know, her performance here is all the more poignant considering the dark tragedy that would end her life in the short years to come. But for now, she is a heavenly creature, moving with her companion over the threshold of a castle that has not been occupied for well over two hundred years.

"You are striking, especially here, my dear Marguerite," the man says, speaking for all of us. He places a hand on her face and she leans into it, smiling. "I am so thankful you agreed to come."

"Where else would I be, if not our future home, with you, sweetest Quentin?" she says.

"Our present home, the home of my ancestors, and soon a home for our children," Quentin says. They kiss, and the shot fades to black.

What follows is a smattering of montage: the servants and local labor work at the direction of the couple to restore the great house, one room at a time. The effort would require years or more to complete, but their priority is on securing the leaks in the roof, jettisoning the accumulated debris, cleaning out the cobwebs, and scattering the various birds and vermin that have claimed Castle Orlock as their own. Throughout this, the couple flirt and fawn over one another, lighthearted and cloying in these saccharine displays. But we need not suffer long.

There is a brief scene set on the main stair landing, with the lovers meeting beneath the watchful eyes of the ancient Orlock. Marguerite naturally despises the portrait and wishes it struck to pieces; Quentin, recognizing his own features, deduces that this must be a painting of the great Count Orlock himself, the mad wizard to whom all of his family's ill reputation is attached.

"Little is really known about him, save for his reputation for depravity and his alliance with devils," Quentin says, his reverence tinged with amusement. "If the townsfolk still tell the stories, I will need to work tirelessly to restore my family's name."

"We shall be good to them," Marguerite says. "Look, there are so many who are willing to work for you, here, even now." She stage-gestures beyond the landing but, finding that they are alone in the great hall, starts in surprise. She catches herself, running her hands over her dress.

"Coin is tight these days," Quentin says, eyes expressing worry for his wife. "None who are willing to come to our castle will linger past sunset, even at the promise of greater payment."

The scene ends in a long shot, with the young couple staring out from the landing across the opulent and soon-to-be-restored glory of the main hall. Orlock's countenance looms above them, a satisfied smirk creeping along his painted face, his eyes alight with mischief. The black cat is noticeably absent from the painting.

Thus are the seeds planted for Gothic resurrection.

Quentin descends a long and winding stair, his solitary candle flickering, threatening to go out. It is here that he first encounters the cat in a classic (or derivative, depending on your perspective) jumpscare fake-out. The creature leaps out from the darkness to elicit a cry of fear from the castle's new master. When Quentin recovers, he allows a halfhearted laugh at his own expense, then raises the candle to spread light in the stairwell.

"Let's get a good look at such a creature as might produce in me a mortal terror," he says. "Ah, a young tom, with shining coat and lustrous eyes. You have supped well in mine castle, have you, cat? Do you roam these halls with familiarity and prestige as its true master, and see me as interloper and pretender? If so, good sir, lead on, and reveal to me your manse's secrets."

The cat, having received its due respect, offers a friendly mewl and bounds down the stairs. Together they reach the bottom of the stairwell, where a great wooden door clasped in black metal awaits. The door swings open to reveal a spiral stone stair along the walls of a cylindrical chamber. The cat leads on and Quentin does not hesitate. The stairs lead them down into Orlock's laboratory, which now stands in terrible disarray after generations of disuse. Despite the state of the lab, Quentin is obviously impressed. He spends some time righting fallen tables, chairs, and glass equipment, going so far as to restore a peculiar golden idol to its demonic throne on the far side of the room. Soon he calls for the servants and the workers, who, despite some initial reservations and vague gestures against evil, set to work cleaning the dust, broken glass, splintered wood, and vermin scat from the chamber.

"The laboratory is a happy discovery, as it will prove to be the ideal location for my research, far as we are from the prying eyes and meddlesome censures of the reactionaries at the institute," Quentin says over dinner. He and his love sit at a long table in the main hall, eating beneath the watchful gaze of Orlock's portrait. Their high-backed chairs emphasize the scale of the room, of the castle, of history itself, weighing down on them. "Should I find success—"

"*When* you find success, my love," Marguerite interjects.

"Yes, thank you. *When* my theories are proven, we will have enough capital to restore the castle in totality. We won't have to be content with a few rooms, or have to choose between the walls and the roof."

"I care less about money, and more about your well-being," she says.

"My work is my well-being."

"So you say, and so I accept. But…"

"But?"

"When shall we be married?" She emphasizes this by placing

her fork on the table, then reaching for her glass of red wine with her left hand. "When will you consider your work to be in a state sufficient to turn your mind and your body toward matters of domesticity?"

"My love for you is not conditioned upon the vulgar religious order of the day, nor the petty concerns of men."

"But what about *my* petty concerns?" she says. Quentin sees now that he has been caught by his own carelessness.

"My love. When this phase of the project is complete, you shall have all that you want and more," he says. "I merely must demonstrate, in replicable conditions, the truth of the matter: that the mind exists in a higher state as well as a material one. That our thoughts are generated in the interstitial, connected to the ether even as anchored to the fleshy brain, yes, but merely tethered for a short while at birth, and freed upon death. There will be research to follow, of course. There always is. But once I have established this foundation, the world will be mine. Ours. And I shall give you the wedding you desire, and children should you wish, and provide for our family all the days of our lives and beyond. In this, I shall be your servant."

She smiles at this, all traces of her doubt evaporated by his pretty words. She turns to the servants who linger at the edge of the great hall.

"Leave us. Return only when summoned, and not a moment before."

Shadows move along the edge of the room, disappearing through swinging doors.

Marguerite stands up, pushing her chair back. She pulls a comb from her hair, releasing her locks in a great flood. She walks, slowly, around the kitchen table, finding her man looking up at her, at her bosom, and her hands are upon him, and his upon her, and they are soon joined with one another upon the great table, under the watchful, painted eyes of Orlock the ancient.

Science and philosophy texts intermingle with the occult tomes discovered in the lab, both vying for Quentin's voracious appetite for knowledge. Candles grow low and are replaced. Glassware is cleaned and restored to use, bubbling over with strange liquids set above strange fire. Animal corpses are subject to the ministrations of careful blade work; a white lab coat becomes a butcher's apron. Marguerite haunts the halls as a lonely specter, her eyes on her betrothed from a distance. Her only companions are the servants in their duty, as the townsfolk barely acknowledge her when she is about the village. They dare not speak with the lady of the great house unless spoken to first, and then only in formal obligation.

Quentin is elated, flummoxed, despairing. The drink comes in greater and greater quantities, and this of course does nothing to improve the quality of his work. He burns a scroll of his own notes, dozens of hours of work turned to ash and smoke, and he starts over. It is only when he returns to the great occult texts of his ancestor that his interest is piqued, his instincts as a researcher aflame with inspiration.

"Fanciful implementation, but the core ideas are sound philosophy," he whispers while paging through a book in his lab. But...not his lab—he is suddenly on the great stair, beneath the portrait of his ancestor, Orlock, whose blue eyes are upon him, unwavering. "Perhaps my great-great-grandfather had found some thread of truth among his forays into the dark."

Quentin, alarmed at his transposition, jolts suddenly as a great *slap* is heard on the landing behind him. Lying there, as still as can be, is another tome, a book that is without dust but is still clearly old, if well cared-for. He bends down to take his doom in his hands.

It is a journal. The journal of one Count Gregorie Orlock, master of the black arts. Quentin sits right where he is, out of time and place, and flips open the book, eager to discover what secrets it contains. It is through deliciously overwrought voiceover that Count Orlock tells his tale, and through footage of the events described—events shown through a haze of gel, fog, and vivid psychedelic effects.

> It is through the most strenuous of ritualistic practice that I have at last made contact with what Christendom might understand as a demon, but that I know to be a spirit of the other-world, no more terrifying due to its strange nature than a creature of the deep sea or dark jungle. After my initial attempts at conjure failed, I persisted, and the entity did appear in my laboratory as a strange and curious shadow, with eyes of deep red that burned into my soul. It took very little time for it to learn my language, engaging me by pointing to the various implements and instruments of my work and demanding words of explanation. The real breakthrough came, however, when I provided it with a book on the basics of alchemical theory, which it devoured in under an hour's time. After this effort, the thing withdrew, but I summoned it the following night, and it could speak to me in a halting, clumsy Latin. But it had words enough to make demands, to which I immediately acquiesced.
>
> It demanded corpses.
>
> That the plague had been circling round the village now seemed suddenly a happy and fortuitous event. The graveyards are full and the fresh earth is shallow.
>
> Upon consuming the brains, its mannerisms

and language would improve, as if absorbing knowledge of human language, customs, and culture through digestion. It is at this time that my house servantry waned. The smell from the laboratory and the bone pit was no doubt awful, but I had become largely inured to it. Perhaps some of the cleverer ones suspected my secret business and left quietly due to superstition and self-aggrandizing morality. If so, they are fools. Soon I will have new servants, and they will be bound to me with true loyalty—not merely some base need of coin for potatoes in their pots.

When we could finally hold a scientific conversation, the shade and I, it explained to me with some amusement that I had been performing the ritual correctly all along, but that it chose to appear only when my commitment was evident. It complimented me on striving to be more than some mere dilettante, some soft-handed aristocrat playing at Black Mass. No, what it desired was a partner, not a rote magician. And I could prove myself further by bringing it—her—a live specimen on which to dine.

Orlock and his tallest, strongest servant venture to the village below, where they offer coin to a prostitute plying her trade on the edge of town. She is seduced with wine and gifts of chocolate, then taken to the lab, the abattoir-to-be. When the shadow emerges from behind an altar laden with candles and steaming glasswork, the horror of her utter lack of comprehension is expressed through a confused parade of makeup-caked facial expressions.

The scene of consumption is a spectacular series of gore effects shots in lush Technicolor excess. Geysers of vivid blood erupt across the screen. The organs are real, certainly and clearly, so much so that censors in the United Kingdom wanted the sequence cut entirely, and rumors persisted for years about their origin, despite the producers' (halfhearted) statements that they were sheep's guts, that *of course* they were, how could they be anything else? The discolored latex appliance on the woman's neck and upper torso is visible in the high-definition transfer of the film, but this technical accident is forgivable considering the bounty of gore revealed by the clawing attacks of shadow-fingers that the restoration otherwise enlivens.

It is after these heinous moments of grim spectacle that the shadow becomes more *solid*, more real, its shape taking on feminine qualities, its face that of the prostitute's but restored to a youthful, luxurious vigor. Lacking the ravages of malnutrition and physical violence that defined the woman's life, her true, holy beauty as intended by God shines through. It—she—turns her attention to Orlock, who has retreated into a corner of the lab, handkerchief over his face, eyes wide in shock, but unable to look away. Her lips are red with blood. She saunters up to him, layers of shadow peeling off in torn membranes of black latex, until she is naked before him. She reaches for him and laughs wickedly at his arousal, and takes him, there, in the company of bones likewise stripped naked save for errant ribbons of blood.

> *Her seduction of me was complete. I was her willing servant in all things. As long as I kept her fed, she taught me secrets of the divine and the damned, shortcutting a hundred years of natural philosophy research to plumb the secrets of the world beyond ours. I learned of orders of creation above and below, and saw the stars move in strange and impossible patterns. I saw the end of humanity, and its beginning, and the conquest of the insect-men to come, and the waves of extinction and evolution that will follow their empire, ad infinitum, until the*

very end of time. I saw, in fleeting glimpses, the shame-inducing face of God—if one could condense that boundless, terrifying energy to a single idea—peeking out at us through veils erected by the demon to protect us from His gaze, and I realized then how childish my pretensions of devil worship once were. I was truly damned, but in a way that Luciferians could only vaguely sense, and that they would have recoiled from, had they seen the truth of the madness at the heart of our dark and impossible world-upon-worlds.

Our work had a destination, an endpoint. To join my lover, fully and truly, we would need to sever my soul's biological component, a precise snipping of my body, which, while providing me inordinate sexual pleasures in the embrace of the demon, had grown vestigial for the expansive power and pleasures that lay beyond this material realm. The final ritual, which I have developed with my mistress, is outlined below. I need only practice, and practice, and once more demonstrate my persistence, my true and all-burning desire to transcend my mortal shell and join her forever in unholy union within the dead and haunted spiral-city beyond the firmament, where the curtains of this wretched passion play are drawn back and the stage itself stands revealed.

Quentin, finding untold inspiration in the fanciful tales of his ancestor's journal, takes to dressing in the man's clothes, drinking his ancient wine, and forgoing meals with his beloved Marguerite. The black cat returns, spotted about various scenes, quiet and still in the background, watching, watching. It speaks, once, in a brief scene in which Quentin finds himself staring up at the portrait of his ancestor at some dark and foul midnight hour.

"Let me serve you, as I served the former master of this house," the familiar says, slithering up to Quentin. "Your illustrious ancestor, who even now frolics among devils and demons and angels, invites you to join him at bacchanal. Your work will complete his, and exceed even your wildest dreams, young master."

Corpses are, of course, the raw material of this line of research.

Set on this bloody course, Quentin dons a strange, twisted mask—a variation on a classic red devil, with a beard not unlike Orlock's and piercing, painted blue eyes. The ceremonial knives in the lab remain up to their cutting task, long and sharp even over the dusty centuries. Time is curved here, and what needs to work still does. The conclusion works backward through time, shaping the course of events to bring about its own birth. And so the thieving of bodies begins anew but, denied the convenience of a plague, necessitates murder.

Quentin stalks the village in his devil's mask, preying upon the vagrants first. When his knifework is done, he collects their bodies and stacks them like cordwood in a wagon secreted at the edge of town. Over the nights to come, the killing escalates, as the vagrants are few and poor stock for research into the potentials of the human mind. Next are lonely travelers or servants returning home late upon the fog-strewn byways outside of town. Rumors begin to spread about the devil of the road. Those servants who have yet to realize the evil at the heart of their new master pay for their loyalty with their lives, meeting death at the end of ancient knives. Then there is a more bold collection: Quentin invades the home of the village bürgermeister, a portly and privileged sod, who makes a poor defense against the masked fiend. His family, grown fat upon his corruption and the labor of their neighbors, pays the knife price of scientific advancement.

The number of dead is unclear, and the sequences of killing are brief and dreamlike, without much setup, with minimal dialogue, accompanied by a pulsing, low, semi-musical soundtrack. There is something primal at work here, and as grotesque as these scenes are—rivaling even the slasher films that would emerge in only a few more years' time—their appeal to and capture of audience attention is undeniable.

After these nights of terror grow beyond rumor and spill out into open horror and lament, a group of villagers descends on the constabulary, demanding an inquest. The chief spends little time talking the villagers out of their fears, instead offering threats of imprisonment or worse. When his threats are not persuasive enough to disperse the townsfolk, the constables assault the crowd, clubs and blades swinging, maiming and injuring many and arresting several more. The hangings are shot in one long, continuous take from afar, with a crowd littered about the gallows while the sun retires from a purple and pink-slashed sky. This petty revenge dressed up as *order* is not lost on the villagers, who scheme and skulk in the shadows. Instead of returning the bodies to their grieving families, the constables pile them high in a wagon bound for the castle. A young man and woman from the village spy the cart arriving at the dreadful house and watch as goblins drag the corpses inside. The two villagers flee before they are spotted, but we, of course, follow the dark servants inside and witness the fate of the dead.

The bodies are sliced open, their organs and bones removed, cleaned, and cataloged. Their parts are dumped into barrels of bubbling chemicals of preservation, manned by green-faced freaks who emerge from shadowy corners of the laboratory, obeying telepathic orders from the black cat who lounges over the lab from its post on the stair, or upon the bookshelves, or among the glassware, or at the base of the golden demon-idol. Sometimes, the cat is in multiple places at once.

The body parts are withdrawn from the chemical soups by metal tongs. Quentin calls forth demons among sputtering candles and the light of torches held by his inhuman servants. He consults anatomical charts, taking notes on brain and organ size with gleaming metal calipers. From human skulls he drinks terrible potions concocted from essential saltes. He is driven to great leaps of inspiration, recording his notes on an ever-crowded chalkboard of arcane symbols and scrawled Latin of doomful portent.

Marguerite emerges to beg her betrothed to return from his journey of madness. She is a reminder of lost humanity, of the world of men and God beyond, reaching out for a lost soul. But her behavior is languid, her words slow and unsteady. Whether she is being actively drugged or is merely exhausted by her lover's descent into deviltry is not clear.

Refusing her dinner meal, keeps herself awake well into the night, praying to God to deliver them both from the schemes of the Dark One, who she has seen moving freely about the castle during the dark watches. Strange noises from the shadows dog her prayers and tittering laughter answers her cries of fear until, finally, diminutive goblins burst forth from beneath her bed, knives silver and gleaming in sputtering candlelight, to make a butchery of the beauty. They drain her blood into a chalice.

The final reel contains yet more horrors, suitably escalated by filmmakers striving for shock. Back in the village, the chief constable orders further hangings in a desperate and cruel bid to manage the people, who openly call for violence against the young Lord Orlock.

When a young man's betrothed is beaten to death by leering constables in the middle of the street in a sexually charged scene, he does not stand idly by and wait for her corpse to be subjected to the degenerate will of his lord. No, this young man takes a sickle into his own hands, this tool of labor, and wields it as a weapon.

The constabulary do not see it coming—and one of them sees nothing at all, as the young man drives the blade into his oppressor's eyes with one, two deft strikes. Blood flies and the mewling pain echoes throughout the village square; the ropes of the gallows swing and snap with the weight of dead bodies.

Others join the fray. Torches are lit, pitchforks emerge from bales of hay, knives are drawn up from drawers. Men, women, and children descend on the constables, who swing their clubs and swords in futile defense. The brutes enforcing the ruling order are soon swept under the rising tide of popular revolt, eyes plucked out, hands chopped off, heads scalped. Their bloodied remains are thrown upon the gallows platforms, which are set aflame. These dead will not be subjected to the perversions of the master of Demon Castle Orlock.

Meanwhile, in the darkness of the laboratory, Quentin labors feverishly to complete the ultimate ritual. Torches blaze to life, held aloft by goblin hands; strange orbs of energy and snakes of ectoplasm illuminate the dark corners of the dungeon; the black cat rests on the stairs, eyes trained on the young sorcerer.

The fruit of his labors is piled before him on a great surgical table. A twisted mass of bodies, ruined flesh remade into the vague impression of a gargoyle's great head—bodies for lips and bones for teeth; black cavities for eyes that burn with a strange fire; broken legs for horns and ears; curtains of flesh and walls of bone giving structure to a hideous face. The sight is nauseating and permitted on screen for only brief moments at a time, generally out of focus or framed poorly, inviting the audience's imagination to supply the truly horrific details, at least for now. Hanging crookedly on the wall behind the corpse-head and Quentin is the great portrait of Orlock himself, summoned to the lab for the culmination of his death's work.

Quentin removes the strange mask but dons the decrepit purple robes of his ancestor. A manservant comes forward with a chalice dripping with blood, liquid and fresh, and young Orlock accepts it with all the reverence of a devout Catholic at communion. He raises the chalice high.

"Oh, spirits of the other-world! Oh, damned and devils alike! I,

Quentin von Gorefield the Second, the true and rightful heir of Count Orlock himself, invoke my familial privilege! I accept my inheritance of power and damnation!"

Lightning crashes at the most opportune time. It covers the sounds of the mob approaching the castle.

Quentin drains the chalice, his beloved's blood running down his cheeks and neck. He drops the cup and holds his arms out wide.

"I summon thee, spirits of Castle Orlock! I have built the golem, completed the binding ritual, and now invoke thy presence for contract!" Lightning crashes again, and all the torches blow out.

From the dark corners of the chamber comes that familiar, feminine laughter heard at the beginning of the film. The shadow-demon emerges from the dark, whispering sweet nothings into Quentin's ear, wrapping its arms around his chest, running its hands down into his pants.

"*I bid you welcome, young Orlock,*" it says, voice fluctuating between Orlock's prostitute-victim and Marguerite. It settles on Quentin' murdered lover, finding the voice and form to be more suitable for its purposes. "*I bid you take what is yours by right. Join me now, in unholy matrimony...*"

Quentin is not surprised to see the face of his murdered woman before him. Quite the contrary: he is aroused to new heights of passion. Marguerite has become a pretty wrapper over the present he intends to open, pliant and submissive, just as he always wanted her.

"Let us give our child life," the demon says, removing its black shawl of shadow and revealing the naked body beneath.

As the sorcerer and the demon join before the writhing mass of horror constructed from the dead, the mob reaches the castle. The sealed gate presents a stoic face of defense. But when roused from its slumber, the working class makes for a fearsome and clever army, and soon ropes and ladders are produced. The adventurous young, so eager for righteous violence, are the first to scale the walls, making leaps of faith to seize stone outcroppings or hang from perching gargoyles. Then they are over the wall, and it is but a matter of descent to the other side, and the vanguard is within the walls of the nobleman's redoubt. The crowd erupts in a cheer as the gate opens. The villagers flood the castle grounds.

The mob rushes toward the main keep, torches ablaze, farming tools and kitchen utensils turned weapons of revolution. Fire is everywhere, set in whatever will take it: trees, bales of hay, abandoned wagons and carts that not so long ago ferried the corpses of their murdered neighbors. The moon is blood-red, hanging low in the sky.

The crowd crashes against the closed door of the castle, expecting an extended test of strength to breach the inner halls. What they find, instead, are unbarred doors and the wide, expansive main hall within. Here they find more fuel eager for the touch of flame: familial banners, portraits of dead ancestors (save Orlock's), the dining table and high-backed chairs, long since disused by a loving couple torn asunder.

The villagers pour into the castle's many rooms, setting them ablaze and grabbing treasures for themselves: fine clothing, the lady's jewelry, gold coins, even pots and pans from the kitchen. In Marguerite's room, her rotted corpse remains, picked clean of flesh and organs, but her red-stained bones stand mute witness to the theft of its worldly possessions. If God is just, her spirit is in Heaven, ignorant of this defilement.

In the dungeon below, Quentin's attention is drawn to the clamor above. The distraction is momentary, as the demon who has assumed the form of Marguerite returns his focus to the task at hand. She holds his face between her hands as she rides him to completion, her face a mask of madness, her lips smeared with blood.

Lightning crashes as the lovers complete the ritual—it breaches the ceiling above, runs through the walls, sending stones tumbling out and spikes from the laboratory's domed ceiling down to the mass of meat and bone fashioned into the face of a great monster. And how that monster roars. Aroused to un-life, the bodies churn and twist. Individuals have been fashioned into musculature for this aggregate horror. Its bone-teeth snap, its leg-jaws twist and writhe, its eye sockets churn with a terrible blue fire.

Quentin laughs maniacally. He is a man who has pushed himself into the country of lunacy and finds it to his liking. Black smoke pours through the door at the top of the laboratory's winding stair, and fire spreads along the roof of the chamber. The door is blown open with a burst of fire and waves of smoke, and the consumption of the laboratory commences. Flames chew through wooden supports and burn along the walls, threatening the stability of the entire castle.

The inferno brings down stones and collapses walls. The invading mob flees, as so many of them are caught suddenly within the reach of fire now burning uncontrolled. Those who linger for treasure and spoil find Castle Orlock to be their tomb. The villagers pour back out of the keep's main door and gather at the front gate to watch the fire purify the ancient fortress.

But evil is not finished. A great roar rumbles through the air, interrupting the celebration. The sound is unlike any ever heard by peasant ears: a great bellowing like a lion with the reverberating undertones of a furious whale song, filtered through the endless earthen catacombs of a subterranean world leading up to the surface from Hell itself.

The front doors to the castle blow open with a burst of flame, and the gargoyle head of corpses slithers forward, eyes alight in blue, bodies-as-structure aflame and flesh melting. Its horns are bodies, twisted together and bent into broken-bone configurations that call to mind a bull's horns and a deer's antlers, pulsating with blood, turning to blackened, withered ruin under the searing touch of fire. Men and women faint and shriek at the sight, but the head slides forward, pushed along by grafted hands and feet and arms beneath its great, blood-dripping bulk. The mouth opens, and fire erupts outward in a great arc, incinerating a few unlucky men who did not have the good sense to step back in the face of cosmic evil made manifest.

Those who can, flee, and those who do not are consumed in the last, raging moments of the head-of-corpses, their vile deaths among the final tragedies of the film's conclusion. But one greater woe remains: the end of the castle itself. It is a monument to architecture and the strength of the village below, built by generations of the villagers' ancestors and thus belonging to them, their inheritance, denied to them by a cruel and unjust order of power. But burn the castle does, its towers toppling under pressures mundane and supernatural, spirits screaming as walls collapse and floors and ceilings fall away. We see one final shot of Quentin, who, in the embrace of his melting shadow-bride, laughs like a madman. Just before he is buried and burned alive, he offers one final line of dialogue.

"I have completed your work, grandfather," he says, angling to look upon the askew portrait of Orlock, likewise aflame. "Together, we have conquered death…"

30

The deep sleep of exhaustion should have carried Kneale well into the mid-morning or beyond. But his mind recognized the need for preparation, for action. There was a battle to fight.

He afforded himself the luxury of a shower, of a clean field uniform—black and brown cargo pants, long-sleeved sweat-wicking shirt, jet-black ballcap, fresh socks and underwear. The mess tent was open. The cooking staff dutifully fried up eggs and brewed coffee. Cast and crew wandered the grounds, rising slowly well after the sun. Kneale didn't believe he could turn them into an army. But he hoped he could help them survive.

He checked on Alvira first, finding her outside of her tent showered, rested, and resetting the magazines, knives, flares, and stakes in her tactical vest. He gave her an approving nod and she responded with the same, no words needing to be exchanged. This was a veteran who understood that shortcuts lead to death.

Kneale stopped at the makeup tent next, finding Nike and her team drinking coffee.

"How can we help?" Nike asked.

"We'll need more of these," Kneale said, holding up a stake. "As many as you can make for the crew." *It might help them think they have a chance against that thing.*

"We can do that."

Kneale found Renee, Terence, Daniel, and Christopher standing in front of the castle, likewise nursing coffee or cigarettes. It was strange seeing so many of the cast and crew up at such a relatively early hour—most of them usually slept through a good portion of the day, considering the long hours required for the night shoots.

"Here he is," Renee said. The group turned to him. Kneale had not had time to formulate much of a plan. There was not enough daylight for a full-scale assessment of the castle ground's defenses, or to train the crew for personal combat. The truth of the matter was, if the vampire was half as strong as it had shown itself to be the night before, most of the people here were going to die.

"The crew should remain inside the castle, behind locked doors and barricades," Kneale said. "I'll need Daniel and Christopher to reinforce the salt circle outside the walls and set up new lines where they can."

"Such a creature may find a way through our defenses," Christopher said. "There is only so much we can do."

"Then do what you can," Kneale said. "If we can slow it down, or limit its avenues of appraoch, we might have a chance."

"And what about you and Alvira?" Renee asked. "If we're all inside the castle, where will you be?"

"Killing it," Kneale said. "Or at least slowing it down until sunrise. If we can't stop this thing tonight, and you all somehow survive until morning, you'll have to get the hell out of here, movie be damned."

"So it all comes down to you, then," Renee said, a statement more than a question. She turned to Terence. "She was right about what would happen."

"She usually is," Terence said. He looked at Kneale. "Usually."

"We intend to join you for the fight, should it come to that," Christopher said. Daniel nodded, his hand running over the ceremonial bone-knife strapped to his hip.

"I don't just want to throw bodies at the thing," Kneale said.

"We need to be smarter. We need to protect ourselves while finding ways to make it bleed."

Christopher produced the pistol he had fired the previous night. It was a heavy hunk of metal, its wooden grip faded but polished. The six-shooter's barrel held a patent date of 1858. Something else was etched into the barrel and the cylinder—runic carvings obscured by the daylight.

"On loan from an old friend," he said. "This will harm whatever the night can throw at us. I guarantee it."

"Holy water, garlic, talismans, and even bullets will slow the creature down," Daniel said, "but only a stake through the heart, followed by removing the head and burning both will guarantee its destruction."

"Then we draw it into the open, here, in the courtyard," Kneale said. "I have some ideas to that effect, but I'm going to need the crew's help."

Renee glanced at Terence, who gave her a subtle nod.

"We got work to do," she said. "Now what do you need from me?"

Nike's team scrounged for branches and fastened them into spears or stakes to hand out to anyone who would take one, followed by a few minutes of training with Daniel, who gave pointers on how to drive them into and through the chest cavity of a target. Others cleared the tents and vehicles from the center of the castle courtyard and grounds, moving them against the walls to create more open space. They closed up the connexes and drove the prop truck up to the main gate, closing off that entrance—from the ground, at least. Christopher walked the perimeter with a bag of salt to reinforce those lines of defense. Alvira worked with a couple of PAs and the kitchen staff to fill glass bottles with alcohol and rags. Kathleen and her crew erected overhead light setups near the castle itself, running wires and prepping the generators. Terence slung garlic over the garden gate, then tied it off with a great chain that he doused in holy water. He would spend all night keeping watch if he had to, and he would fire off a flare should the walls be breached from this side of the castle.

The energy of the crew was positive and proactive. Giving them something to do in the face of the uncertainty ahead made a difference. Kneale couldn't be sure how many of these people understood what they were up against. He wasn't sure he understood, for that matter. All he knew was that he had lost Pore to things that shouldn't be, and that their retreat, terrifying and difficult as it had been, was in all likelihood permitted by a foe who spared their lives out of curiosity or cruel playfulness. They would make that bloodsucking freak pay for its mistake.

In the hours before nightfall, the cast and crew gathered in the dungeon of the castle. Dailies of the production played on the wall in place of one of the classic movies: shots of the woods, of Christopher and Peter squaring off against Daniel-as-vampire, of Yvonne and Andrea exploring the haunted castle by candlelight.

There they were, among the others, in the flesh: Yvonne attending to Andrea, who lay on a portable air mattress in the corner of the dungeon, writhing against layers of blankets. Kneale offered Yvonne a cup of coffee; she accepted it with a gracious smile. Andrea, eyes closed and face pulled tight in pain, was oblivious to him.

"How is she?"

"She's undergoing the change," Yvonne said, wiping a cloth

against her friend's forehead. "She's in a lot of pain. We have to keep her out of the light."

"If we kill this thing, she goes back to normal, right? It stops the infection?"

Yvonne shrugged. "I know what the others have said, what they speculate," she said. "Having some familiarity with the occult comes with the job when you work with New Camlough, but that doesn't mean I'm an expert—or anyone else here is. Not really."

"Daniel and Christopher seem to be pretty knowledgeable."

"And you and Alvira seem pretty capable," Yvonne said. "I hope you four can work together to keep her—all of us—safe."

"I will," Kneale said. "Or die trying."

"You're an actor now, remember?" Yvonne said, giving him a sly smile. "You're under contract. You're not *allowed* to die. So you have no choice but to succeed."

Andrea stirred. Yvonne leaned in close.

"What was that? Andrea, honey, we're here for you."

"...Kneale here?"

"Yes."

Andrea's eyes snapped open. Bloodshot, red. The contrast with her pale skin made Kneale recoil.

"Alan Kneale." Her words had a slight lisp, as if some physical property of her mouth had changed. The easy beauty of her face had drained away, replaced by sallow skin and shadows dogging her eyes. Yet Kneale found he could not look away, as much as he wanted to. "I let you live," she said, her voice dropping low, her Irish accent giving way to something else, to *someone* else. "I let you live so I could watch you die. Tonight. Tonight." She offered him a grotesque leer, her upper teeth pursed over her bottom lip, sharp and grating.

Kneale pulled away from her hateful gaze. She offered a tepid laugh that degenerated into a coughing fit.

"I should go," he said.

Yvonne nodded.

"I'll save you for last," Andrea said, her voice still not her own, dogging Kneale's hurried steps away from her and out of the basement. "*I'll be sure to kill you slow!*"

31

Night arrived on a wave of humidity. The sky threatened to break out in rain, but the lightning and thunder kept their distance and the forest fell into awed silence.

Kneale and Alvira sat atop the roof of the castle, a view of the recently cleared courtyard before them. Light rigs set along different sections of the wall illuminated the forest floor in several directions.

Alvira finished triple-checking her tactical vest, satisfied that her magazines, knife, stakes, and flashlight were all accessible. She slipped it over her head and onto her shoulders.

"The only thing missing is armor plates," she said. "Never thought I'd miss that stuff, but here we are." She donned the wreath of garlic next, shaking her head in disbelief as she did so. "At least we'll smell like Grandma's cooking when we die."

Kneale swept his binos across the wall. Night had fallen on the wilderness, but with it came a dreadful, rolling bank of fog, alive with the rising moon's blue-grey light. It absorbed the illumination shed by the light rigs set atop the walls, diffusing it, helping the forest keep its dark secrets. The fog stayed clear of the three makeshift altars maintained by Christopher and Daniel, which were freshly stocked with candles that even now burned bright. Kneale didn't understand how salt, fire, and garlic could keep something so powerful at bay. Maybe they wouldn't. Maybe they would all be dead by sunrise.

"You ready for this, Six?"

Kneale lowered the binoculars.

"No one's ever ready for a fight if they don't understand the enemy's capabilities or strengths," he said. "But we've survived so far. And the fight will be on our terms, not his."

"I thought it would be safer back home," Alvira said, her hands nervously moving across her rifle. "I figured, after a few years, I could throttle down. I could feel calm again. Like I wasn't constantly under threat." She shook her head. "Sometimes I feel like it's more dangerous to live here than it was to be a soldier over there."

Kneale grunted in acknowledgment.

"Things are going to shit out there," she said. "There's something on the air. Smells like the end."

The minutes crawled by, accumulating into hours. The cold night air alleviated the uncomfortable humidity a touch, but threatened to drain the heat from them. Christopher called in hourly radio checks from the defensive position in the garden, where he, Daniel, Terence, and Renee kept watch on the north wall and back gate.

Kneale was the first to notice the animals.

They were shadows, moving low to the ground, keeping to the trees at first. But they grew bolder, slinking up to the walls, disappearing from view, hugging tight to the perimeter. A group approached from the south, their eyes catching reflective light from one of Kathleen's rigs set up near the front gate. Kneale pulled up the radio.

"Coyotes along the south wall," he said.

"Acknowledged," Christopher said over the radio. "Our producer informs me that they are likely scouts. A recon-by-coyote."

Kneale smirked. Sure, why not.

"Then hold tight. Both entrances are secured, so they shouldn't pose a threat. Just keep your eyes open."

"They crossed the salt lines, then?" Christopher asked.

"Roger," Kneale said.

"Interesting."

After some time, the coyotes disappeared. Whether they had wandered off by some angle they couldn't cover or whether they were still there, pressed low and tight against the walls and awaiting some mysterious command, Kneale couldn't say. He pulled up the radio to ask if Christopher and his team could see or hear anything at ground level, but he discovered that his radio offered only an impatient *chirp* when he pressed the transmit button.

"Try yours." Alvira pulled her handheld up.

"Any station this net, radio check, over." The same chirp was her only response. "It's not the batteries. I just changed them."

"Unless they've been drained," Kneale said. Before they could troubleshoot, a burst of air blew across the roof, cold and strong. Kneale and Alvira crouched low against the lip of the wall, the air churning above them, something great and chaotic passing just overhead, so close they could touch it.

The swarm of bats twisted through the air over their position, rising to coil around the castle's central tower before flowing back out into the night sky. They smelled of deep earth and hot animal breath. When they had passed over, Kneale lifted his head over the break in the battlements to peer back down into the courtyard and toward the front gate. Countless twin sets of light, spread out among the trees that surrounded the castle, stared up at him through the rising fog. The coyotes had revealed themselves, and their eyes were on them.

"Air recon," Alvira said, wiping at her short hair. "Goddamn. Who is that?" She pointed down to the courtyard, where several figures moved through the fog like ghosts in a dream. They walked with a slow and unsteady gait, like drunks emerging from an all-night bender, or the dead rising to walk for the first time in a hundred years.

Kneale tried the radio again, but a crash of static was his only answer. He leaned over the wall with his binoculars to get a better look. What he saw didn't make much sense. The figures were dressed in frayed and rotting suits or dresses, and their heads were covered in a smattering of desiccated hair. Their faces were ill-defined in a way not accounted for by the distance, dark, and fog. No. Their sorry state was due to the natural decomposition of time spent in the grave.

"Walking corpses," Kneale said. "Inside the perimeter." Alvira pulled up her own binos.

"I think you're right," she said. "How did they get inside the perimeter? Did they scale the walls?"

"Something we missed."

"There. Graveyard." Alvira pointed to the break in the wall on the eastern side, where a tall metal gate hung loose on its hinges, swinging back and forth in the cold wind. A gust drew out a wave of red and orange leaves. Branches obscured the area, but a shambling corpse emerging from under the stone archway confirmed Alvira's guess. More dead followed, stumbling and slow, their clothes old and torn, their bodies covered from skulls to splitting shoes in rotting earth and writhing worms.

"I didn't think—I didn't think it would be…" Kneale managed, his words catching in his throat. Adrenaline churned through his nervous system.

"Doesn't matter," Alvira said. "They're massing in front of the castle. Having themselves a little formation."

About two dozen bodies had exhumed themselves from their nominally eternal resting places, and most of them were in rough shape. Nearly all of them were stripped bare of skin and hair, their eyes long ago disintegrated or consumed by vermin, their bones cracking under the effort simply to stand. Individually, Kneale figured they were not much of a threat. But as a pack, they could cause some trouble. If they fought like the skeletons in the library, they might be surprisingly capable. Or…

"How much energy would it take to reanimate a single corpse, let alone a small army of zombies?" Kneale said.

"That's the kind of fucked-up question Daniel or Christopher might be able to answer," Alvira said, shaking her head. "I'm a little out of my depth here."

The zombies turned toward the castle, all at once.

"And how much energy would it take to control them, especially at a distance?"

Kneale pulled his binos back up to his face and scanned the walls. Seeing nothing, he shifted his focus up to the tree line. Something small caught his eye: a glimmer of light, a subtle movement of shadow.

"Check out the trees, south by southwest," he said. "I think I saw some of those spooklights floating around. Put some glass on it."

Alvira searched for a moment, then focused on something that caught her eye.

"Looks like a shape—rectangle, wood. Those lights hover around it, separating it from the trees and the dark."

"It's the coffin," Kneale said. "That's our target. That's our boy."

"What's it waiting for?"

"Maybe it can't breach the perimeter. Maybe Christopher and Daniel's preparations are keeping it out."

"So, we just do this every night until one of us blinks?"

"Maybe. They might be able to finish the film within the castle grounds," Kneale said. "We can exfil during the day."

Alvira pointed to the coffin floating in the dark.

"And what's keeping that thing from following us home or finding us again? Or deciding that it's worth the trouble to try us in the daylight?"

Kneale didn't have an answer for that.

"Just knowing that it's out here, knowing that it knows my

face—yours, too—makes me think we're probably not safe, even if we leave," Alvira said. "I don't need another demon keeping me awake at night."

Kneale shifted his binoculars back down to the horde gathering below. Their dead faces were all bone and shadow, worm and dripping mucus, dirt and death.

"What's he going to do with all of them?" he said.

"Storm the castle," Alvira said. "We should open fire, now."

As if in response, the zombies all looked up at the same time, a coordinated *snap* of neck bones that reverberated across the courtyard. Then they turned just as suddenly, executing a military-style about-face to the southern wall, their backs to Kneale and Alvira. The corpses marched together, spread out and walking in a straight line. But several steps later, the crowd coalesced and advanced toward a point on the far side of the grounds.

"They're going for the prop truck," Kneale said.

"Why?"

"Take precise shots," he said, setting down his binos and lifting his rifle over the battlement. He leaned against the cool stone into the weapon's buttstock. "Aim for the head, like in the movies."

"Why the truck? What's going on?"

"It's blocking the main gate."

"So? They can't drive. Can they? Are the keys in it?"

"I don't want to find out," Kneale said. He lined up the lead corpse in his optics and squeezed the trigger.

32

Firing the weapon was a comforting, familiar sensation. Seeing the impact of his round on the head of a walking corpse gave Kneale a rush of excitement that counteracted the nervous pounding of adrenaline. The feeling amplified as the corpse fell forward, face down, its ruined head an exploded-out mess of goop and black ichor. It did not rise again.

"Headshots are effective," Kneale said.

"Acquiring targets," Alvira said. She fired—one, two shots. She clipped one of the zombies near the front of the column in the shoulder. It shuddered and stumbled but kept its balance. The corpse resumed its course toward the truck.

"Slow is smooth, and smooth is fast," Kneale said. "Ease into the trigger squeeze, don't pull. The shot should surprise you."

"Roger that, drill sergeant," she said, lining up her rifle for another go. One shot this time, followed by a fist clenched in victory. Her target tumbled down, lifeless once more.

"Nice shot," Kneale said. He lined up another zombie head in his sights. The dead advanced and fell, one shot at a time. The smell of burned powder hung over the air. Soon there were only a handful of the dead left, but they were only a few meters from the prop truck. Alvira pulled back from the wall for a magazine change. Kneale guessed he had two, maybe three rounds left. He lined up a shot on the one closest to the truck. He fired, missed, clipping the truck's door. He exhaled, focused on his breathing, and acquired the target one more time.

A swarm of black claws and fleshy membrane obscured the target. The bats had returned, drawn back by their master in a bid to keep the marksmen from completing their desperate work. Kneale threw his arm up to clear them from the air like annoying flies, smacking their little brown bodies and dry wings. The swarm squealed and shrieked.

A shot exploded next to him, followed by two more. Kneale produced his knife, then slashed wildly upwards into the maelstrom of teeth and wings. Bat blood slicked along the blade and spurted onto his hand and arm, acrid and hot. The spell broke and the swarm dissipated, self-control returned to the animals as the fingers of their dark master loosed their hold on their shallow minds. They fled into the sky, just in time for Kneale to see the door to the prop truck slam shut. Alvira kept firing, pouring rounds into the cab.

They wouldn't leave the keys in it, Kneale thought. *No way.*

The truck started with a heavy growl. Its running lights burned harsh and bright. Metal-on-metal sound, followed by the bright red illumination of its reverse lights, heralded their doom. Alvira fired off another round, which ricocheted harmlessly off the truck.

"Hold your fire," Kneale said. "We'll need the rounds."

The truck backed up, then angled its trailer toward them and the castle in a clumsy half-circle. One of the zombies had managed to get back on its feet, only to be caught by the rear bumper of the truck and knocked to the earth again. Its head popped under a heavy tire, releasing a burst of grey slush.

The driver—or, rather, the vampire psychically controlling its body—shifted the truck into drive. The engine roared as the zombie pressed the remains of its foot onto the gas pedal. The vehicle careened forward, smashing the gate open and barreling through the wall, dislodging stone and metal gate. The truck popped up over the debris, teetered on its passenger-side tires, then fell into the crumbling wall. It crashed to the earth with a great *slam* and a groan of metal.

When the truck had settled, there was noise and movement from the cab. The driver's-side door, facing the sky, popped open. The living corpse pulled itself up over the edge of the overturned cab. Its head exploded in a mess of gore as a bullet passed through with hateful precision.

"Fuck *you!*" Alvira shouted. She set her rifle back down. She held up her fist in triumph.

"Nice shot."

"Only a minute too late."

They scanned the wreckage of the truck and gate. The wind rustled through the forest. Trees leaned over the walls, branches scratching at stone. The overturned truck ceased idling, its engine noise running down into liquid gurgles and the hissing of escaping gases. Smoke and sputtering light leaked out from beneath the hood, hinting at the fire within. The air grew acrid with burning fuel. Flames emerged from the cracks in the metal to climb high into the night air, a summoning signal for enemies approaching in the dark.

Four coffins appeared in the haze of smoke and the gloom of night, floating on invisible currents of power. They were raw collections of grey tree branches and planks cannibalized from the cabins around the hidden lake, held together by rusted strands of barbed wire. Caskets of necessity. They floated through the breach in the wall, one by one, passing through the kiss of fire and into the courtyard.

"The truck and wall debris must have overrun the salt circle," Kneale said. He sat down behind his rifle, angling the barrel toward the floating procession of the dead. "Go time."

"Hell of a last stand," Alvira said, counting the remaining magazines stacked between them. She touched a nearby crate covered in a blanket for self-assurance. Glass bottles clinked within.

PROJECT VAMPIRE KILLER

The four coffins hovered above the tangle of ruined bodies. The engine fire of the downed prop truck rose high and wide, illuminating the courtyard in its hungry, poisoned glow. Kneale stared at the flames and saw other fires on other battlefields. Burn pits churning through plastic and batteries; fire chewing through metal and blood-soaked uniforms; the noxious, poison fumes of human shit mixed with diesel and stirred by young men and women whose futures would be curtailed by diagnoses delivered by stern-faced doctors and administrators saying *the VA does not consider this service-related and will not cover the cost of treatment.*

The coffins rotated, their bolted-on lids flapping open toward the ground, disgorging their payload before returning to the woods.

The bodies within *plopped* onto the ground, just four more corpses among others. But these rose again, summoned to resurrection not by the trumpet call of angels but by forces malign and sinister. In contrast to the zombies, these creatures retained much of their skin, faces, hair, and features—their deaths having occurred much more recently. Two women, two men, wearing contemporary clothing, but soaked through with gore and moist earth.

"I've seen them before," Kneale said, dread creeping into his voice. "From the tapes in the woods."

"What?"

"They're—they *were*—a film crew, shooting a movie nearby," he said. "I wasn't sure if—"

The vampires bared radioactive-green fangs. The defenders of the castle opened fire.

33

The 5.56-millimeter rounds had an effect: knocking the bloodsucking freaks down, rending their flesh, splitting open their faces. But they rose back up as quickly as they were felled.

"Grenades!" Kneale shouted. He kept firing, hoping to keep their targets pinned down just a few moments longer.

Alvira tore off the blanket covering the crate to reveal eight wine bottles, emptied of their original contents and refilled with kerosene. She grabbed one and produced her lighter, alighting the rag hanging out like a tongue.

"Here." She held up the flaming bottle to Kneale. He set down his rifle, took the bottle, pointed with his off-hand at the monsters below, and threw. The glass container spun end over end down a near-perfect arc, its *Finger Lakes Wine Country* label showing its face to the dark sky before shattering against the cold earth. The flames climbed along the rag and spread rapidly along the fuel exposed to air. The fire found the clothing of the undead and began its quick work.

"Another!"

Alvira lit the next Molotov cocktail and handed it to Kneale, whose second toss was even more on the mark than the first. The glass bottle landed against the face of the largest of the four monsters, a scarred-face man who had played the killer in the horror movie that preceded their own. He took the blow without reaction, the glass shattering over his forehead, the fuel cascading down his face, the fire burning across his head and upper torso. He held up his hands before him, as if confused, and then fell to his knees as the flames crawled over and consumed his skin. The scream he let loose was that of a dying animal, alone and afraid, its final moments spent in despair and agony.

"Hold," Kneale said. "Cavalry's here." From the east side of the house, Daniel and Christopher rushed forward, flashlight beams snaking over the courtyard. Christopher paused to take aim with his old-style six-shooter. Strange runes glowed a vibrant plethora of colors, illuminated by scant moonlight sneaking through the clouds. He fired a single round in an explosion of stinking gunpowder and flame. The mewling undead stuntman suffered the full force of the shot, his melting head exploding in a shower of jellied brains and gibbed skull plate. Smoke rose from the remains of his blood-spurting neck.

The undead moved with preternatural speed, their bodies leaving a trail of glowing shadow and smoke, their movement impossible to react to with human reflexes.

Kneale tossed a rope ladder over the edge of the wall, then double-checked that the upper rungs were securely bolted in place. He slung his rifle over his back and dropped down over the side, trusting his boot to find the next rung, and the next.

As Alvira reached the ladder, the swarm of bats returned, all screeching menace and a whirlwind of teeth. They cut across her face, tearing into her cheeks and going for her left eye. She combat-crawled back toward the crate. As the swarm chewed through the air overhead, she grabbed for a long, wooden torch wrapped in old rags and dipped in kerosene. The lighter's flame found easy purchase. Squinting through the tears of her bloody eye, she thrust the burning torch into the swarm.

Kneale stepped off the ladder and into the courtyard, then swung his rifle around to take aim. Two of the vampires had closed the distance with Christopher and Daniel, locking the actors in their deadly grip. The third lingered behind, her back and long hair aflame. He fired twice. At least one of the rounds found its target. Kneale let his rifle drop to its shoulder strap and produced a new weapon. The vampire, bent with pain and fury, reached him in a blaze of shadow and fire. Her fingernails were razor-sharp claws that she buried in his neck, her glowing-green teeth extended for the kill.

Kneale raised the weapon at the last possible moment, his reaction time almost a tick too slow, extending the stake point-first up from his chest. The rush of the vampire's body colliding with his own almost broke his grip, but he held fast, keeping the point up and on target.

The vampire pulled her face and fangs back. Confusion passed over her eyes: first, at the wreath of garlic draped over Kneale's neck, then at the vile blood leaking from the hole in her chest. Kneale rode an adrenaline spike to shove the stake in further, her rib cage cracking and her lungs and heart bursting. She let out a low, painful moan. For one fleeting moment, light and vigor returned to her pale face, to her eyes, to her hair, and the vibrant actress who once was had returned from the depths of the monster she had become. Then she was gone again, unlife and life alike fleeing this husk, her time here complete. She was off to her next role, on a stage set upon the distant shore.

The body crumpled and contracted, as if all the moisture had drained from it in a single instance. Skin wrinkled along bone; muscle shriveled; rigor mortis set in with a burst of dust and dried blood. Kneale shoved the desiccated corpse off, leaving the stake embedded in its chest, just to be safe.

The two remaining vampires still held Daniel and Christopher in deathgrips. Kneale rushed toward them, prepared to match their deaths with his own in defense of the castle. The smell of incense punched through the fog of killing and combat, reminding him of churches with sky-high ceilings, of men in vestments intoning ritualistic prayers, of pews packed full with relatives and community members to mark a confirmation, a wedding, a funeral.

Renee and Terence emerged from the far side of the castle, swinging censers that teemed with incense smoke. The censers were gold-plated, domed containers on slim chains that clinked pleasantly with each swing, emitting the heavy vapor in lazy trails that lingered in the night air. The effect of the miasma was immediate. The vampires released their victims, sending Daniel and Christopher reeling to collapse into the dirt. The night creatures howled and coughed, spitting up mouthfuls of their victims' blood and clawing at the air. A Molotov cocktail landed close, releasing a swarm of fresh fire upon them. Atop the castle, Alvira stood tall, torch in hand, blood streaming down her face. She released a guttural battle cry of triumph.

Kneale emptied his magazine into the burning vampires. The night air was choked with their cries and with the smell of burning flesh. Kneale produced another stake, his hands now accustomed to its shape, weight, and power. He was upon the nearest bloodsucker in no time at all, knocking it back to the ground with a backhanded swipe of the stake's pointed tip. He dropped a boot on its neck, pressing tight, *tighter*, choking the air out of it. There was no recognition of humanity in its snarling, flame-crowned face, but only hate, only hunger, only evil.

Kneale drove the stake down into its chest with the full force of his adrenaline-strength, breathing the incense in like sweet forest air, his heart pumping the very lifeblood on which these foul creatures sought to feed. The creature's rib cage cracked open like wet cardboard. Gore and dark blood splattered against Kneale's madness-twisted face, pushing him into further acts of strength and rage as the thing died again.

His victory was almost cut short by the swiping claws of the last vampire. She rushed toward him in a shadowy blaze of cold terror. A flash of light and sharpened bone slashed through the night air, carried forward on currents of incense smoke by the sure hand of a trained stage fighter. The whalebone knife sliced across the vampire's throat, splitting her neck with uncanny precision. She tumbled forward into Kneale, hands grasping at her wound. Renee and Terence, still gripping the censers nearby, shouted encouragements to violence. Daniel and Alvira were all knives and stakes and burning torch, flashing and piercing bloodless skin, slicing and destroying undead flesh, smashing out sharpened teeth and breaking crooked fingers raised in ill-suited defense. The murder was rhythmic, primal; returning a once-human body to a natural state of death as an act of mercy, of exorcism, consecrated in a wash of arterial spray and cleansing fire.

34

When the killing was done, they were left with blood on their hands and faces and with gore dripping from their weapons.

"Check on Christopher!" Kneale shouted. Renee and Terence set down their censers, which spilled out rolling waves of smoke. They reached their comrade, who lay motionless in the dirt.

"Are you alright?" Kneale put his hands on Alvira's shoulders. Her face was covered in streaks of black blood and bile. Her whole body shook with adrenaline overload.

"Yeah," she said, her eyes wide and her smile quivering. There was blood on her teeth. "We did it, Six. We're killers. *Vampire* killers. Can you believe that shit?"

Kneale turned to Daniel.

"Are you hurt?"

"Fangs broke the skin, but did not puncture a vein," the actor said, angling his neck for Kneale to see the shallow wound. "Christopher was not so lucky." The clinking of chains drew their attention back toward the gate.

The great coffin floated over the flames that consumed the prop truck. A jet of fuel spurted out to catch fire in a burst of heraldry, announcing the arrival of death itself. The size, shape, and decorative nature of the coffin confirmed it as the very same one Kneale's team had encountered below. It was the coffin of the master.

"He's dead," Renee said, all emotion drained from her voice. Christopher's head was in her hands, eyes shut by her soft touch. Terence, ever the director, produced a handheld digital camera from his satchel, flipping the viewscreen open and popping the cap off the lens to capture the approach of the master vampire's coffin.

"We have to destroy the bodies," Daniel said, not taking his eyes from the approaching threat. "Including Christopher. It's what he'd want us to do."

"We can do that if we live through the night," Kneale said. He changed the magazine out on his rifle. Alvira mirrored him. Daniel popped his neck, stomped his feet, one-two, then held the blade out before him. "You two should get inside the castle." Renee and Terence wasted no time returning to the stone fortress.

The coffin drifted to a slow halt just a dozen meters away. The earth writhed with worms, maggots, and great rats feasting on the burning remains of the undead. A blanket of pulsing, green fog could not hide their wicked activities from the eyes of the living. A great gust of deep-autumn wind carried the stench of decay and rot.

Light erupted from the cracks in the coffin, outlining its lid and suffusing its contours with malignant energy. The lid swung open. The master floated up, hands crossed over his chest, body perfectly still as it rose.

Nosferatu emerged from his coffin to stalk the crew of the ship.

Its face was less human than before, and more monster, all grey flesh twisted into a heavy, bat-like brow over wide, inhuman eyes that were portals to a realm of fire; chin sharp, nose long and proud, cheekbones high, skin taut, head bald, ears pointed and wide. Before and beneath it lay the carnage wrought by the vampire killers upon its servants. Anger—or amusement—passed over its face, before its eyes settled on Kneale.

I know your stench.

It turned to Alvira.

And yours. Where is my bride?

Then, to Daniel:

Bring me the one whom my heart desires, and I shall let thee live.

Something drew its attention away from the three warriors. It raised part of its upper lip to reveal a long and crimson-stained fang, before its body exploded in a concussive wave of wing and claw, of teeth and wide ears. Bats, fat and grotesque, flowed over them in a wave of noxious mammal-smell, all dirt and blood-encrusted fur and rotting guts, mouths yawning open in insatiable hunger. The swarm reached Terence and Renee at the entrance of the castle, where it coalesced into shadow, within which fog and wing melted together to form a grey hand. It reached out to grab the director by the neck. Terence gasped and choked, dropping his handheld camera. Renee backed away, her eyes flashing with terror and wonder.

Kneale reacted first. He crossed the gore-soaked courtyard in no time at all, raising the wooden point of a stake high just as the vampire flicked its semi-material wrist, dislodging Terence's skull from his spinal column in a burst of blood and popping flesh. The director's spirit lingered on for several moments as his eyes rolled in confusion, his mouth dropping open, slack, unable to find the breath to speak in the final moments before death.

Kneale leaped forward, stake held aloft. But in that leap, the master's eye found his, and the world faded away, leaving only the internal realm of fog and memory rushing up to claim him.

35

The air inside the Humvee cab was hot, tinged by the smell of diesel fuel and full of dust and sand. Nothing about it was comforting, but it was familiar. It was a long way—and a long time—from the cold autumnal killing field before a castle in upstate New York.

The unimproved road stretched out before him—before *them*, his soldiers in the Humvee with him, Kneale in the front passenger seat, hand on the radio set, watching the sides of the road for explosives, a simmering core of fear and loneliness where his heart used to be. Kneale spent a lot of time here, on this road or ones like it, with these soldiers or others.

The master did not find this memory to his liking. The sun was ever-present, a howling menace that dominated the sky. The heat was almost as bad, draining the life from even these day-dwelling cattle. The master could survive under such conditions, of course, but his strength would be low and his abilities beneath a threshold of what was required. No, this would not do at all. So he brought Kneale elsewhere.

The air in the apartment smelled of beer bottles left open for days on end and a garbage bag in the kitchen in need of disposal. Kneale was still in his black field outfit, his tactical vest weighing on his shoulders, his face flecked with dirt and blood. It was daylight out, or at least he thought it was, with light peeking through the down-turned blinds of the living room's large window. Yes, a little light was necessary for the illusion. The *impression* of day was acceptable. The master would find a way to keep him from looking or going outside. This place—this room—would do nicely. It was, in many ways, already a tomb.

Kneale stood up. His legs were weary and his back ached. He wondered why he was so filthy, why he hadn't changed or taken off his gear. Instinct brought his hand to the TV remote. He pointed it at the large, black screen that sat on the dust bunny–ridden entertainment center. The TV was wrong, its proportions misaligned, the subtle curve of its screen warped in a sickly configuration, more overtly a scrying stone than a simple means of entertainment. It wouldn't turn on. Kneale dropped the remote, then reached for the handful of magazines on the coffee table. They had names and covers he didn't recognize, slashes of color and impressions of form. Was that a woman in a bathing suit, implied by waves of dark flesh tone and bright highlights? Was this one a car magazine, with the boxy dimensions of a vehicle dominating the page? Kneale didn't even like cars. Why would he have a car magazine, let alone keep it on his coffee table? Why did the titles of these magazines appear as jumbled collections of half-letters, moving in and out of alignment, refusing all efforts at recognition?

Instinct pushed him to drop the magazines and step quickly out of the living room and into the kitchen. The window above the sink was nuclear-bright. Kneale headed straight for it. The master would have to shift before that searing pain bore through Kneale's eyes and into the vampire's mind. He had to find true darkness.

He found it buried under a mountain of weary, lonely nights alone. Beneath the refuse of potential, under blankets of bitterness and resentment. The master found the widest, hungriest, blackest sky imaginable, littered with mere pinpricks of unfamiliar starlight and far from the burning gaze of the damnable sun.

Kneale stood under the haunted Colorado night sky and

shivered—not from the chill air, but from recognition. The Nathan Ranch in Meeker, Colorado. Confusion and instinctual resistance rose in him, but the master worked quickly, recognizing the mistake in not vetting the memory. There, in Kneale's hands, was the familiar weight of the night-vision monocular he carried with him. There, on Kneale's hip, was the Motorola handheld radio, its tall antenna reaching up along his torso. There, on the road before him at the base of this valley, was one of the reliable pickup trucks the Observer/Experiencers drove out into the field, kitted out with enough food, water, and fuel for several days.

Kneale reached down to the handheld to run a quick radio check, to hear a human voice, to ground himself in this place. Before he transmitted, a voice spoke to him from the radio.

You are supposed to be here, Alan Kneale. You volunteered, remember? You are paid well for what you do, and this work is simple, and far safer than anything you ever did in the Army.

"Yeah, that's right," Kneale said, trying out his own mouth, his tongue, seeing if they could still form words, words of his own voice. "This is the best-paying gig I ever had."

You have only seen a few strange lights, a few ghostly figures that could have been the fog, or your mind playing tricks...what with the stories the others tell. There is no reason to be fearful here. The night is so welcoming.

"Yeah." The light from the moon illuminated the plain in all directions. Night cloaked the distant mountains in shadow, but they rose high against the stars in sharp profile, beautiful testament to the glory of creation.

"The mountains were pretty in Afghanistan, too," a man said, speaking from the dark. He walked out of shadows that unzipped around him. The face was familiar. His attire matched Kneale's. *We must work together*, Kneale thought. All soldiers, contractors, and field spooks tended to look the same after a while. There was no reason Kneale should recognize this man over any other.

"This place is dangerous, isn't it?" the man said. His voice belonged elsewhere, beyond, taken out of this world and into the next. What was he doing *back here*?

The man looked around, then studied Kneale's uniform and equipment. "This is Colorado, right? Where things really went sideways for you."

Kneale wanted to speak but couldn't. He was trapped on stage, in a play where an interloper had entered the scene off-mark and off-script. The audience hadn't caught on, yet. Sweat broke out along Kneale's forehead. He would have to think of something to keep the glamour alive. Otherwise they—*the master*—might realize something was amiss.

"We didn't know, not at first," the man said. "About you being on the Colorado op. Me and Alvira, we had heard rumors. I knew someone who did a rotation here, but he never saw anything strange. But you saw plenty strange, didn't you? You were here at the end. Or near enough the end to have gotten the picture. Were you here when it happened? When the whole thing blew up?"

Kneale shook his head, *no*.

"I was on a three-day leave," Kneale said. "It was a bad two weeks leading up to the…to the end. I saw a lot. Experienced a lot. We all did. When I came back, the camp was deserted. Trucks and equipment were smashed, the trailers were ransacked, all the science staff and the other O/Es were missing. I just left. I just drove away."

"Before you left," the man said, stepping closer, his face known, his voice clear, clearer even than the sensation of being *here*, in this memory of a place, "did you see enough to believe? To believe in spirits? In the supernatural?"

"Yes," Kneale said, tears gathering at the corners of his eyes. "That's a good word for them. *Spirits*. I can't really tell you what that might mean, though."

"And I can't tell you much more, except to say that I'm a *spirit*, too, but not quite like what you saw here in Colorado, and not quite like what you've seen in the woods where you are now, in

New York." He paused, letting his words linger in the air like so many ghosts. When the man breathed and spoke, no white air escaped his lips. The landscape and sky appeared behind him, *through him*, blurry in detail beyond his semi-transparent form. He held up his hands. "I am not a threat, but the spirit that brought you here is. You have to resist it. You're a soldier, Six. You have to get back to the fight. The one at the castle."

Kneale nodded, the tears rushing down his cheeks. Something deep within his heart stirred with warmth, with a refutation of the fear that had dogged him ever since he was old enough to understand death. The fear that there was nothing beyond it.

"I died in that dungeon hell, but I'm here with you, now. I've been to other places, too, and I'm anxious to get back. I came here because I will never leave a fallen comrade." He held out a half-visible hand, flickering now with blue light along its edges.

The jig was up. The audience understood now that this was off-script, that this wasn't a memory at all, but something different. A threat. This man did not emerge from Kneale's memories. This conversation never happened. This man was something else, something *more*, substantial and alien in a way that the master did not think possible.

No, he whispered. *NO*, he commanded.

Kneale shook off the voice, so insistent, so terrifying. He reached out. The hands of the living and the dead met. The curtain came crashing down.

36

Dirt. In his mouth, pushed up his nostrils, flowing into his ears. Encasing him in cold rot. Panic fired across synapses, spreading to every fiber of his consciousness. He struggled. He pushed. Pore spoke once more, and then was gone forever:

Fight.

Kneale pumped his legs and thrashed his arms. The earth's invincible, iron-tight grip was an illusion. He broke free. He clawed at the dirt above him, pulling down one fistful of rock and soil at a time, his feet finding purchase, pushing him upwards inch by inch. The dirt drifted down over his nose and mouth, releasing pockets of air that fueled his lungs for the next volley of effort.

Fingers burst through the surface, emerging through the membrane of the grave into the world of the living. The night sky was hidden by the great canopy of withered trees, their multicolored leaves obscuring the stars and the moon. Kneale pulled himself out of the muck, chest heaving for breath, soil rolling out from between his lips. He moaned in pain and victory, emerging fully formed from the womb of the earth. He rolled onto his back as the branches above warped and twisted. Film distortion cascaded along the bubbling veneer of this simulacrum, revealing its analog origins, the substrate beyond the surface. What he saw was merely photosensitive chemicals applied to tape, the images captured long ago and played back for his benefit, or for the benefit of others. Nearby stood the dolmen, its stones haunted by glowing blue spooklights that orbited above and around each pillar and the great cap in fearful symmetries.

You are different, the master said. *You are a killer.*

Kneale's whole body was worn out, burning with exhaustion, but he pushed himself to his feet all the same.

You are better suited for this world than most. You understand what is asked of you as a living creature. In a world of suffering and hunger, you use your teeth and claws.

Kneale raised his fists before him. His eyes searched the rocks and the trees beyond for the vampire.

What sane and loving God would make feeding the foundational principle of life? Have you considered that? The destruction of other living things, to keep other living things living. A house of cards that is now crashing down in our present age.

"Come on, you son of a bitch," Kneale said. "I'm ready. I'm ready."

A true predator, when faced with threat, does not lie down to die.

"Let's finish this, you fuck."

If I were to leave you as you are, you would already be finished. Your body is past its prime, your mind harrowed unto near madness through decades spent in the practice of violence. But no matter how strong you are, eventually the disease, the insects, the entropy—it all catches up with you. Because the world was built for those things. For the killers. For the carrion-feeders. For me.

Kneale found himself drawn toward the dolmen. The stones sputtered, the tape well-worn from repeat viewings of this part. His thoughts were a staccato series of interrupted patterns, overlain with animal kingdom imagery of coyotes chasing down a young deer, of flies swarming over the face of a crying baby, of waves crashing against the skyscrapers of a starkly familiar city.

What a cruel joke, then, to create thinking animals and place them within seas of pain and loss. What cruelty, leveled upon us by God. Because God is cruelty. God desires cruelty, selfishness, strength. Become as I Am, all of those things. Together, joined in undeath—or become meek and decay. The feeders shall inherit the earth. I could be your companion. Your master, your teacher. Your lover, if that would suit you. I will teach you the secret song of the night, sung unto the Black Goat of the Wood. We shall sing on All Hallows' Eve and Walpurgisnacht, and on every damnable Christian feast day beyond and between, deep into the charnel house of the future. Endless nights will flow together along a river of death to the end of the world. No possession nor secret rite shall be denied to you. No meal, no kill, no ripe body shall be out of your reach.

Kneale had heard seductions like this before. Back on the ranch. Transmissions from the goblin world. Voices promising joy and an end to pain. Promising *transcendence*. Needling away at his sanity.

The vampire stood atop the dolmen. Its bare torso was grey and smooth, its long, thin arms wrapped up to grasp its shoulders. Its pale face held a narrow chin, sharp nose, and terrible, illuminated eyes, eyes that bore into him and held his own, even against his will.

"Where are we?" Kneale asked, approaching slowly. He laid a hand on one of the stones, which sputtered and went blurry at his touch.

Do you know that human thought exists in higher dimensional space? Thought emerges from planes not intuited by human scientists. The brain—that goop encased in blood and held in place by your fragile skull—is a transceiver. It doesn't produce thought any more than a radio device creates the music revealed through its speakers.

Kneale ran his hands through his tactical vest, searching for weapons. Rifle, gone. Flare, gone. Garlic necklace and stakes—all gone.

I will turn several of the others and kill the rest. The offspring you slaughtered were weak, denied nourishment in this remote place. But the many here—down below, cowering in the dungeons of the castle—they will serve as blood stock for a new cadre. Would you join me in the feast, or be fed upon?

"Fuck you," Kneale said, summoning his anger. He thought about the violence he would visit upon this walking corpse given the chance—given the proper *tool*. A tool in his *hands*.

The smallest of frowns passed over the vampire's gaunt face. Twin fangs slid over pale lips.

It is death for you, then. There is nothing beyond this world. Just blackness. An eternity of suffocation, of vile darkness beyond even my tolerance. I have no appetite for oblivion. It seems you desire to be prey, to suffer death. So be it.

Kneale willed the dolmen to maintain its form. He pulled himself up onto the covering stone. Perhaps the monster was right. Maybe he did desire death. His life didn't matter. It had not mattered for a long time.

Curiosity turned to amusement as the creature pursed its lips. It bared its long and terrible fangs, inviting attack, excited by the unexpected, by the sheer novelty of this creature's brazen gesture toward futility.

Behold, I am become death. Eater of your world.

Kneale willed himself to a solid footing atop the dolmen. He summoned his fury and his fear, localizing it around his right hand, within his fist, until it was a physical thing, or whatever passed for *physical* in a place like this. The stake materialized, and so did something else. The rosary in his breast pocket, beneath the tactical vest. A gift from Christopher, now a gift from the dead. *Memento mori.* He retrieved it and wrapped the beads around the sharpened piece of wood. The crucifix glowed in delirious anti-light. The metal face of the forsaken Christ cried tears of despair.

The creature made no move to avoid the incoming attack. The stake sliced through the ether, a thing of fog and mist-become-wood, piercing the creature's chest with a sound like ripping paper.

The puncture grew into tears that arced around the vampire, through the air, through the forest itself. Spiraling red orbs of nauseating light poured out of the membrane. The rush became a river, and the dolmen stones were submerged, the clearing flooded, now drowned in blood. Kneale was carried high, higher, up beyond the canopy, tossed back and forth among red waves of cosmic blood all the way back to the castle. The flood carried him above the walls and towers. The sky was revealed to him as a hungry, wet mouth filled to impossible volumes with teeth built to razor through whole species, whole ecosystems, entire levels of reality itself.

37

The vampire caught Kneale mid-leap. The material world was a terrifying rush of sensation, of pain, of cold, of fear pumping through his veins. This was his reality again, or close enough to it.

Smoke rose from the creature's grip on Kneale's neck. Burning flesh-smell, combined with the pleasant aroma of roasting garlic. The wreath caught fire, and the vampire released Kneale, tossing him back a dozen feet. He landed on his back, dropping the stake to slap out the tiny flames that danced along his shirt.

Gunfire erupted from nearby. The vampire held its hands out, fleshy palms sagging and burning as if from acid. Flecks of flesh and black blood exploded from its shoulders and torso as Alvira's rounds flew true. It reached down, slow and deliberate, to grab Terence's severed head and toss it at Alvira. It landed with a *crunch* against her face. She fired a round into the black sky as she fell back.

Kneale grabbed an empty magazine from his cargo pants pocket and set it out before him. He took the flare from his kit, popping the cap off and placing it on the bottom of the baton. Using both hands, he brought the open flare down on the magazine, metal-on-metal, once, *twice*, third time the charm. The flare ignited with a burst of chemical-burn smell and a *whoosh* of velocity, the rising star hitting its apotheosis in the stretch of sky

PROJECT VAMPIRE KILLER

just over the castle's tallest tower. The projectile exploded into a falling sprite of green light, illuminating the courtyard, the castle, the walls, and the woods beyond with its verdant glow. It fell, drifting slowly, hissing and emitting sparks as it returned to earth.

Across the courtyard, lights erupted. From the castle walls, illumination poured down. From within the windows, vibrant, movie-set glow burst out. The lights blinded Kneale and the others, showering them in an irresistible suffusion of night-for-day. The synthetic sunrise was overwhelming. The vampire screamed in frustrated agony.

There was a shattering of glass and the smell of candle smoke.

"Now! Kill it! Kill it!"

Kneale blinked toward the sound of the voice. Daniel, the actor-turned-vampire-killer, tossed a glass vial at the terror. It broke apart on impact, spreading blue flame wherever its water splashed against the creature's vile skin, made pale and revealed as malnourished and disfigured in the blinding light of Kathleen's greatest achievement as director of photography. Daniel raised Christopher's occult six-shooter and fired a glowing round directly into the master's chest, knocking it off balance with an explosion of grey flesh and black blood.

The vampire screamed in unholy terror. Its fury was echoed by sparks exploding out from the many light rigs arrayed across the courtyard. Bulbs burst and generators fell silent. Metal groaned and warped, joining the cacophony.

Kneale found the stake wrapped in the rosary and pushed himself to his feet, one last time. Legs pumped and arms raised. Through the blue fire and the flailing limbs of the vampire, an eye emerged to meet Kneale's, to facilitate a connection that was a shadow of its former power.

We can live forever. And if we cannot, God owes us all a goddamn apology.

With two hands on the wooden stake, Kneale drove its sharp point into the chest of the vampire. Its rib cage split with a clap of thunder and a surge of black air and blacker goo pouring out in a great rush. Pair after pair of mold-encrusted hands emerged from the broken bone and split flesh, pushing their way up, dragging with them screaming phantasms of vaporous form and shadow.

The dread light fell from the vampire's eyes, and it knew death, personally and truly, and, if such a thing could be said to still have a soul, it was surely ferried toward judgment.

38

Nike provided the bone saw, salvaged from her burned-out prop truck. Kneale had to do the work. The vampire was his kill, after all. The solemn and grotesque duty of removing its head fell to him. It was grisly labor, carried out on a folding table set up among the splattered and charred remains of the master's undead army scattered around the courtyard. The cast and crew of *Hierarchies of Blood* filed by to watch, orderly and silent, like German villagers in a World War II film paraded out to see firsthand the atrocities carried out in their names. Renee organized a working party to shovel up the spattered, burned, and shot-to-shit remains of the zombies, depositing them back into the graves from which they first arose. Alvira and Daniel stood watch nearby, their silent presence fulfilling some ritualistic warrior-sentry roles that Kneale did not consciously understand but that his instinct recognized as just and right.

The vampire's flesh was withered and tough. The corpse was old, much older in true death than in its corrupted undeath. Its arms were twisted tightly, wrists bent forward, all the skin dried up, its muscles contracted. The teeth of the saw moved through the blood-drenched throat and caught on the spine, releasing a smell that gave Kneale a furious stomachache. Yvonne attended him with bottles of water poured into a basin in which he could rinse his hands of the dark blood. Kneale resolved to burn his clothes after he was finished. But the tool did its job, and the head did come off, finally.

Alvira filled its exposed and ruined esophagus with garlic, then placed a garlic bulb in the decapitated head's open mouth. Daniel took the head, as he had the others belonging to the fallen vampires. Production assistants loaded the corpse of the master vampire onto a stretcher. Kneale led them to the dolmen.

The vampires' bodies burned atop grey branches, stacks of scripts, and coffin wood. The stones superheated. The bones turned to ash in the light of the morning sun. The wind carried away swaths of the blackened flakes. The stake—still wrapped in rosary beads—remained.

They burned Christopher and Terence atop the dolmen later that day, after the ashes of the monsters had disappeared into the wind and the rocks had been cleansed with the remaining holy water. Kneale was too exhausted to question this. Whether they had friends and family who would miss them was, he suspected, irrelevant. Working for New Camlough was not a typical gig in the filmmaking industry. He understood that now. They had all signed on to something bigger than themselves. They belonged to the production, even and especially in death.

During the ceremony, Alvira stood next to him as the corpses burned, set to the flame by Daniel's torch, their spirits cleansed and released through prayers spoken by Yvonne in a language neither of them recognized.

"Some pistol," Alvira said, holding Christopher's borrowed six-shooter. The runic carvings along the barrel and cylinder glowed purple in the light of the funeral pyre. "Really does a number on the undead."

"He said it belonged to a friend. We should try and return it."

"I remember him saying something about a lawman in the Southern Tier," Alvira said. "Said he had his own public-access TV show about all this spooky-ass shit. Can you imagine that?"

Kneale shook his head. "We've encountered weirder things."

"Do you think we should go back for Pore's remains? To burn or bury them?"

Kneale stared at the bodies overrun by flame, ceremonially wrapped in stark-white bandages turning to ash. That Renee filmed the proceedings should have been a sacrilege, but it felt natural and right, as if she was documenting something holy.

"He doesn't need it," Kneale said. "His spirit escaped the vampire. He won't turn. He's beyond that."

The bodies burned. The pistol shimmered, lightweight and cool in Alvira's hands.

Kneale emerged from his trailer well after nightfall the next day. The shower had failed to make him feel clean. Something in the water stuck to his skin like sediment. His muscles burned with fatigue and his back cried out for relief. Fresh clothes and a new pair of boots were poor defense against the cold of night.

He found Renee and Yvonne in the castle's dining room, production binders in hand, consulting with unit leaders and crew. Kathleen and her team had been busy pulling the surviving light rigs down from around the courtyard and getting them prepared for continuing production inside the castle. Daniel drifted through the halls, a phantom in full vampire attire and makeup. A fluttering of white dress and lilting laughter echoed across the old stones, chilling and familiar.

"Alvira's still crashed out," Renee said, scribbling notes in her binder. "She's asleep in one of the bedrooms on the floors above, if you need her."

"No, she can rest. I'm surprised to see everyone back to work. How are you filming without a director?"

"The crew are resilient," Renee said. "New Camlough doesn't just hire anyone. There has to be an underlying passion for the work. There's always an understudy, someone who can step into the role ahead of them. That's how it is in the military, isn't it?"

Yvonne stood up straight. She wore conservative hiking clothes in stark contrast to her usual elegant and revealing costumes designed for maximum on-screen impact.

"I shadowed Terence when I could," Yvonne said. "I know how to deal with actors. A woman's career as an actress is only so long, before the roles dry up and your agent stops calling. I intend to be a part of this game for as long as I can, in front of the camera or otherwise."

"Smart," Kneale said. "How's our other female lead?"

"She's taking to the change well," Renee said. "She'll be in one of tonight's scenes, actually. We're filming out at the dolmen, if you'd like to see her."

Kneale's eyes went wide.

"The change."

"Yes."

"We just killed several vampires, and now you want Andrea to become one? I thought the whole point of killing the master was to save her from the infection."

Renee stood up straight, turning her full attention from her notes to Kneale.

"Andrea is our friend and colleague," she said, choosing her words carefully. "We will support her during this time of great personal change and growth. Her turning will suit the production and the company."

"Haven't you ever had anything bad happen to you that made

you tougher, that set you up for something better?" Yvonne asked. "I'd think the experiences you had as a soldier tempered you."

"Or, perhaps, your experiences at the haunted ranch in Colorado," Renee said. "Surely you see now that your time there prepared you for what you've faced here. What you've achieved."

"She's going to become a monster," Kneale said, his core going ice cold. "Like the ones we destroyed. She's a threat."

"Not if we take the right precautions," Renee said, her voice going low, as if she were concerned that others might hear. "She need not go feral."

"But the master is dead. I thought that would solve things."

"Maybe the infection has proceeded beyond that stage, or there's been a mutation."

"What does that mean?"

"It means she's becoming something new. Just as you have." She glanced at her watch. "If you'd like to see her, be at the rocks at midnight. We have something special planned. Something not in the script."

"I'm tired, Renee. I don't know if I want to see anything special ever again."

Renee and Yvonne both gave him predatory smiles—wolves who, in some twisted fairy tale, knew their trick had worked. The bait was taken.

"You know that's not true, not anymore," Renee said. She leaned in close and spoke in a hushed voice. "You're starting to *like* all this spooky-ass shit, aren't you?"

39

In the expert hands of Kathleen and her lighting team, the dolmen became a shrine of religious ecstasy. Soft white light cascaded down from above, while purple- and green-tinged illumination colored the fog rolling beneath the stone cap. The whir of the industrial-strength fog machines and the generators that powered the setup was a comforting, synthetic hum in the dark and menacing wood.

Around the pillars of rock stood actors in occult robes of makeshift finery, assembled in haste by Nike. They stood in a loose circle around the illuminated dolmen, holding long candles lit with flames that grasped for the night sky. Atop the stone cap was the center of their attention and the focus of their prayers: Andrea, dressed in purest virginal white, as if adorned for her wedding. Her skin, normally light, was almost totally devoid of color due to both the work of the cinematographer's lights and her advanced condition. Such ethereal beauty was only heightened by the contradiction in color that were her eyes and lips: both had adopted the countenance of purest, bloodiest red, in a shade well-suited to pop on camera, digital or otherwise.

Those eyes swept the scene before her, observing the extras arrayed in worship and the crew behind them set to capture the scene. Then she looked into the woods beyond, to the castle, to the endless sky swirling with stars above, alighted in configurations and brightness previously unknown to her. The forest and sky spoke to her in a thousand-thousand competing markers of signal, her renewed mind quickly adapting to reorganize and recognize it all. The numbing rush became a comforting rhythm, and then actionable information of various import. She grew aware of the advanced age of the remaining leaves on the trees, and could calculate, with a degree of effortless certainty, the precise number of hours left before they would break free from their branches to take temporary flight. She knew the number and relative health of the coyote pack that circled the castle and dolmen, and knew how long ago they had last fed on live prey. She tasted the carrion breath of the turkey vultures perched on low-hanging branches nearby, counting down the days before they migrated in advance of the coming winter. She felt the writhing of earthworms and many-legged things in the soil beneath the sacred stone and rocks upon which she stood, their dumb but purposeful gyrations attuned to the pumping of her own black heart. She saw her fellow cast and crew as nervous systems alight with flickering illumination, for which she felt the first pangs of ravenous hunger, and she knew that light for what it really was.

She understood, with a stark degree of clarity, the true source of her vampiric desire. The light of consciousness, of life, of interconnected systems of mind and body, was cultivated from the interior divine spark of God, the *Imago Dei* itself, that which sets the animal human apart from its brethren. Upon reaching this understanding, her heart was filled with a potent mixture of longing and self-hate, which her vampiric nature synthesized into anger, into rage, into want. She had been turned into something that could never truly know reunion with its creator, and thus was doomed to lust after and imbibe the most base and mean symbol of salvation: blood. It was blood she would feed upon, yes, but it was what the blood represented that drove her to hunger and, in the dim and distant future, inevitable madness.

As her friend—did that word still hold meaning for her?—

called out *action* and the camera operators approached the tableau, she toyed with the idea of ignoring the role they had asked her to play and instead turn her energies to killing everyone here.

Andrea decided instead to placate those who claimed to know and love her, riding the rising wave of crackling energy that gathered within the tattered remains of her inmost spirit. She sculpted that energy into stones, and from those stones built columns and an archway—a gate—and raised that gate over cursed and haunted soil.

The worms and many-legged things played their roles as well, hitting their marks with feverish burrowing. The bones were easy to find. They did not resist the gentle encouragement to rise, to move through the churning layers of earth. They found one another near the surface, coming together with the force of magnetized materials, one, two, three at a time, until they were the frames of bodies again.

The remains of jaws opened in declarations of joy and fealty to their new queen, their arms held aloft in supplication and worship. Andrea accepted their tribute, going so far as to favor them with a flash of fang. The cast, to its credit, held their positions among the rising dead for as long as humanly tolerable, backing away slowly only when they recognized the *specialness* of the special effect, and upon seeing the great skull and blood-red eyes of the dead lodestar appear in the heavens. The great vision of her own skull, duplicated above but shorn of flesh, revealing razor-sharp vampire's teeth, eyes looking down upon them, seeing, seeing *more*, through them, into them, beyond them, floated in semi-transparent splendor. Skeletal hands likewise appeared beneath it, mirroring Andrea's own movements, fingers interwoven at the tips to form the steeple of an unholy church.

The coyote pack howled. The carrion birds screamed their insane songs. Small, inhuman creatures danced their goblin dance just beyond the limits of the movie set's lights.

The crew rolled the cameras for as long as they could tolerate the anti-miracle. They wept openly, terrified but transfixed, as Andrea rose into the air and the dolmen itself shuddered and vibrated with a searing beam of light. Great, black bat's wings tore through the back of her dress, sending out a shower of dark blood. They spread wide and loomed large like the hands of the devil herself, and pumped slow and heavy, keeping her aloft.

Kneale and Renee fell to their knees, as did the others, to weep tears of blood and terror.

POST-PRODUCTION

40

The darkness drew him deeper into its folds. Kneale slept in blissful, unfeeling darkness. The world was shadow and endless, but also coming to an end, and in that end was peace. If an afterlife was closed to him, Kneale hoped this was what death was like.

But he was not dead. Not yet. The monsters could still find him, even if he could not find himself.

Hello, Alan.

The voice was soft lace and warm, smooth candle wax, dribbling over him. It drew him out of that pleasant null and back to the world of the conscious and all of its attendant terrors.

You saved me. You saved me from becoming a slave to that creature. The voice again, like pure sex, now. His heart pumped blood in a fast and deliberate rhythm. His hands opened and shut, grasping for soft flesh.

I am changed now. You were too late for that, but I forgive you. I forgive you because what I have become is greater than what I was, but I am free of that vile creature's influence. For that, I have you to thank.

Kneale opened his eyes. The darkness of the trailer was a living shroud, making the space darker than it should have been in the fleeting hour before sunrise. A part of him still craved the embrace of oblivion, but another, hotter part of him burned for her.

You deserve a reward. A token of my appreciation.

He sat upright, the tangled blankets falling to the floor. His bare chest accepted the kiss of the cold air, made colder in the presence of the specter lingering at the edge of the bed: Andrea, the majority of her white gown purposefully torn away for him to see. She ran her delicate hands over her legs, her arms, her chest. But it was her eyes that held him. Eyes, bloodiest red, burning into his own, into his brain, embedding themselves as permanent memory, as the very definition of beauty, of compulsion. Under the full weight of her psychic and physical presence, Kneale was drawn to the revenant before him as a leaf is drawn into the air by a late October wind.

You deserve my kiss, Andrea said, or thought, and Kneale thought it, too.

I deserve your kiss.

You want my kiss.

Yes, I want your kiss.

You want to be like me. To sing the secret song of the night. To be a soldier once more. My soldier.

Yes.

Then come to me, my love. You have always had eyes for me. Now, let me give you new eyes. To see in the dark, and all the endless nights ahead.

Kneale shifted up to his knees and moved toward her. He wanted nothing more than to meet this vision of terror and beauty in the air, to be entwined in her arms, to smell her smell, to kiss her, and to have her kiss his neck, and drive her teeth deep into his flesh.

Andrea held out her arms, her hair flowing in whispering strands of ethereal beauty, her eyes and lips coaxing him forward, her vampire's teeth emerging in response to his arousal.

"That's enough, Andrea," a voice said.

An interloper, Andrea said-thought. *She is jealous. She would place herself between us.*

The smell of sex and sweat on the air was joined by gun oil. A shotgun racked, metal-on-metal, a slug fed into a chamber. Light glimmered off a silver crucifix at the end of a rosary, held out from the darkness.

She cannot give you what I can give you, Alan. No woman can. You will spend the rest of your days pining for the pleasures I offer, and will never find them. Not without me.

Something landed on the bed before Kneale. Twin bulbs of garlic, their cloves opened by a pocketknife to release their scent. Overpowering the animal-lust within him. A slap in the face.

Andrea hissed and withdrew. Kneale's stomach dropped in disappointment. It was a feeling of immense loss, of disappointment without measure, of erotic promises unfulfilled. When Andrea spoke again, she used her voice and spoke from just down the hall.

"I was just having a bit of fun with him," she said. "He was enjoying himself. Weren't you, Alan?"

His throat was too dry to speak. Part of him—the disciplined part, the one concerned with self-preservation over petty lusts—reached for the garlic bulbs, holding them up to his face. Instinct curled his hands around them, holding on to those pungent totems of life.

"If you are jealous, perhaps you would like to join us?" The heat of Andrea's mind shifted away from Kneale, focusing on Alvira like the intense beam of a searchlight.

When Alvira spoke, her voice quivered, but she held her calm.

"Ah, no. Kneale ordered me to keep watch. Figured it would be a good idea."

"I have a few good ideas of my own," Andrea purred.

"Andrea," Kneale managed, his throat and tongue finally taking orders from him again. "Please. Leave us. This isn't what I want."

"You could have fooled me," she teased.

"Go. Go, now."

"As you wish."

Andrea floated out of the room, her regress a whisper in the night. Shadows withdrew with her. The erotic press of darkness and humidity relented, signaling her departure. When she was gone, Alvira secured the trailer door's lock. Kneale fell back onto his bed, breathing heavily.

"You okay, Six?"

"Just throw a bucket of cold water over me."

"I might need some of that myself," Alvira said. "I wasn't expecting her to…have that effect on me. The other one—the master—wasn't like that."

"No," Kneale admitted. "No, she's different. More dangerous."

"Should we do something about it?"

Kneale thought about that question for a moment.

"No, Renee wants her alive."

"*Undead*, you mean. We're still following orders, then?"

"That's what we do," Kneale said.

"Yeah. I suppose so." She made to leave.

"Hey. Thanks."

She shrugged in the dark.

"You'd do the same for me. You might have to."

"Yeah."

"This is what you wanted. Right?"

"I'm not sure," Kneale said.

"Yeah," Alvira said, opening the door. "Me neither."

After she left, the door swung closed behind her. Kneale knew he should probably lock it again, but he stayed in bed. His mind swam with possibilities, with ways that night's events could have gone differently, or might still. He drifted off to sleep, Andrea's smiling, wicked face appearing behind his eyelids, the curves of her body, the smell of her hair, the silky touch of her voice lapping at his will.

Whenever you want me…

…you can be mine.

41

Daniel handed him the skull, pure white, shorn of all flesh. The surface was cool to the touch, and parts of it were surprisingly springy and soft. Kneale turned it over in his hands, bringing it face to face with himself. The eye sockets were narrower than he expected and the frontispiece was sleek like a predator's skull. Its twin pair of vampire's teeth remained sharp and pure.

"A well-deserved trophy for our head vampire killer," Daniel said. "That one is the master. I gifted one to Alvira and kept one for myself, and presented two to Kathleen and Nike for their support in the final battle. It's remarkable we suffered so few casualties. A testament to your leadership."

Kneale said nothing, preferring instead to focus on the skull. He was not good with praise. He preferred new tasks, new objectives. Keep his mind working, keep his hands busy. Keep his mind from reflecting on what he had done. Daniel frowned, expecting, perhaps, at least a *thank you* for boiling and cleaning the skull.

"They'll be starting the film soon." He headed into the keep through the great front door, opening the portal to a world of warmth and candlelight in contrast to the icy late-October night air.

"I'm not in the mood for a horror movie," Kneale said.

"Renee promised us something special tonight. A celebration of our victory, and for completing production. Besides, it's Halloween, a night best spent in good company in the warm, soft light of the screen."

Kneale made to sit in the back of the dungeon-theater, but Renee caught him with a look and gestured for him to join her near the front. Kneale's head swam with visions of Andrea's ghostly beauty, with thoughts of terrible violence, with the oppressive darkness of the forest, with the glow of the dolmen.

Renee patted the seat next to her.

"Should you check your bank account, you'll find a nice little bonus as a thank-you for helping us reach the end of production," she said. "The hard part is over. Now we just need you on-site as we finish editing and post-production processing. We'll be out of here by early December, maybe before the first heavy snowfall."

"Good," Kneale said. "I'm ready to get back to civilization."

"I thought soldiers never tired of the field," she said.

"On the contrary," Kneale said, "I hate the woods."

Renee laughed. "I can't blame you."

"She came for me last night."

"Who?"

"She tried to turn me."

"If that were true, you'd be one of the living dead," Renee said. "She was toying with you."

"I didn't appreciate it."

"Are you sure? She was a beautiful woman before she turned. Now, she's practically a goddess."

"You know what I mean."

"But she offered herself to you? Her kiss. Her gift. And you declined?"

"Sort of, yeah."

"Not many are given such an offer. Fewer still refuse it."

"You hired me to kill those things," Kneale said. "And now you're surprised I didn't become one?"

"When we hired you, I was sure you'd be like all the others: inflexible, overconfident, not open to new experiences. But you've proven yourself more than a good soldier. You're someone I can count on, and someone who understands the scope of our work. Someone adaptable."

"You once said that this film is a weapon," Kneale said. "What did you mean by that?"

Renee crossed her arms, letting the hum of the cast and crew filing into the dungeon wash over them.

"What do you know about psychological warfare? About intelligence service operations in Europe, the UK, even in the good ol' USA? Some of what they did in the twentieth century went public, but the horrors of our own time remained classified. Nine-Eleven changed everything, as you know firsthand."

"I was just a trigger puller. Still am."

"Of course, but you asked, and some awareness of who you work for and what you're doing is necessary going forward. Playing the polite-but-ignorant grunt doesn't suit our relationship any more, and won't serve our ends. Should you go looking, you may discover that there's a disproportionate number of occultists involved in intelligence, media, and national policy work. All swearing secret oaths, attending strange religious rituals in the woods of northern California, having sex parties on remote islands and at sites of sacred power, obsessed with strange lights in the sky, eugenics, and the occult. Obsessed with the phenomena occurring at a certain haunted ranch in northern Colorado, for example."

Renee pressed a finger to his forehead.

"Would-be apostles of the dark, all of them. They make a big show of the national elections. The corporate media convinces us that there are stakes for the common person, but there aren't. Things always get worse. It's all austerity for us, bailouts for the wealthy, and war on our streets and abroad. It's a big club, Kneale, and we ain't in it."

"You're a conspiracy theorist."

"A nice bit of wordplay out of Langley, meant to lump thinking people in with the fringe lunatics espousing the terrors of the lizard people, or the imminent assumption of a resurrected JFK Jr. to the throne. No, I'm a political *pragmatist,* because I understand who it is I work for, and what power really is. Who wields it, and why."

"What does all this have to do with our movie?"

"You may begin to recognize the systems of control at work in national media discourse, in pop culture, in our increasingly calcified economic structures," Renee said. "Our film is simply one tool among many in a grand tapestry that our betters have woven, sometimes in concert, often at odds. Ah, there she is."

Renee nodded to Yvonne, who stood now at the front of the crowd, illuminating her face from below with her cell phone flashlight. The actress-turned-director smiled, then clapped her hands together.

"Good evening, cast and crew of *Hierarchies of Blood,*" she said, projecting her voice with the volume and force of an experienced stage actress. "I would like to be the first to congratulate you on officially wrapping production."

Scattered applause became a resonant flood, all cheers and shouted celebrations, echoing back in on themselves in the stone sub-level. Yvonne held up her hands to quiet the crowd.

"We mourn those we have lost on this production. But we acknowledge their sacrifice on our behalf, in pursuit of an art that can—and will—change the world. *Cinéma goblin* is not just an idea. It is the next evolution in filmmaking, in art itself. We are—

among visionaries like Monty Blackwood and the artists behind *The Secret Goatman Spookshow*—its pioneering practitioners."

There was that phrase again. *Cinéma goblin.* Kneale still did not fully grasp it, not really, but he now understood what it was to incorporate the real with the unreal, the true horror with the horror fiction.

"I'm not the director Terence was, not yet, but I appreciate the cast and crew coming together under incredible circumstances to help me—us—complete this film," Yvonne said. "For the projects to come, let us grow together. Let us sharpen our skills. Let us honor the spirits of the lost." She smiled and clasped her hands together, her actress's timing impeccable. She had the makings of a leader. "Tonight's feature is one of Terence's favorite movies. In honor of his legacy, of which we are all a part, I present to you *Behold the Undead of Dracula.*"

More applause. Yvonne bowed and stepped away from the wall. The projector—an authentic, ancient machine—turned its reels. The sound system crackled to life.

42

BEHOLD THE UNDEAD OF DRACULA
*COPYRIGHT MCMLXXIV
BY CAMLOUGH STUDIOS, INC.*

The audience in the dungeon experiences *Behold the Undead of Dracula* as a psychedelic thrum whose artistry and efficacy are augmented by the intoxicating cannabis smoke-filled air, by their exhaustion, by their grief. They see the film as it was always meant to be seen: not as a standard Eurotrash shocker, but as a parade of Gothic horrors that points to the dark truths of the contemporary world.

A sorceress, dressed in stately robes and adorned with golden jewelry marking her as a woman of power and importance, drains a bejeweled chalice of blood into a patch of dirt at the center of a stone chamber. Pillars of mortared stone support crumbling walls and a domed ceiling, at the top of which a stained glass window depicts a battle between a great, bat-like devil creature and his armored paladin foes.

She lifts the chalice high, then sticks her tattooed fingers into the bowl, collecting scattered remnants of blood that she flicks around the sunken level of dirt. What blood remains she drinks, letting the ichor flow down her lily-white face and stain her lips, chin, and bare neck. She tosses the empty cup aside.

"I call upon thee now, oh King of the Night! I summon thee back from Death, who cannot hold you, but is your servant! I rend open the gates of the underworld for liberation! I entreat Hell itself to vomit up its great prince, you, o adversary of adversaries! Return to us, to me, upon this mortal plane, oh great lord! Arise, Demon Lord Dracula!"

The soundtrack's horns and synthesizer strike harsh notes of triumph. The fanfare precedes the rumbling of earth and the displacement of soil before the woman's feet. Pressure builds beneath the surface of the pit upon which she stands, and soon the rotted remnants of an ancient coffin surface from the black dirt, the muck and dark soil rolling off of it in waves. The sorceress's eyes go wide with lustful rapture, and she slowly backs out of the dirt pit, climbing back up to a circular stone platform. The coffin is followed by four more that emerge from the ring of dread earth.

The voice that speaks from within projects its voice without, words echoing across the chamber, throughout the ruined castle, among the trees of the haunted forest beyond, and in the minds of the audience that watches in rapture within their own castle in another land, in another time.

Who would summon Vlad Dracul, Lord of the Night and Master of Death?

The woman, entranced by the results of her blood magic, pushes awe aside to kneel on the stone floor, her face pressed down between her hands.

"I do, on behalf of your enemy, humanity, who stands upon the brink of destruction." The response is slow in coming, but when the voice speaks again, it is softened by interest.

Explain yourself, child.

"We approach a period of social and technological apocalypse," she says. "We seek to destroy ourselves, utterly and fully. Or, rather, those that rule us do."

What concern is that of mine?

"A concern of glory, my lord," she says, risking a glance upwards. The other coffins—all four of them—likewise stand upright, floating in the air with the master's casket. Fingernails scratch against the rotted wood. Women moan and writhe within. "This world stands on the brink of destruction, on a series of brinks, stretching far into the future. Only one so wise and powerful as yourself might save it from tipping over. Only the great Dracula can save humanity from the artificial cataclysms it has built for itself. Can you imagine a greater irony, that one such as you, conquering and uniting humanity under a campaign of true terror, might bring about the peace that his enemy has long promised but never delivered? Can you imagine a greater insult to God himself than to achieve what he refuses to do?"

Thunder crashes; clouds obscure the full moon. Such blasphemous conspiracies are too much for even the moon to bear witness.

"I would need an army."

The voice of the dread dark lord comes from desiccated lips now, speaking from within his grand coffin of rot. "I will need men. And blood enough to feed my cadre of generals."

The other coffins quiver with the outward pushing of limbs and the ecstatic moaning of women.

"Yes, blood!" they cry. "Blood, for us!"

The sorceress risks speaking once more.

"There is one who can build you this army," she says, not taking her eyes from the bulging, brittle planks of wood. "A descendant of the greatest natural philosopher of his time, a man with the blood and brilliance of Frankenstein. He needs only the resources and direction of a noble patron." She stands up now, knowing that she has the dark lord's interest, knowing also that if she fails to convince him, it will be her death—and, perhaps, the death of all mankind.

"He will build for you an army of the dead, nigh invincible to the terrible weapons of mankind, needing not food nor water nor rest, but only the direction of your generals. Your army will spread across Europe, and from there also into Asia, and Africa, and beyond. A world war fought by corpse-soldiers, perfectly loyal, against the diseased and ill-kept militaries of a fractured world. Let me be your servant, Lord Dracula, and you shall have the peace and prosperity of an endless, earthly kingdom that Christ himself refused, thus condemning his children to millennia of death and suffering."

The great coffin explodes, wood flying like shrapnel. The others follow suit, revealing their occupants. Dracula, resplendent in a black and crimson double-breasted suit with signature wide collar and great, silken black cape; and his brides who are to be his generals, in stark-white dresses stained with blood, their varying skin tones overlain with a pallor that only serves to emphasize their terrible beauty.

The camera moves in on a track, tilting upward, Lord Dracula's handsome features cast in light from below and shadow from above, a sculpted and great eyebrow raised in interest.

"Tell me about this...*Frankenstein*," he says, running his tongue along his bottom lip, revealing his great fangs.

And so the film's plot is established, and the reasoning for the half-dozen or so supernatural setpieces that follow are justified. Werewolves traipse through London, slaughtering workers at a munitions factory; Hamburg is beset by winged devils who set flame to government buildings; malignant ghosts harry a market in Paris, disrupting agricultural trade; Rome's streets are flooded with the living dead in a mockery of Resurrection Day to demoralize the Church. Ominous signs and portents gather in the heavens; whole graveyards suffer disinterment in the countryside outside of Darmstadt, and within the ruined Castle Frankenstein itself, a young descendant of the mad doctor rekindles a forbidden fork of philosophical research. His youthful hands are guided to his work by his lover, a woman of pale but familiar countenance, odd appetites, and generous sexual proclivities—all in service to the true Master, whom Frankenstein knows only as the Patron.

But while Europe's incest-ridden royalty and ruling classes offer their people nothing as the wave of evil rises, individual heroes emerge in each country, guided by their knowledge of the occult to resist the tide of darkness. Recruited by famed but discredited occult scholar Professor Marshal Phillips, they join together in a mad odyssey across the continent to collect its few remaining artifacts of supernatural power.

The diverse and charming cast of Irish theater character actors and Camlough Studios mainstays—including familiar faces from both *Witch Hell* and *Dr. Orlock's Castle of Terror*—battle rubber-monster terrors and sneak their way through Gothic set piece locations as Dracula's army assails the continent.

At New Forest, the heroes barely survive a psychedelia-infused encounter with the resident Witch-Cult, eking out their victory on the astral plane and stealing away with the coven's Grimoire.

They lose a member of their party in the Museum of Celtic History, as their Prussian-born thief, Gunther, seizes the Staff of Moloch and entreats the dark gods to zap him off of the material plane.

"I will see the terrible face of the gods, the only gods that entreat with humankind!" he intones in the moments before his body is disintegrated by lightning crashing through the stained glass ceiling window above. This is one of the film's more grotesque special effects, as a dummy stand-in covered in putty is melted by a controlled electrical fire.

Professor Phillips's solemn intonation that "To oppose evil is to live" is small comfort in the presence of Gunther's still-smoking remains, his eyeballs liquefied, his skin melted into a crispy puddle on the museum floor. The party's prize is the Chalice of St. Patrick, a humble cup of immense holy power.

Mid-film, the party journeys by rail into haunted Hungary, communicated via map and animated route lines overlain with historical stock footage of Eastern European train stations flooded with refugees. The female lead, played by Mara Pengrave—another victim of a real-life tragedy to come—wields a torch as she descends into a local catacomb, followed closely by the others. In the depths they encounter Roman legionnaires cursed to living death, for they carry the Lance of Longinus, that dread weapon that pierced the side of Christ. The walking, armored corpses menace the explorers, but Pengrave's training as a stage sword fighter is put to good use here, and her character dispatches several of the undead with a shining, silver sword of an ancient paladin. She cuts the Spear of Destiny from the hands of a dust-ridden warrior, and the party flees the catacombs with their prize.

The face of a devil on a skeleton key, pressed into a lock embedded in a wine cellar door, permits entrance into the labyrinthine catacombs beneath the derelict Shelley Estate. Darkness lies within, as do the glowing red eyes and flashing claws of wolf-men in tattered Austrian Commando uniforms. They stalk the dark corridors, revealed in flashes of torchlight carried by the party's doomed hirelings—whose bodies collapse in a slurry of liquid gore as the werewolves attack. But swords and bullets plated with silver are sterner stuff, and after the chaotic melees of the delve into the endless cellar, the Shield of King Arthur is theirs.

Villages burn and castles are razed. Armies of the living dead cobbled together by young Doctor Frankenstein and led by Dracula's generals spread terror across Europe.

With time working against them, Professor Phillips leads the ragtag band of four warriors—each character written in broad strokes to express the national character of their homes in Ireland, France, Italy, and Canada—into deepest Darmstadt, where Castle Frankenstein and the occult war engine of Dracula's ever-growing army of the undead awaits.

With the zombified soldiers of young Frankenstein patrolling the grounds and manning the gates, a direct assault is impossible. What the party lacks in numbers it makes up for in guile. They

PROJECT VAMPIRE KILLER

commandeer a pair of wagons laden with fresh bodies bound for the resurrection lab. Two disguise themselves as lowly farmers, their faces covered in black mud and wrapped in tattered rags. The others hide among the rotting corpses of the shipment, covering themselves with death. Malnourished horses draw them up the great hill upon which the castle looms, where dark stones and towers are set against a purple-red sky.

Decomposing revenants wielding rust-covered swords and wearing the armor of armies long since disbanded stare dumbly into the sky as the wagon passes through their checkpoint. Now that they are beyond the walls and within the castle grounds, the subterfuge's greatest test awaits. Dreadful figures with burning red eyes and clad in black robes—demonic agents of Dracula himself—inspect the cargo as it rolls in. These vile creatures of living darkness ignore the wagon drivers entirely, preferring instead to evaluate the quality and quantity of the raw material bound for the mad doctor's processing station. They press pitchforks into the corpse-piles and wave burning torches over the bodies. Flames and bloody tongs press dangerously close to the faces of our hiding heroes, conveniently lit and shown in close-up within the corpse pile to emphasize the drama. Professor Phillips, covered by bodies mutilated and dismembered by some unspeakable violence, is pierced by one such probe. He bites down on his bandage-wrapped hand, stifling the scream he so desperately wants to release. It is an act of tremendous willpower, emphasized by the close-up of his wounds oozing out rivers of fresh blood.

But the test is passed and the inspectors are satisfied. They wave clawed hands at the drivers, who guide their cargo through another gate into a smaller, more secluded courtyard. It is here that the heroes emerge from beneath the camouflage of death and rot, springing to life with swords raised and pistols bared. The inhuman servants of the castle prove little challenge to the invaders, and their heads and limbs are soon severed in geysers of jet-black blood.

With the film's runtime winding down and the production's budget long ago evaporated in a haze of practical makeup effects, monster costumes, and elaborate composite painting shots, a jarring cut reveals the heroes in the depths of the Frankenstein resurrection lab, where the young descendant of the original mad doctor finds the interlopers unwelcome company. Extras, crew members, and dummies alike are piled atop the tables borrowed from previous sets, productions, and craft services, all splattered with what remains of the production's fake blood stocks and caked in grey powder for passing effect. Careful inspection reveals a number of these props as on loan from the *Witch Hell* and *Dr. Orlock's Castle of Terror* collections.

The confrontation is obviated by stilted, confusing cuts due to missing or degraded footage, as well as the unfortunate lack of multiple takes and appropriate scene coverage. The grand reveal of Frankenstein's ultimate creation, Uber-Stein, is an abortive, brief series of shots of a giant golem's head obscured by a curtain but backlit in profile, soon consumed by a fire set by a torch-wielding hero. As for Frankenstein himself, his obsessive occult pursuits have left him physically weak and unable to overcome even the diminished prowess of the aged and wounded Professor Phillips. The two struggle within the lab, knocking over shelves of stage-glass beakers containing foaming and fogging chemicals. The combatants roll through a burner and their clothes alight with flame, then they tumble through a glass window conveniently posted at the far side of the lab. The portal is composited into the establishing-shot painting of the grand castle, which we return to just in time to see them plummet to the dark mountainside below.

Another awkward cut reveals the others fleeing from the fire in the laboratory and the cries of an immolated Uber-Stein. They ascend more rounded staircases in a series of reused shots from before, cleverly cut to exclude the now-deceased Professor Phillips.

PROJECT VAMPIRE KILLER

Finally they reach the forbidden tower where Dracula's coffin lies in repose. As a stock-footage sun sets and the countryside falls into (day-for-)night, the candelabras set around the coffin spring to unholy life, flame and sparks raising dreadful shadows. The moon rises, low and near enough to touch.

Something within the coffin stirs. Our heroes step back—swords, pistols, and torches raised—just before the lid explodes upwards with great force. A geyser of black smoke and fluttering bats shoots up to the ceiling of the stone chamber, snuffing out candles and torches alike.

When the smoke clears, the bats swarm back together above the coffin in a charming hand-animated special effect. They coalesce into the form of a tall and stately man. A final, terrible burst of purple energy splits the air, and Dracula stands before them. He is handsome and tall, his wide shoulders home to a cape of deepest black and regal purple fabric with blood-red trim and a wide, open flare of collar about his pale neck. A black coat hangs over a formal, willowy white shirt, which highlights a crimson medallion hanging from a gold chain upon his breast. It is not clear where the shadows end and his body begins.

The dark lord does not speak, preferring instead to hold each of the four interlopers with his dreadful gaze. They have the mental fortitude to resist his glare, and the good sense to produce the powerful artifacts that they have gathered at great cost to themselves: the Chalice of St. Patrick, which they quickly fill with holy water; the New Forest Grimoire, whose various spells may yet prove deadly to the Count; King Arthur's Shield, held aloft to reflect holy light upon the dread vampyr, and the Lance of Longinus, sent probing toward Dracula's side, whose powerful defensive swipes are turned back by the spear's tip, now searing hot.

Points of magic light and energy flow from the grimoire, peppering the ghastly lord with stings he cannot block. Holy water thrown from the chalice lands unerringly upon the count's face, sending his flesh sloughing off in putty-like strands. The shield becomes a ram, knocking him from his feet, sending him back down into his coffin. Our heroine wields the spear and it strikes true, piercing his side as it pierced the Lord's, releasing a torrent of blood and water from opened heart and split lung.

While this sequence is impressive in its rapid, kinetic action and editing, and the special effects, however brief, do not disappoint, the battle is somewhat anticlimactic, due in no small part to having been filmed by the handful of crew willing to work overtime to complete the film. The actor portraying Dracula pours his all into the close-ups, in which he delivers the vampire's final monologue.

"I meant to save you from yourselves," Dracula says, tears of blood streaming down his face. "A great war is coming, and then another, and another, until history itself is ground under the wheels of your bloodlust. Your hate for one another will destroy you. Your hate will destroy us all. I offered you escape from the torture rack of history. You have answered my offer of freedom with your own deaths. My expiration is the murder of your future."

The spear probes deeper. A wooden stake pierces his chest. A hammer nails it in place. Blood vomits up from Dracula's red lips, spattering across the ceiling and defying gravity to pool there.

This should be the part of the horror movie where the vampire is vanquished, when the sun rises, when the world is returned to light and the promise of life. But in *Behold the Undead of Dracula*, we get none of that. We have the death of a monster, yes. But in his death, in his failure to conquer Europe and unite it under a single banner, we have, instead, the promise of darkness. Of impending doom.

The bloody twentieth century lies ahead of our heroes. Beyond that, the twenty-first, full of its own cataclysmic horrors—some known to the audience, most yet to be revealed.

43

There were nights of brief snow that soon melted off, but no lasting accumulation. That suited Kneale fine. It afforded him more opportunities to hike deep into the woods to be alone, to listen to the wind moving through the trees, to see the animals and birds about their business, and to seek the spooklights that appeared with less and less frequency. November truly is the Gothic month, absent the garish Halloween colors of fall foliage. It was grey skies and bare branches, icy winds, and lonely stretches of forest. The castle was larger than ever, with new towers, wider walls, and curious rooms that emerged at strange junctions of hallway, unbidden and unremembered, yet covered in dust and the disuse of long marches of time.

The rush of constant activity of the film production had given way to a persistent, eerie silence both within the great castle and on its fallow grounds. The tents were long gone, with only a handful of vehicles, trailers, and the burned-out remains of the prop truck near the front gate. The vast majority of the cast and crew had departed shortly after production finished, with only Renee, Yvonne, Kathleen, Alvira, Kneale, and a small team of PAs still on-site. Renee and Yvonne spent their days and nights locked in the editing room deep within the castle, with Kathleen taking shifts to color-correct the footage as necessary. A musician arrived from Belfast for the soundtrack, bringing with him synthesizers, drum machines, and various electronic paraphernalia. His equipment produced haunting melodies and synthesizer harmonies, creating the electronic ghosts that would haunt *Hierarchies of Blood*. Kneale did not bother to wonder why the musician had to be in-person for his contribution. Of course he had to be here. Of course he had to walk the grounds, the halls of the castle, the trails of the wood. He had to touch the stones of the dolmen and lie atop the cap, and stare into the swirling night sky as his lungs filled with that special cannabis smoke.

Kneale became a ghost, lingering at the door to the editing room to watch the women work, walking through the woods with Alvira or by himself, or simply staring at the ceiling in his trailer for hours on end, failing to find sleep. They were paid well to do nothing, and therefore had nothing to complain about.

As for Andrea, she had taken to nights-long journeys away from the castle. Where she went and what she was up to was a mystery to Kneale—one he was determined not to solve.

The sky was black and the forest was cloaked in wavering shadow. Headlight beams were knives cutting through the murk. Kneale held up his hand in greeting and to defend his eyes from the light. After the limousines rolled past the wreckage of the prop truck, he and Alvira closed the repaired gate, securing it against the night. The vehicles cut straight across the courtyard at a deliberate pace, guided forward by Renee, who stood near the entrance to the castle and held a pair of red glow sticks as beacons in the dark.

When Kneale and Alvira caught up with the vehicles, the party emerged. Even in the dark, Kneale could tell they were older. A slight stoop to their bodies, slow movements, overwhelming clouds of perfume and cologne. Kneale had done a little VIP protection work in the past and knew what was expected of him: polite deference to everything they might say, an expectation that he was a go-fer as well as a trigger puller, and silence, above all. He repeated these rules to Alvira as they waited at the periphery for some signal or acknowledgment from Renee. That nod came and they approached—their dark fatigues and corded sweaters in stark contrast to the suits and dresses of the honored guests.

"Barbara Malgrave, this is our head of security, Alan Kneale, and his second, Carmen Alvira."

The shortest person among the crowd turned to greet him. Her eyes were large and the brightest brown, illuminated with a peculiar sheen. Her night-black hair was held up in a bun, not a strand out of place. Her cheekbones were high, her face symmetrical, her forehead wide. She was beautiful, and had been even more so in decades past, but the luster had merely shifted into a stateliness in her advanced age. She moved with the grace of someone used to being in charge of every situation in which she found herself. She extended a hand to Kneale and shook firmly and with confidence, even if her skin was thin as paper. As her eyes met his, Kneale had the sensation of fingers running over his prefrontal cortex. Then, satisfied or bored, the older woman offered her hand and winning smile to Alvira.

"Ms. Malgrave is one of the principal founders and head of the board of New Camlough Studios," Renee said. "She is serving as executive producer on *Hierarchies of Blood*."

"And many more to come, I should hope," she said, her voice velvet, tinged with the remnants of an almost-purged continental accent. "Mr. Kneale, Ms. Alvira, I have heard much about both of you and would like to offer my personal gratitude for your efforts to keep my production safe. I am told that without you—and the sacrifice of one of your compatriots, among others—we would have lost many more to that fiend that stalked these dire and haunted woods."

Kneale lowered his head.

"We are honored to serve, ma'am," he said. Usually the business types and senior officer shitheads loved that kind of sniveling reverie for what was, at the end of it, bloody work for people like him. For people like Pore.

Malgrave flared her eyes wide, then offered a smirk.

"Speak plainly with me, Mr. Kneale, always," she said.

"Of course, ma'am," he said, not sure what she meant, or if he had made a mistake.

She smiled wider. She liked using her authority to put people off-balance, then.

"You will both join me, I think, for the screening. Is it ready?"

"It is, ma'am," Renee said. "The projector and sound system are undergoing final preparations. We can head below at your convenience."

Malgrave clapped her hands.

"Wonderful. Join us for the preview of *Hierarchies of Blood*. I trust you are both in the mood for a good horror film. Let us see if my money—and my faith in Renee—has conjured one."

44

Short, failing candles burned low on bronze sconces, lighting the path through the halls to the door that guarded the castle's sublevel, down the winding stone stair, and into the gloom of the dungeon itself. The VIPs and their escorts found their seats in silence as shadows crawled through the dark places of the great house, always seeking, always restless. Orange and black lights splashed illumination against the far-right corner of the wide room, where the composer and a woman Kneale hadn't seen before were clad in purple robes with black hoods drawn. They tinkered with electronica and handled wires, their half-hidden faces aglow in the soft light of their equipment's many illuminated buttons and displays. Black speakers stood as totems on either side of their synthesizer keyboard stands, open laptops, and drum machines.

Malgrave took her seat several rows back, near the middle, just beyond the twin support columns of mortar and stone that framed the white fabric screen hung on the wall ahead. The others spread out among the disparate rows. Malgrave insisted that Alvira sit to her left and that Kneale sit at her right hand. The security contractors waited in awkward silence, declining to make small talk unless spoken to themselves. Renee directed a handful of production assistants—all dressed in uniform black—to finalize preparations for the projector, assist the musicians, and work the nearby popcorn machine that snapped and sizzled with the first fruits of movie manna. Two of the assistants moved through the rows, offering their esteemed audience tall, stemmed glasses of dark liquors. Malgrave accepted hers with a subtle nod of acknowledgment, but her eyes remained fixed on the white rectangle that would soon show the results of her investment. Alvira and Kneale were not offered drinks.

"You have questions for me," Malgrave said, her face angled a degree toward Kneale. He hesitated, not wanting to interrupt her.

"Asking questions isn't part of my job, ma'am."

"No, it is not. But your job is to do what I tell you, and I am granting you this indulgence, because it pleases me to do so. You have earned some insight into our project. As the master vampire slayer, you are first among a small group of very rare, very special individuals. I reward faithful service. Has your service been faithful?"

"Yes, ma'am."

Malgrave remained silent for a moment. She was not one to repeat herself. But the offer felt temporary, like an idle distraction for a woman whose attention would soon be wholly focused on the film. He would cut right to it, then.

"I don't really keep up with movies, but I know that this kind of thing went out of fashion decades ago," Kneale said. "Spooky castles and vampires were quaint when I was a kid. Why make this movie? No offense if this is what you like, ma'am. You can do with your money as you please. But as a mainstream movie? It doesn't add up."

Malgrave smiled.

"Do you believe in sin, Mr. Kneale?"

Ah, so that was her angle. A religious nut. Not uncommon among the upper echelons of defense industry moneyed types, he had discovered. He must have missed the *go forth and sell weapons to thy neighbor* bit in Sunday school.

"That question is above my pay grade," he said. She made a noise that might have been a laugh.

"I speak of the mass distribution of trauma and of hatred—the all-encompassing, all-infecting influence of *sin*, sin on a societal scale. The mass occult rituals of genocide, of war, of exploitation, of pollution, of human trafficking, of storing up riches for yourself while people suffer and die in the streets at home and in the killing fields abroad. I am talking about the influence that satanic miasma has on people up and down the societal strata. Human minds can be primed to respond to select Jungian archetypal representations as conveyed through precise patterns of light and sound. Imagine grand resonance fields generated by factors of ritual, of hidden energies harnessed to occult ends, embedded within these images and sounds, within these films. These *horror movies*. Imagine the workings of strange men and women, cloaked in shadow, discovering the processes behind the veneer of normative reality, and turning them to their own ends through the magic of cinema."

Kneale frowned. That was a lot to take in.

"Politics aren't really my thing, ma'am," Kneale said. "Never seemed relevant."

"Indeed. You are a good soldier precisely because you have not reflected much on the consequences of and the forces behind your chosen trade. You strike me as a man who simply *does*, and does what is necessary, for his own ends and for those whom he serves. Introspection does not serve a butcher." She paused to take a long sip from her tall drink. "What you might think of as *good*, pleasurable, or even tolerable in life is far outweighed by suffering and humanity's endless, harrowing evil," she said. "To say nothing of disease, of natural disasters, of hunger. One can only conclude that God is mad, or psychotic, or wholly absent. One might also conclude, perhaps, that God *hates* us, and, even if he offers us a limited window of salvation, he is responsible for the annihilation or eternal suffering of the vast majority of humanity throughout all time. Can you imagine being condemned to eternity in some burning prison because you didn't pick the precise faith tradition, or for other choices wholly beyond your control, including but not limited to Calvinist pre-election of the saints? What crime justifies endless torment or annihilation? Is this logical? Is this justice?

"We are left with alternative explanations, of course. Perhaps we are pieces of God, split into a billion-billion pieces, subjecting ourselves to endless suffering down a haunted river of time, just as a madman bangs his own head against the wall of his asylum cell until he falls unconscious, only to rise again and recommit to his project of self-harm. Perhaps, as the anti-theists and materialists hold, our suffering has no meaning at all, and that we clamber about and howl in the face of an indifferent void. Can you imagine? How dreadful. How boring."

The candles went out around the dungeon one by one, casting the chamber into further darkness.

"There is another explanation, one that I cannot prove but that I hold as likely true as any other. We might consider the harrowing state of existence for most living, self-aware creatures as a sort of morality play, a grand drama of history. *The* drama. The only show in town. Perhaps, then, it is our lot in life to think, do, and suffer under evil, under sin, as characters set on their courses by a writer-director who is hidden from us. If we are players on a stage, or actors in front of an invisible camera, that camera being the eye of God, are we to be held liable for the lines he has written for us, the blocking he has established, of the personal preferences and perversions of a production aesthetic tailored to deliver a lurid commercial product to a discreet market? Perhaps, Mr. Kneale, we are merely actors in the *Grand Guignol* cosmic."

Her words were tinged with sulfur. There was something deeply unsettling about what she was saying, even if they had an aura of truth about them. But there were counterarguments to be made—examples of love, of forgiveness, of charity. Of mercy. Hope. *Or were there?*

"Tell me," Malgrave said, running her finger along the rim of her glass. "How much *hope* and *love* have you found in your own life? What you have, you earned by force of will and strength. What slim comforts you maintain were born of service to cruelty and violence, at great cost to yourself and others. Where is the *hope* in that?"

    Had she anticipated his counterarguments?

Did she read my thoughts?

    "Consider what I said about us being actors—all of us, bound to fate, bound to the meandering plot and contrivances of some hack horror writer. We act then, blindly, but hitting our marks all the same, as if by fate. Would you wonder, then, what would happen if we actors were to realize that we were affecting a drama? Would you wonder what we might be capable of should we discover that the backdrop of our lives is a matte painting, that our clothes are cheap props, that our conflicts and pain are affectations? By seeing through the illusion of our drama, we might enact new ones. Imagine rituals that could reshape the order of the play, of the film, of the world—rituals designed by the greatest sorcerers and scientists of every age who strained to see through the cracks in the firmament, past the curtain, beyond the veneer of the stage under the set lighting. Imagine the actors—no, the *characters*—seizing the production equipment and producing a new film, one of their own design."

    "So, *Hierarchies of Blood*—you believe that we made a movie within a movie," Kneale said. "I think I'm beginning to see the metaphor."

    Malgrave's eyebrows arched.

    "Your lack of imagination, even after all you've seen and done, disappoints me, Mr. Kneale. I am not speaking in metaphors. If I am to be an actor, my willpower will overcome that of our silent director. Through *cinéma goblin*, we generate new scenes, a new cinema, writ in the radioactive wash of the quantum undergirding of reality itself. We leverage real forces you might understand as the supernatural or the occult. Real horror, real *power* drawn from beyond the veil, interlaced with the symbolism and staccato rhythms of subliminal suggestion. Psycho-spiritual warfare through horror movies. A film within our own film, that subverts and redirects the flow of light and sound, of the projector itself. A rebellion on a small scale that will explode outward in radiating gyres of chaos. *That* is my work now. That has been your work as part of this production, off-screen and on."

"You give me too much credit, ma'am. I'm only in one scene."

"If the crew—or the fictional characters they create—were to rebel against the director, against the script, there might be mechanisms in place to resist them, no? Would not others step in, summoned to improv in the moment, to salvage the scene? Someone emerging to call *cut*, to reset and try again or, failing that, otherwise remove the rebellious elements?"

Renee worked the projector at the front of the room. A laptop screen illuminated her face. The film would be starting any moment.

"The vampire," Kneale said.

"You and the other vampire killers prevented an improvisation meant to restore the balance of the script," Malgrave said. "Did you know that some of the earliest films featured spooks, spirits, and devils? That the earliest practitioners of the form were, in fact, sorcerers and alchemists seeking to make new worlds from the crumbs of creation itself? They could not have anticipated how wildly they would succeed. For so many, the world is defined by and confined to screens, whether those we carry with us, those in our homes, or those of our minds. We conjured devils, and the devils have a grip on our souls. We make new devils in our own image. We don their costumery. We subvert them. We become them."

Kneale thought of his brief on-screen role as a malignant creature dancing atop a stretch of wall. He wondered if the scene would make the final cut.

"So, filmmakers are sorcerers?"

"Much of it started in Europe, but their alchemical art found its truest and most successful permutation in America, far from the watchful eye of the old masters of the witch-haunted continent. They drew their power from hundreds of years of genocide and death—a grand sacrifice on an unbelievable scale, all endorsed by the religious establishment for maximum dramatic irony. They created new hierarchies of blood with evil gods and demons, drawn from the raw ether of the substrate on which all existence rests. Imagine thinking you had created a new art form, only to discover that you had replicated the elemental superstructure of reality itself."

Her face had adopted an insidious glow, her eyes gone black, her teeth stark white in the radiation of the projector's light. The musicians began their solemn work, their synthesizers and electronic instruments laden with the opening notes of doom.

"If I watch this film, what will happen to me?"

"Not everything is directed at you, nor is every Hollywood enterprise some nefarious plot of the Skull and Bones society or the Order of the Night Moose. But some films *are* weapons, mimetic viruses waiting to explode into the subconscious of chosen audiences."

She turned to face him, her eyes wholly black, her fangs stretching down over blood-red lips. She pointed to the projected image appearing on the dungeon wall before them.

"This is a stake we will bury deep in the chest of the world," she said. "We use the Gothic to re-stage the possibilities of history, calling back to a time before the future was closed off to us. Before it was closed off to you."

She put her hand on his chin, holding him in place, as if for a kiss. He shuddered, turning away from her leering visage. His body flooded with adrenaline, his limbs shaking. She retracted her hand. His stomach turned, and, although his body cried out in mortal fear, he was fixed to his seat. Between rapid breaths of animal terror, he managed to speak his final questions.

"Wouldn't you want me dead? For killing one of your own?"

"The one you killed had gone feral, living alone and feeding on animals, on hikers and vagrants. It meant to stop me, to halt my insurrection, whether it understood that or not. I should hope that if I ever reached such a degenerated state, someone like you would come along and end my embarrassment."

In an act of mercy, she released her fearful grip on his panicking nervous system. He felt command of his body return to him in a rush of pinpricks, as if his whole body had fallen asleep. The thrum of blood and the beating of his heart in his ears was painful.

"I give you a choice, Mr. Kneale. You can return to your old life. Or you can help us make movies. Our project was a success thanks to your efforts: the film is complete, and we have produced vampire killers. Now, you are an instrument of true terror. You have worked for me before, you know. This offer is a promotion of sorts."

The Ranch, he thought. *Colorado.*

"Yes, indeed," she said. "The Observer/Experiencer program has been of great interest to those who seek to unbound the restraints of reality, of the story in which we find ourselves. The Nathan Ranch is not a mystery I have been able to solve, despite the efforts of men and women like you, and the best scientists money can skim from the defense industry. It resists all efforts for study. Actively. Perhaps I should try a more direct approach, like Alexander at Gordium. Perhaps I will, yet, and you will be a part of that effort. But, ah, my film begins. The spell is cast."

The music swelled. The electric notes of a synthesized theremin warbled over the grumbling of a reverb-laden church organ. A monotonous bass line snapped and hummed beneath it all. Faux static popped and hissed, like the degradation of a recording committed to vinyl half a century ago. On the screen, the words "NEW CAMLOUGH STUDIOS PRESENTS" appeared in an elaborate, hand-drawn typeface, calling to mind the artful credit presentations of old. "A FILM BY TERENCE PRIMROSE" drew applause, as did "CHRISTOPHER BELGRAVIA" in the cast credits. The other names and titles were all familiar to Kneale, having spent production among them. He knew Pore's name would be saved for the credits roll at the end of the film, where it would appear not far from his own.

Someone appeared next to him, holding out a tray not of drinks, but of slender, rolled cylinders that gave off a familiar and pungent aroma.

"A sacrament borne from Colorado soil, birthed from the sky and grown not too far from the place where you chased ghosts and looked for cracks in the world," Malgrave said, her eyes on the credits, finding her own name there, near the end. "Did you know that sufficient concentrations of meteorite debris can effectively change the soil composition of, say, a cannabis plant field? That those alien elements when processed through the natural growth cycle of high-strength psychotropic plants can produce flowers of not only great potency, but of profound psycho-spiritual effects?"

Kneale took one of the joints. The tray floated to Malgrave, who took two, handing one to Alvira and keeping one for herself. A metal lighter appeared, flicking open with fire.

"Sorcery is ever pharmakeia, but intent determines the outcome," Malgrave said between lungfuls of smoke. Beside her, Alvira coughed. The lighter floated before him, held by a shadow.

"Your role as head of security on this particular production is at an end, Mr. Kneale. Whether you mean to continue in my employ is an open question. Your lines are not yet written. You have broken out from the iron grip of the director. What will be your next performance, I wonder?"

Her eyes glowed then, red irises at the center of veins of crimson. On screen, familiar actors in period costumes trudged through upstate New York forest standing in for European countryside.

We must find shelter before nightfall.

I am not so superstitious.
Perhaps you should be.

Eyes, awash with blood, appeared in half-transparency over the trees, over the forest, over the whole makeshift Gothic world within a world.

Kneale's shaking hand brought the joint to his lips. The tip caught fire and he inhaled. His mouth and lungs filled with the swirling smoke. His third eye was permitted to crack open. He could see the filmstrip itself—or was it the flickering pages of a book?—moving over everything before him, containing him, encompassing everything that ever was or would be.

Hierarchies of Blood grew expansive; a series of semi-familiar scenes and faces, cut together with transformative, expert craft to produce something new. Magic, alive, a creature of its own, like the features of a friend on their child's face. Here, within this insurrection against nature, Daniel was transformed into a terrifying vampire who stood on the precipice between charisma and terror. Peter and Christopher embodied brave and stalwart defenders of Christendom. Yvonne and Andrea grew more alluring and powerful than any women Kneale had ever seen, even and especially as evil overtook them. The camera transformed them all—and him, too, for he was there, *here*, a creature of the night himself, draped in the countenance of evil, dancing upon the castle walls, a horrifying specter who haunted the grounds, threatening damnation to any who might fall under his spell.

But it was the castle that dominated the space, that conquered every frame. Resplendent in its towers, its inner halls, its dungeon. Candle and torchlight cast it in a stately, awe-inspired glow. Shadows danced and tumbled. Strange shapes clambered over the stones in darkness. Spooklights scuttled around its contours. Always, the castle, a castle at the center of all things.

There was blood, of course. Every bite, every kill, was an orgasmic explosion of crimson liquid, of arterial spray of operatic embellishment. The gore effects were sublime, all practical, in-camera effects wrought by Nike's skilled makeup team and captured by Kathleen's lighting and lens work. Spectacle, shock, and blood-drenched faces twisted in competing ecstasies of pleasure and pain. If the vampires made victims, it was not clear from the expressions of the humans upon whom they fed. The juxtaposition of the sexual and the violent was emphasized all the more by the ejaculate nature of the blood, spurting out in squishy, rhythmic bursts.

As the smoke transformed Kneale's mind into an attenuated receptor, time compressed. He experienced a sliver of the film's true occult potential. At the dolmen, the horrors that gesticulated and reveled in the shadow were no less frightening on camera than they had been the night that they captured the event. Andrea was no less terrifying, floating as she was, becoming now the queen of blood, of the forest, the ruler of the night-things and the arch-succubus of the castle. The goblins welcomed her ascension with spastic reverie. On both sides of the screen, the audience wept tears of blood. Their emotions, augmented by the smoke, the live music, and the ritualistic nature of the film itself, were attuned to the sensuous Technicolor-inspired horrors of *Hierarchies of Blood*. Their minds and spirits vibrated in concert and harmony with the spell woven by the film, by the cast and crew, by Kneale, even, in his own small contributions.

Blood spread across the final, closing frames. Blood dripped from the projection, splattering against the floor. Blood flowed in great rivers around the audience's feet. The flood washed away the stones of the dungeon, of the columns and walls, until the audience found themselves on city streets, cobblestone and rough-hewn rock, statuary faded and lacking facial detail but implying beings with great wings and weaponry, long since lost to endless stretches of collapsing time. The street was one of many, the stone buildings around them abandoned and dark. The city wrapped in on itself with impossible dimensions, revealing its great shape.

A spiral. A dead city: a city of the dead, a necropolis at the heart of time, where the sky was hideous and alien, swirling with the detritus of cosmic graveyards, of stars rotted out and forgotten. At its center, the great castle.

Kneale saw. He understood.

This is what their—*his*—vampire movie might be about. What it all might mean in the end.

45

The stones of the dolmen flickered and warped, insubstantial, objects held together in waves of light sent from an unseen projector. The trees shimmered and moved, and their attendant darkness glimmered under the same effect. The wind was a soft, persistent scratch along the lo-fi audio track. Imperfections in the film appeared as spots of light at the edges of Kneale's vision. He would have laughed, had the effect not been so terrifying. The spooklights were ghosts, after all. Ghosts of decay, of signal. Imperfections in the strip. Cracks in the façade.

He had marks to hit, lines to deliver.

The moon hung low, a great crescent shape of artificiality. Blood red. Kneale reached the stone formation and ran his hands along the cap and a pillar. The dolmen thrummed with energy, with the rhythmic mechanisms of the unseen projector, the projector behind the world, or, at least, the projector behind his own mind.

"Beautiful, isn't it?" Renee said, coming in right on time. She appeared next to him, her hands on the stones, eyes turned to the matte-painting sky. "The effects are temporary, but I like to think that this is how they see the world all the time. We are so rarely permitted glimpses of the underlying plastic base and halide, of the truth behind the truth, beyond the walls of static."

Kneale focused on the dolmen, on the rough, abrasive

sensations along the palms of his hands and his fingertips, distant and cold in the light of the truth.

"I saw a city, and our castle stood at its heart," Kneale said. "It was not the first time."

Renee waited the proper number of beats. It was a rhythm they had developed after working together for so long.

"The ancient city," she said, her voice almost a whisper. She took a half-step towards him, subtle, caught only by a well-placed lens, perhaps, to emphasize the quiet drama. The awe she felt in discussing the topic. The conspiracy at the heart of all conspiracies. "It's the only city. It sits at the heart of time, at its beginning, and at its end."

The stones warped and the soft murmur of the night wind rippled and bent. The cut was jarring. An imperfection that created a sudden shift in the scene, the leading context lost. The conversation had shifted.

"You envy them," Kneale said, his face turned toward the sickle moon.

"Don't you?" Renee asked, eyebrows raised, glasses reflecting moonlight in close-up. "The power they have…Forget politics and culture. They have the means to conquer death itself."

"I killed their kind," Kneale said. "You had a hand in that, too. They won't forget that, will they?"

Renee held her arms close to her chest. Her breath was a ghost slipping from her lips.

"You destroyed an enemy of our mistress, as she hoped you would," she said. "You're an asset to her, now. Valuable. Hers, if you wish to be."

"I don't know what else I could be." Kneale took his eyes from the moon. Its red glow had transferred to the stones of the dolmen. Warmth radiated from them in rising waves.

"We begin pre-production on New Camlough's next film after the holidays are over," Renee said. "Take some time off, get drunk, get laid. Whatever it takes. We need to be ready. The undead always rise again, the full moon always returns. Now, we make films for select audiences. But she has plans for mass-market releases. She wants to take the ritual to the next level."

"To what end?"

"Hers," Renee said. "She's a monster, but she's better than some, than most. The others—well, you've seen what they can be like."

"What if I told someone?" Kneale said. The stones grew warmer as he pressed his hands into them. A familiar, recognizable heat. He gave a small shove, just to see what would happen. The stones responded with a rippling pushback. Kneale caught sight of a flash of white, a sputtering black pattern. Film dislodged from track. Ink flashing along fluttering pages of white. Some mad synthesis between the two modes.

"It would not go well for you, or for anyone you've ever known or loved."

"Is that a threat?" Kneale said these words too fast, too close on the heels of Renee's lines. He had to get himself back into the moment. They could recover. They always did. Somehow, he felt like they always said and did what was asked of them. They were professionals, after all.

"I couldn't threaten a man like you," Renee said. There was a tinge of confusion at the edge of her words, quickly suppressed. No, she would trust him, and she would keep the scene going. "I'm just…trying to give you some friendly counsel. You're in a new world now. The old rules don't apply here. You should focus on surviving, not on trying to upend a system that was in place before you were born, and that'll be here long after we're all dead. It'll probably outlast *her*, too."

She lingered, counting out the beats, *one, two, three*. Cut to Kneale in close-up, head bowed over the stones, his hands floating above them, done testing their limits.

"You, Alvira, Daniel. You're the first vampire killers I've ever known," Renee said. "I was starting to suspect they were mythological, that no one could accomplish what you did. You're a symbol, now. That's a powerful thing. A dangerous thing. You'll need to be careful."

"If I keep working for her," Kneale said.

"You might be interested in what we're working on next," she said. "It's a mad scientist picture, inspired by the works of H.P. Lovecraft and Clark Ashton Smith. Flesh golems and the zombified dead returned to life by way of a terrible, bio-organic resonance machine. There's some derelict industrial property in Rochester that we're scouting. Yvonne has some interesting ideas that we might incorporate into the script. We'll find a way to get Andrea involved, too, of course. She'll be our special guest star. She has to be."

"I figured you'd want to pack up and head back to New York City or LA after all this."

"Western New York is perfect," Renee said. "Post-industrial skyline, grey clouds for mood and lighting, the memory of a prosperous past hanging over everything like a shroud. What could be more Gothic than the Rust Belt?" She tilted her head as an invitation to follow. She led him away from the stones, from that weak point in the firmament, from the sore he could not stop poking.

"Yvonne should direct," he said, as they walked back toward the castle. "She deserves it."

"Indeed. She can work with Andrea. Influence her."

"Can she control her?"

"No. No one can control Andrea but Andrea. But friendship transcends undeath, it would seem. And horror always benefits from a woman's touch. They'll make a good team for the films to come." She waited a moment before continuing. "Something didn't fit for me, you know. About your story."

"What story?"

"You said Andrea was in your trailer that night. That she tried to seduce you. To turn you."

"Yes. So?"

"Vampires can't enter unless invited," Renee said, speaking softly. "You have to let them in."

They left the stones behind. They approached the castle. The walls were tall and impregnable. The towers stood proud. Crimson and purple banners, recently restored, flapped in the cold breeze of early December. Candles burned behind the stained glass windows along each face of the great fortress, sending shadows and light forth to dance. The light, shadow, and sound projections that underpinned the world, that gave life to reality itself, flickered and danced, too. This stretch of film drew to an end, accompanied by rising music, the harmonies of horror that drove the action of history and drama according to rhyme, meter, structure, and script—or, in our case, novel.

In the final moments of the last reel, the great castle was mighty and robust, a stone herald of the glorious Gothic ascendant once more, now and forever. Amen.

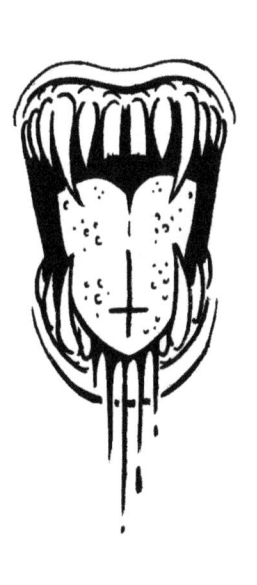

Acknowledgments

Thank you to James R. Moore, whose Black Mountain Transmitter project music has accompanied countless writing sessions of mine. Many of the films he recommended and shared over the past few years informed this novel directly.

Steve Grinstead's edits helped this book take its final and most fearsome form. He is a professional editor of impressive background and talent, and I was lucky to work with him here. Here's hoping he decides to edit a few more horror novels.

Thank you to Bonnie and Tracy for providing our family a temporary home while we moved back from Colorado to upstate New York, and for giving me a space in which to work on the novel for several months. A good portion of *Project Vampire Killer* was written and revised in that makeshift office in their basement, and the woods out back offered great inspiration for a novel set in the wilds of upstate.

Thank you to my wife Jess for her uncompromising support of my writing, as always.

Artist Hellish Maggot provided perfect cover art for this book. I'm certain there's more than a few readers who will be drawn in by its grotesque beauty.

Mat Fitzsimmons has been a constant reader and contributor, providing yet another excellent section break icon here.

Thank you to Matthew M. Bartlett, Max Booth III, Tom Breen, Jared Collins, S.L. Edwards, Gemma Files, Orrin Grey, Christopher

Slatsky, Sean M. Thompson, and those other writers and artists who have publicly and privately supported my work in recent years. Your encouragement means everything to me. Double thanks to Mer Whinery, who provided his name and endorsement for the back cover.

Thanks to Ellen Datlow for selecting some of my fiction to appear in *The Best Horror of the Year* as I was writing this novel, as that honor helped motivate me to see this to completion.

Thanks to Sam Reader, whose glowing reviews at Tor Nightfire represented mainstream recognition of my very idiosyncratic and very indie books.

I am deeply grateful to the many and various artists, writers, actors, game developers, and filmmakers who have and continue to make the vampire one of the most compelling figures across human culture, to include but not limited to: Hitoshi Akamatsu, Roy Ward Baker, Mario Bava, Kathryn Bigelow, Julie Carmen, John Carpenter, Change Cheh, Francis Ford Coppolla, Tom Cruise, Peter Cushing, Willem DaFoe, Terence Fisher, Sadie Frost, Jenette Goldstein, Lance Henrikson, Werner Herzog, Tobe Hooper, John Hough, Leif Jonker, Stephen King, Klaus Kinski, Christopher Lee, Mathilda May, E. Elias Merhige, F.W. Murnau, Reggie Nadler, Paul Naschy, Tom Holland, Gary Oldman, Amando de Ossorio, Bill Paxton, Brad Pitt, Ingrid Pitt, Anne Rice, Jean Rollin, Chris Sarandon, Wesley Snipes, Max Schrek, Masahiro Ueno, and Tommy Lee Wallace, among others. Bram Stoker, of course, holds a special place of honor above all.

Thanks also to John L. Flynn, whose unrivaled *Cinematic Vampires* was a formative inspiration and reference text for this novel. And thank you to Stefanie Spivack for giving me a copy back in 2019, which planted the seeds of *PVK*.

Finally, thank you to every reader who has supported my previous work, whether with a purchase, a friendly message online, or a conversation at a convention or over coffee. *Project Vampire Killer*, alongside *The Haunting of Camp Winter Falcon*, marks a thematic conclusion of this leg of my writing journey. Thank you for being part of that. More to come sooner rather than later.

Gothic Horror Forever!

About the Author

Jonathan Raab is the author of *The Haunting of Camp Winter Falcon*, *The Secret Goatman Spookshow and Other Psychological Warfare Operations*, *The Crypt of Blood: A Halloween TV Special*, and more. His short fiction has appeared in numerous magazines and anthologies, including *The Best Horror of the Year, Volume Fourteen*. He lives in Gothic upstate New York with his wife, son, and a dog named Egon. You can keep up with his new projects at www.muzzlelandpress.com.

Printed in the USA
CPSIA information can be obtained
at www.ICGtesting.com
CBHW050012190824
13302CB00053B/1278